RUNNING WILD

ANTONY TREW has had three careers: sailor, business executive, writer. The first was the sea. Returning to it during the Second World War he served with the South African and Royal navies in the South Atlantic, the Mediterranean and the Western Approaches where he commanded the escort destroyer HMS *Walker*, principally employed on Russian convoys. He was awarded the DSC.

After the war he resumed his work with the Automobile Association of South Africa of which he was Director General and in his spare time wrote the best-selling novel, *Two Hours to Darkness*. On the strength of it he retired early and embarked on a third and highly successful career as a writer.

He now lives in Weybridge, Surrey.

Available in Fontana by the same author

Death of a Supertanker
Two Hours to Darkness
The White Schooner
The Antonov Project
Sea Fever

ANTONY TREW

Running Wild

FONTANA/Collins

First published by William Collins Sons & Co. Ltd 1982
First issued in Fontana Paperbacks 1983

Made and printed in Great Britain by
William Collins Sons & Co. Ltd, Glasgow

ONE

A noise woke him, somebody knocking, then Mrs Barnes' plaintive, 'Wake up, André. Telephone. Public call-box.'

He switched on the light, rubbed his eyes. Twenty minutes past midnight. Christ! Who could it be? So late. Naked, he got out of bed, slipped on shorts and a T-shirt and made for the phone.

'Disgraceful.' Mrs Barnes, plump in a faded dressing gown, her grey hair compressed under its net, glared at him as he passed. 'Waking respectable people in the middle of the night. You tell your friend he should be ashamed of himself.'

'Yes,' he nodded compliantly, picked up the phone. 'Who is it?'

'Listen, I'm stuck.' It was Goddy's voice. Hoarse, slight underlying foreign accent. 'Break down. Gear-box trouble. Need your help. It's urgent. Team work necessary.' The forced laugh, the code words hidden in the simple statement, sent a cold shiver down André's spine.

'Gear-box trouble,' he repeated, frowning at Mrs Barnes. 'Where are you?'

'Just down the road from Max's place. Make it snappy. It's late.'

'I'll say it's late.' André scowled for Mrs Barnes' benefit. 'You put me in bad with my landlady. Be with you soon.' He replaced the phone, turned to Mrs Barnes. 'One of my UCT mates. Bob Meyer. Car's broken down. Gear-box trouble. Have to go and help him.'

'Where?'

'Camps Bay,' André lied. Camps Bay was at least ten miles from Max's place and on the opposite side of the Peninsula.

Mrs Barnes, arms folded across her bosom, shook her head. 'You young people. Always in some sort of trouble. Camps Bay! It's miles away. And don't you be late, André. You've got an early lecture tomorrow.' Mrs Barnes was not only landlady to the three undergraduates of the University of Cape Town who boarded with her but their surrogate mother. She was a caring person whose abrupt and disapproving manner concealed a warm heart.

Within a few minutes André, now in jeans, jersey and a denim jacket, was on his way. He stopped the Mini at a call-box, dialled a number. It seemed a long time before he heard Pippa's, 'Who's that?'

'Me,' he said. 'Ted's had a breakdown. Gear-box trouble. I'm on my way to help him. Like to come?' Ted was Goddy's code name. 'Team work's necessary.'

There was a moment's silence before she spoke. 'Gear-box trouble. Oh dear, poor Ted.' The way she said it he knew she was scared.

'Of course I'll come,' she went on. 'Keep you company. Be ready in a few minutes.'

'Great,' he said. 'Be with you soon.' He got back into the Mini and headed for the block of flats off the main road in Rondebosch where she lived. As he drove he thought about Goddy's phone call. What on earth had happened? Had to be an emergency. Something dangerous? A knot of pain formed deep in his stomach. Gear-box trouble, team work necessary, Max's place. Frightening words: *gear-box*, code name for the Security Police; *team-work*, the cell of three to which he, Goddy and Pippa belonged. *Max's place*, code name for one of four top priority rendezvous, to be used only in the most urgent circumstances.

He turned on to the main road, drove on past the Baxter Theatre. It was raining, wet and cold, and but for occasional cars coming from the Cape Town direction he had the road to himself. Turning left, he drove a short distance up the slope and parked in Soforth's Lane. There were no street lights so he didn't see Pippa until she stepped from the shadows of a hedge.

She got into the car.

'Brilliant,' he said.

'What's wrong, André?' He couldn't see her face but her voice told of her anxiety. He pulled her close, kissed her. 'Don't know, Pips. But we soon will. He's at Max's place.'

'Max's place! Oh God. As bad as that.' She said it despairingly.

He backed the Mini out of the lane, turned and headed towards the freeway which linked Table Bay and False Bay across the neck of the Peninsula. There was a clearing in the sky ahead and Table Mountain, bathed in half moonlight, loomed huge and sombre, a swirl of cloud strung like a scarf along its upper slopes. They joined the freeway, turned left and passed the university buildings they knew so well. At the road fork above Newlands they carried on into Rhodes Drive, following the winding climbing road past Kirstenbosch towards Constantia Nek. Here on the higher slopes of the mountain there was little traffic at that hour but approaching a bend soon after Kirstenbosch the Mini's headlights picked up a police car parked at the roadside. Pippa said, 'Oh heavens!'

André, his heart beating faster, patted her knee. 'Not to worry, Pips. Nothing to do with us.'

For some time after that he concentrated on the rear view mirror but there was no sign of headlights. 'You can relax,' he said. 'They're not following.'

'Thank God for that.' She laughed nervously.

During the journey they discussed Goddy's phone call, hazarded guesses about what had happened, arrived at no conclusions.

'He must be in dead trouble. That's for sure,' André said.

'But what sort of trouble?'

'We'll soon know. No future in guessing.'

After that they were silent, each engrossed in their troubled thoughts.

As the Mini purred through a night curtained with rain Pippa was thinking of the beginning of it all – of how she'd got involved. It had really started with that first meeting with Goddy in Stefan Carralin's rooms. Stefan, doing a post-graduate course in clinical psychology and deeply involved in anti-apartheid activities, had persuaded André and Pippa to join the movement he headed. At first their roles had been passive, little more than attending clandestine meetings where protest measures were discussed. But later Stefan told them that, their credentials having been established within the movement, they were expected to play a more militant part, to make up a cell with a man called Ted. Stefan told them that they could take time to consider this; but since they saw apartheid as something morally indefensible, a form of political violence, they said they didn't need time. They had gone to Stefan's rooms a few nights later and there met Ted for the first time. They had liked him at once and accepted without hesitation the proposal that Ted – alias Goddy – should be their cell leader. Four months had passed since then, and now that they knew him better their liking and respect had grown.

In early middle age, heavily bearded, thick-set with pale limpid eyes, Goddy had shown himself to be a man of strong character; one who could be charming, resolute or ruthless as the occasion demanded. He'd told them early on that 'Goddy' was a nickname, that his real name was Stanislaw Godeska, the son of a Polish émigré to Britain who'd served in the Polish wing of the RAF during the Second World War. Stanislaw said he'd been born and educated in England but lived for many years in Germany. He had come to South Africa in the late seventies to represent a West German firm of scientific instrument makers in whose Dusseldorf factory he'd worked for several years. They knew he did a fair amount of travelling about the Republic, and that he had secured a number of defence contracts from the South African government for the supply of scientific instruments – something, he complained, which went against the grain of his anti-apartheid convictions. 'But a man must live,' he'd said with a half smile, throwing his hands out in a gesture of embarrassment.

For Pippa the slight foreign accent, the limp – relic of a car accident many years earlier – seemed to add to Goddy's charm. Whatever it was, she found him an attractive man.

André's voice broke into her thoughts. 'Wake up Pippa, we're nearly there.'

'I wasn't asleep,' she said. 'Just thinking. What's the time?'

'Five past one.' He turned the Mini left into Southern Cross Drive and not long afterwards pulled off the road on to a dirt track which led between vineyards to a clearing fringed with trees and dense scrub. The half moon had gone behind the clouds and the rain persisted but there was no sign of Goddy or his car. Soon after they'd parked, however, he came from the darkness and opened André's door. 'Thank God you're here,' he said.

Because there was more room there they went across to Goddy's Volkswagen; it was parked in a gap in a thicket of Port Jackson willows. Pippa got into the back, Goddy and André sat in front.

André said, 'So – what's the trouble?'

'I'm on the run.' Goddy's voice was subdued.

'Christ! What's happened?'

'I was driving to my place at midnight – I'd reached the corner just before the driveway – when Aaron stopped me. He said the Security Police were in my flat. Been there, he said, since ten o'clock that night. Ransacking the place – waiting for me.'

'Oh, no, *no*,' Pippa's voice rose.

'Better keep your cool,' warned André. 'Who is Aaron?'

'He's a coloured. Assistant caretaker to the block of flats.

More than that. He's one of us.' Quickly he added, 'Forget I told you that.'

There was silence for a while, beyond it nothing but the patter of rain on the car roof and the sound of their breathing. At last, hesitatingly, André said, 'Anything in the flat which could incriminate Pippa – or me?' He was at once embarrassed, aware that his instinct for self-preservation had taken over.

'Nothing,' said Goddy. 'Absolutely nothing that could incriminate either of you.'

Pippa said, 'What happened after Aaron warned you?'

'I turned the car round and drove on to Wynberg. Phoned André from a call-box there. Came here immediately afterwards.' He hesitated, then spoke with a sense of urgency. 'I've got to get out of the country right away. Absolutely no option. But there are problems. Even if I had them I couldn't use my cheque book or passport. In any case they're in my flat with everything else I've got. So here I am with about forty rands in my pocket, no passport, and the car plus the clothes I stand up in.'

Anxious to make amends for his selfishness, André said, 'I know it's tough on you, Goddy. How can we help? Have you any sort of plan?'

'That's what I want to discuss. Why I wanted you people here. How do I get away? Airports, railway stations, seaports are out for obvious reasons.'

'What about crossing over to Botswana or Zimbabwe – or even Mozambique?'

A rumble of disapproval came from Goddy. 'That's a last resort. Too risky. They watch the borders of neighbouring black states like hawks. Military everywhere. It might work, but the odds are against it.' He paused. 'Unfortunately if they get me they get you. *And* Stefan.' There was something chilling in the way he said that. 'Security Police interrogation will break anyone. They're professionals. They'll have all they want from me in a few days. I've no illusions about that.' He stopped for a moment and they could hear his uneven breathing. 'You know what that would mean for you and Pippa. I have to be frank. No use beating about the bush.'

'Yes. We get the message.' André's voice had taken on a touch of asperity. What Goddy had said sounded more like a threat than a friendly warning. 'So what d'you propose?'

'Look. We're all in this together.' Goddy had become conciliatory. 'We're under great stress. It's important to keep cool, to remain objective. I've had nearly an hour more than you people in which to consider the situation. I *think* there's a plan that will work. And it's one that'll look after all three of us.'

'What's that?' André and Pippa asked the question almost simultaneously.

'*Southwind*. Your father's ketch.'

'*Southwind*,' echoed André. 'How d'you mean?'

'We get away in her. No immigration clearance. No need for passports. No borders to cross. No travel money involved. We sail at night in *Southwind* and no-one's any the wiser.' Goddy's hoarse voice was charged with enthusiasm.

'You mean,' said Pippa, 'that André and I must clear out now? Leave the country?'

'Not necessarily now, but soon. You don't *have* to go. Assess the risks for yourselves. The Security Police are after me. How did they get on to my tracks? Think about that.' He wasn't going to tell these earnest young people that he was pretty sure who had given him away; Marion – it had to be her. He'd always known there was an element of risk there because of what she might have seen that day in her office, but it was a risk that had had to be taken. Maybe he'd handled her too roughly. But the stakes were high and he couldn't have played it any other way.

'We work on a cell basis,' he reminded André and Pippa. 'Should be foolproof. But there are linkmen and there are black activists. Someone's probably blown under interrogation. Can you two pretend you feel safe? You may be at the moment. But in the weeks ahead the SP will be picking up more pieces of the jigsaw, fitting them together. Then what?' He paused, waiting for the words to sink in. 'We work as a team in the same cell. Share the same political philosophy and moral values. Now, if ever, we need each others' support.' Silence then but for the continuing patter of rain on the car, the sound of an aircraft passing overhead and a dog barking somewhere in the distance. 'I leave the decision to you,' he said quietly.

Pippa said, 'Tell us about the *Southwind* plan.'

TWO

It was dark, they were no more than dim shapes in the car, unable to see each other's faces. 'Look, I'll have to be brief. It's late and time is vital.' Goddy's quick speech stressed the urgency. 'This roughly is the idea. The other day, André, you told me that you and your brother were going on a cruise in the coming vac. Taking *Southwind* up to Mossel Bay. You laughed when I said 'watch it – it's winter'. You said that was the challenge. Three hundred and fifty miles each way in weather that could be a bastard. Remember?'

'Yes. That's right. Actually we're off in two weeks' time. Jan's begun to get *Southwind* ready.'

'Where's she lying?'

'In the yacht harbour. Duncan Basin.'

'How long would it take to get her ready for a really long voyage?'

'Depends how long. Where to?'

'Angola or Mozambique.'

Almost before Goddy had finished saying that, André blurted out, 'You can forget them. If we're to clear out in *Southwind* we'll have to get Dad's permission. *Southwind* cost him close on two hundred thousand rands. No way is

he going to agree to us taking her to Angola ...
– or any other communist country. Wh...
certainly won't agree to *any* long voyage u...
skipper. That's another problem. Jan doesn't ...
share our political philosophy. He sees nothing wron...
apartheid. Nor does Dad for that matter.'

Pippa said, 'André's right, Goddy. I can vouch for that.'

'So you sit and wait for the SP.' Goddy spoke with weary
finality. 'God help you – no-one else will.'

'I didn't say that,' protested André.

Pippa said, 'Jan *is* dead keen on sailing. He's a guy who
loves adventure. I think he would see a challenge in helping
us get away even if he did question our motives.'

'Maybe. I don't know.' André sounded doubtful.

The silence which followed was broken by Goddy.
'Right,' he said. 'Would your father agree if the destination
were England?'

'England!' echoed André. 'For God's sake, man. That's
more than six thousand miles of sailing. It'd take a long
time.'

'Better a long time at sea than a long time in solitary
confinement. I don't have to tell you what that's like.' They
could hear Goddy tapping nervously on the steering wheel.
'Surely if you explained things properly to Jan and your
father – the extent to which you're involved, the real danger
you and Pippa are in – he'd agree. Point out that he'd be
running no risks. He's already given permission for the
voyage to Mossel Bay. *Officially* he won't know of the
change of destination. And he certainly must *not* be told
that I'm coming along.'

'Just as well,' said André. 'Dad would throw a fit if he
thought *Southwind* was being used to help . . .' he hesitated. 'To help a wanted man to escape.'

'And he doesn't approve of you,' added Pippa. 'Thinks
you're a bad influence.'

'Quite,' said Goddy. 'That's precisely why he mustn't
know.'

What happens when *Southwind* fails to arrive at Mossel Bay? Thought about that?' asked André.

'Yes, of course. That's the essence of the plan.' In the next ten minutes he had dealt with that point and many others, and when he'd finished his listeners were not only convinced that the escape plan was a sound one but they were beginning to share Goddy's enthusiasm.

Though the ketch was not due to sail for Mossel Bay for another two weeks André thought they could cut this to eight days, *if* Jan and his father agreed. Many more stores would be needed for a voyage to Europe, but he explained how they could be embarked without arousing suspicion. 'I'll see Jan about it first thing in the morning,' he said. 'Before he goes to work. If he's okay, the next thing is to get in touch with Dad in Johannesburg. Then we . . .'

'How?' Goddy interrupted. 'How get in touch with him?'

'I'll ask Jan to phone. No details on the phone, of course.'

'Better not be,' said Goddy. 'Don't forget your training. Always assume a phone-tap.'

'Best plan surely is for Jan to ask his father to fly down here,' suggested Pippa. 'Then they can discuss the thing in detail. Really thrash it out.'

There was general agreement on that. Next they settled the date, time and place when *Southwind* would pick up Goddy for the voyage.

Pippa said, 'Problem. If André's father doesn't agree — if there's some sort of snag — how do we let you know?'

The Pole had thought of that, indeed it seemed he'd thought of just about everything. 'Good point,' he said. 'You use the personal column of *The Cape Times*. Since you must *not* make any notes, we need a simple message easily remembered.' He thought for a moment. 'Tell you what. How about, "Jack. Happy birthday darling. Jill." If I see that I know the voyage is off.' Soberly he added, 'Hope to God I won't see it.'

He picked up the thread again. 'There's another point. You may be forced to change the time or date for the rendezvous. In that case add to the "Jack and Jill" message the words "see you" followed by the new time and date. Got it?'

André said, 'Yah. That's easily remembered.'

The Pole turned towards the back seat. 'Got it, Pippa?'

'Yes. Brilliantly simple. Can't possibly arouse suspicion.'

'That's what I thought,' he said modestly.

'But what happens if you can't make the rendezvous?' asked Andrè.

'Don't wait. Go without me.'

They discussed other things until eventually Goddy said, 'Well, I guess that's about all right now. Just want to thank you two. Can't really put it into words.' His voice trailed away. 'But . . . well . . . anyway, thank you. We'd better go now. You first. I'll follow later. Not wise to have two cars coming out on to the main road together. Might be a car passing.'

Before getting out of Goddy's car they looked through their pockets and managed to muster thirty-seven rands which they handed over to him.

'Thanks a lot,' he said. 'With what I've got that's enough for immediate needs.'

Pippa wondered what those needs were, but said nothing.

They went across to the Mini. The rain had stopped and the moon shone fitfully through gaps in the clouds. The only sound was the occasional put-put of water dropping from the trees.

'Well, this is it. Bye now.' Goddy's hoarse voice was subdued. 'Look after yourselves. See you on the thirtieth – I hope,' he added with a dry laugh.

Pippa said, 'Take care, Goddy. I suppose you can't tell us where you're going?'

He took her hand, kissed her. 'Don't really know. But even if I did I wouldn't tell you. The less you know the better.'

André said, 'The less we blow, you mean.' He exchanged a warm handshake with Goddy and went back to the Mini with Pippa. He started the engine, they waved and the little car moved slowly out of the clearing on to the dirt road.

As soon as the Mini's tail light had disappeared Goddy went back to his car. He opened the boot, took a canvas bag from it and got into the front seat; from the bag he produced a pair of scissors, a battery shaver and a hand mirror.

The canvas bag – always in the boot, ready for the getaway he'd long feared might come – had in it toilet gear, a spare shirt, slacks, underwear, socks and a Walther automatic pistol. Meticulously careful by nature and training, he was aware that he'd been guilty of an act of gross carelessness. When dressing that morning he'd forgotten to transfer from one jacket to another the West German passport issued in the name of Willi Helmut Braun, a document without which he never moved.

Now, when he most needed it, the Security Police would be examining it in his flat; the whole carefully constructed and long nourished escape cover had been destroyed. The recollection of this failure induced a sudden doubt: was he wearing the right shoes? He'd made one serious mistake that day, could he have made another. In the darkness he felt for the buckles. They were the right shoes.

Troubled by these disturbing thoughts he settled himself in the front seat and propped the mirror against the windscreen. With the pencil torch in one hand and scissors in the other he cut off his beard. When he'd done all he could with the scissors he removed what was left with the battery shaver. Having put on sunglasses he examined himself in the mirror. 'Not bad,' he said. 'Can't really recognize myself.' After all those years it was easy to forget what one had looked like without a beard.

He transferred the Walther automatic to the glove box in the dashboard, put the shaver, scissors and mirror back in the bag and stowed it in the boot; from the spare wheel well under the carpeted boot-floor he took out a pair of number

18

plates. In twenty minutes he'd taken off the old CA plates, bolted on the new ones and replaced the licence disc on the windscreen with one which matched the TJ number on the new plates. The disc was a forgery, but only a forensic expert would have known that. He tore the old licence disc into small pieces and scattered them in the brushwood. The grey Volkswagen Golf, one of tens of thousands in the Republic, now appeared to be a Johannesburg registered car and not, as it was, a vehicle registered in Cape Town.

He drove out of the clearing following the dirt road between the vineyards until Southern Cross Drive was reached. There he turned right. It was after two in the morning; the moon, already low in the sky, had gone behind the clouds and it was raining again. He drove on, reached the crossroads, turned right for the Lady's Mile, passed over the Simon van der Stel freeway and made his way down through Bergvliet, Retreat and Rondevlei to the Strandfontein road. Throughout the journey there'd been little traffic; sometimes the headlights of an approaching car, occasionally a parked car, nothing overtaking. He followed the Strandfontein road to its junction with the coast road, crossed over and went on until he reached the lower road which ran parallel to the sea. There he turned left and headed towards Mnandi Beach. Where the road ran close to the beach he stopped the car, went down to the water's edge and hurled the old CA number plates far out into the surf.

It was still raining. Back in the car he headed for Swartklip. After meeting Stefan at the rendezvous beyond Swartklip he would pick up the coast road at Gordon's Bay, then drive on by way of Hangklip and Kleinmond. Once over the bridge at Die Mond he knew a place off the main road where the bush had been cleared years ago to make a camp for road workers. It was a natural hide-out. He intended to drive at night and lie up by day. It was mid-winter and the nights were long. The sun would rise at about seven and set soon after five. He'd spend the coming day in the hide-out. Driving through the night which followed, he reckoned he'd reach Port Elizabeth before dawn on the second day.

Helga would give him sanctuary. There was nowhere else he could go. And she would know how to handle the situation. Keep her cool, do all the right things. She was a remarkable woman. It would be marvellous to see her again. At the moment seeing her was the only thing left to him to which he could look forward.

During the drive back to Rondebosch from Max's place André and Pippa had an urgent discussion about what had happened; at times it bordered on the hysterical.

She said, 'What worries me stiff is where Goddy's going — what'll he do between now and the thirtieth? That's ten days on the run. Anything can happen.'

'That's right,' said André. 'Ten days in which the SP will be going flat out to get him. They have fantastic facilities. They're not stupid.'

'Nor is Goddy.' Pippa's tone was defensive.

'I wouldn't like to be in his shoes.'

'You are — we are — very nearly.' She was close to tears. 'I'm terrified. I mean there's no point in pretending I'm not. The next ten days are going to be hell.'

'I know how you feel, Pips. No use pretending I'm not scared. Of course I am. But dwelling on that sort of thing — I mean discussing our emotions — isn't going to help. We're involved, okay. And we're in danger. But let's take a positive view. We have an escape plan. A very sound one too, and . . .'

'*If* Jan and your father will play.' she interrupted.

'I think they will. Blood's thicker than water. Dad will be furious, but I'm pretty sure he'll do anything to help. As long as he's not involving himself and mother. And he won't be.'

'And Jan?'

'He'll be awkward at first but I don't see him turning

down an opportunity of sailing *Southwind* to Europe. He's an adventurous guy. Hates his job. I know that.'

'Hope you're right, André.' She rested her head against his shoulder and he nudged her hair with his chin. They drove on in silence, André thinking how deeply they were involved in the movement. His thoughts went back to that fateful meeting in Goddy's flat – the night Goddy had asked them if they could provide drawings and notes on how to make a limpet bomb with a timing device. 'Pips should know,' he'd joked. 'She's in third-year physics.'

They had been reluctant at first, scared of the use to which the bombs could be put, but Goddy had assured them they would never be used to endanger life. 'They will be for protest purposes only,' he said. 'Blasts at isolated targets. Verbal protests achieve nothing, you know. Protests must be in a form that make headline news. That's the only thing that counts.'

With some misgivings they'd agreed and in due course Pippa had produced the drawings and notes. As instructed by Goddy she'd given them to André who'd taken them to Stefan Carralin. It was Goddy, as cell leader, who'd insisted on this method of delivery.

What Stefan had done with them, to whom they might have been passed, in what way they might have been used, André had no idea. He was painfully aware that, whatever the answers to these questions might be, he and Pippa were dangerously involved.

André recalled the Pole's chilling warning; *Remember. If they get me they get you.*

If they got Goddy . . .

He shivered.

THREE

Driving towards Swartklip, Goddy thought about Stefan Carralin. He'd been with him when Aaron stopped the car and said the Security Police were in the flat – but for Aaron they would both have walked into the trap. As it was, Stefan's presence had been providential, for it solved an immediate problem which stood in the way of escape. Dear, thin, dedicated, chain-smoking Stefan, thought Goddy; but for you, who knows?

'Thank God you're with me,' he remembered saying as he reversed the Volkswagen and accelerated off towards Wynberg. On the way he dropped Stefan in the back streets of Claremont not far from the flat where the younger man lived. In the course of that short journey they'd made certain urgent plans.

'Sure you can do what's necessary *and* make the rendezvous in two hours' time, Stefan?'

'No problem. I'll be there, don't worry.'

'That's great. Two hours from now, then.'

'What are you going to do in the meantime?'

'Warn André and Pippa. They're at risk now. If the police get me . . .'

'They get them,' finished Stefan, adding with a humourless laugh, 'and me.'

Goddy said, 'Yes. I'm afraid so.'

They compared watches – it was fifteen minutes past midnight. After that Stefan left the car and Goddy had driven on to the rendezvous at Max's place. He'd not told André and Pippa that he'd seen Stefan. To those with whom he worked he gave only essential information. Enough for the tasks they had to carry out, never more.

These thoughts ended as the Volkswagen's headlights picked up a parked car. The third he'd seen on the beach road. Late night lovers? Sometimes police cars checked on them. Every time he passed a parked car his pulse rate jumped.

Soon after crossing the causeway he turned left off the main road to follow a sandy track which twisted its way through dense clumps of Port Jackson willows. After several hundred yards it ended sharply in a clearing. His dimmed headlights were reflected on the wet metallic surfaces of a parked car.

A man got out and walked towards the Volkswagen – a very thin man.

Goddy met him half way. 'Okay, Stefan?'

'Yes. Adbul let me have four cans. About thirty-five litres.' He spoke with a cigarette in his mouth, his voice husky.

'Marvellous, Stefan. Must have at least fifty in the tank still. That's about eighty-five in all. Enough for nine hundred kilometres. That'll do me.'

They transferred the jerry cans to the Volkswagen's boot.

Stefan asked, 'You okay now?' The sentence ended in a spasm of coughing.

Goddy said, 'You'll kill yourself with those bloody cigarettes.'

Stefan ignored the remark. After some discussion about things to be done, he said, 'So I tell Helga to expect you between four and five on the morning of the twenty-fifth.'

'That's right. Use a public call-box.'

'Of course.' Stefan took the cigarette from his mouth, coughed and wheezed before putting it back. 'Do André and Pippa know you're going to Helga?'

'No, definitely not. Only you know that.' Goddy went on to brief Stefan about the radio message. Stefan repeated it three times to make sure he'd got it right. Afterwards he said, 'So I send it about three o'clock on the morning of July the fourth. Right?'

'Right. Unless you hear from André or Pippa to the contrary.'

'Okay.' Stefan coughed again, noisily, cleared his throat. 'Do I return the set to Patrick?'

'Sure, that's the idea.' Goddy put a hand on the thin man's shoulder. 'It helps a lot to know you'll be looking after things here. You're a reliable guy.'

Stefan said, 'Just a minute. I've something for you in the car.' He came back with a Thermos and plastic box. 'Hot coffee. Bread and cheese,' he said.

'Bless you, Stefan. That's really good.' Goddy opened the door of the Volkswagen, got in.

Stefan moved away. 'Be careful,' he called.

Goddy waved. 'There's nothing in the flat to incriminate you – or anyone else – but the SP must have some gen on me. Incidentally, I destroyed that material sent anonymously from Pretoria. Too hot to handle. Very risky. May be a trap. You'd better cool things for a while.'

Stefan said, 'Sure, I'll do that. Good luck to you, Goddy.'

'Guess I'll need it, bye now.'

'So long.'

Goddy turned the Volkswagen in the clearing before driving off into the rain-drenched night. He felt immensely relieved. It was a Saturday. Filling stations had by law to close at night during weekends. Even if they hadn't, the last thing he wanted to do was stop at one. It would have added to the hazards of an already dangerous journey. With the petrol Stefan had brought he could now reach Port Elizabeth.

Mr Bretsmar was a tall man with greying hair and a deeply seamed face. His eyes, set a little too close on either side of a long nose, looked out from under bushy eyebrows with the bright enigmatic expression of an ape. The resemblance was not altogether out of character for Mr Bretsmar's eyes were windows to a complex, calculating and enigmatic mind; one in which business transactions enjoyed a considerable priority over almost all other aspects of his life. Subject to this he was on the whole an amiable man.

At the moment, however, sitting in an armchair in his suite at the Mount Nelson, Cape Town's most prestigious hotel, he was in anything but an amiable mood. He had arrived there that morning after landing at the D. F. Malan Airport on the conclusion of a flight from Johannesburg. Jan had met him and during the drive in to Cape Town broken the news as gently as possible. Since reaching the hotel they had spent more than an hour discussing what had happened; how *Southwind* might be the means of escape if his father would agree. Jan had been stressing the dangers facing André and Pippa because of the activities in which they'd become involved.

'You mean to say, Jan, that André and that girl are actually involved in a terrorist movement?'

'Terrorist is a hard word, Dad. It's an anti-apartheid set-up. An underground movement dedicated to political change. That's how André describes it.'

'Political change my foot,' said Mr Bretsmar derisively. 'Bombs, explosions, sabotage. There's nothing political about that. It's pure unadulterated terrorism. And to think that a son of mine should be involved.' Elbows on knees, he rested his forehead on his hands. 'Christ,' he groaned. 'After all I've done for that boy. Doesn't he realize what this will do to us – to his mother?'

Jan got up, went to the window, looked out towards Table Bay. It was one of those winter days in the Peninsula when the sun shone down from a cloudless sky, the city basking in unseasonal warmth. Though he couldn't see her, *Southwind* was somewhere down there in the yacht harbour. Jan thought of the fantastic adventure which lay ahead if he could get his father's consent. Marvellous winds, running up to the Equator in the south-east Trades, keeping well to the west then, once through the Doldrums, beating up through the north-east Trades till you picked up the westerlies. After that autumnal gales in the North Atlantic. What a challenge! If only he could convince his father.

'I know what a shock this must be to you, Dad. It was to me when André broke the news yesterday. I was in a hell of a state. I mean I was absolutely against the voyage at first. But then he convinced me that it was the only way out if he and Pippa were to be safe.' He paused for a moment to let the words sink in. 'The important thing, Dad, is to get them away as soon as possible.'

Mr Bretsmar looked up, his forehead creased, the small eyes narrowed. 'You realize, Jan, that none of you will be able to come back here? To your own country. You understand that?'

'Yes, Dad. I know that and it hurts. But we can make out over there. You and Mother can come over and see us quite often. We're young and fit. We'll get jobs.'

'Imagine your mother's feelings when she learns that you can never come back?'

'*Never* is a long word, Dad. Things change.'

'I know they do,' said Mr Bretsmar ruefully. 'Look at your brother.' He paused. 'And what about *Southwind*? What's going to happen to her?'

'I've thought about that, Dad. She could be used for charters. There's money in that. I'd skipper her of course. Or I could give sailing instruction in her. There's money in that, too, you know. Or we can sell her.'

'Where? Without exchange control authority. And we'd never get that.'

'There's an active black market in yachts in the Piraeus, Dad.'

'Let me think,' Mr Bretsmar's face went back into his hands. 'Let me think. This is a dreadful situation. I must clear my mind.'

Jan walked about the room, hands in pockets, while his father thought. He, too, was thinking: about the stores that would be needed; how to get them on board discreetly. Food, sailing gear, additional charts, paint – lots of paint – radio spares and a host of other things.

Mr Bretsmar broke the long silence. 'The risks, Jan? Are

you sure I can't be involved. It's not just myself I'm concerned about. I have to think of so much. Your mother, my business reputation, my partner Emil Lutgarten, and other things. Are you quite certain that I'm not personally at risk if I agree to this?'

Jan sighed. 'Quite certain, Dad. I've already stressed that, haven't I? I mean we've gone over the whole thing in detail in the last hour. I repeat, all you've done is given me permission to take *Southwind* to Mossel Bay with André. That's all that you've done. Nothing more. You don't know that Pippa will be on board. You don't know that she and André belong to any underground movement. You know nothing of Goddy – incidentally there's still no mention of him in the papers – so you are one hundred per cent in the clear. If we get moving fast we can get André and Pippa away before the Security Police catch up with Goddy. And I suppose there's always the chance that they won't catch him.'

Mr Bretsmar got up from his chair and joined Jan at the window. 'That bastard Goddy,' he said bitterly. 'Influencing these young people. But for him this would never have happened. I hope the Security Police do get him eventually.' He went over to a cabinet in the corner and poured himself a tot of whisky. 'Like one, Jan?' he asked.

'No thanks, Dad. Too early for me.'

Mr Bretsmar swallowed the whisky, gulped, choked, put down the glass. 'I've made up my mind,' he said hoarsely, dabbing with a handkerchief at streaming eyes. 'It's no good.'

Jan looked round from the window. 'You mean we can't go?'

Mr Bretsmar shook his head. 'No, I don't mean that. I mean I can't refuse André's cry for help. We've got to get him and that girl out of the country. You can take *Southwind*.'

Goddy turned off the National Road before reaching Sir

Lowry's Pass, drove through Gordon's Bay and took the winding mountain road which hugged the cliffs overlooking the sea. He passed Ronan Point, Koel Bay, and came at last to Rooiels Bay. Here he paused briefly to survey the lie of the land, for this was the rendezvous where he would meet André on the 30th of June. After a few minutes he drove on, passed Pringle Bay and followed the road as it swung east. He carried on, leaving Betty's Bay and Stony Point on his right. The rain came and went intermittently, the road wet and shining. Coming out of a sharp bend his headlights revealed a car parked at the side of the road. A man jumped from it, stood in the road and flashed a torch. Goddy's stomach muscles tightened. Police? Breakdown? Hold-up? He slowed down, his instinct urging him to accelerate, to race past whoever or whatever it was. But that would have been dangerous. If it were the police they'd give chase, open fire perhaps. He took the Walther pistol from the glove box and put it on the seat beside him.

Drawing ahead of the parked car he noticed as he passed that a woman was in the passenger seat. The man with the torch came to the Volkswagen's driving window, '*More Meneer* – morning sir,' he said in Afrikaans.

'Sorry. I don't speak Afrikaans,' lied Goddy. He was known to be fluent; if this stranger were questioned by the police he would say the driver of the grey Volkswagen, a clean-shaven man with dark glasses, couldn't speak Afrikaans.

'My car's broken down, sir. We've been here for three hours already. Myself and my wife. Another motorist said he'd get help from Gordon's Bay. But that was two hours ago and nothing has happened.'

'What's the trouble?'

'Fuel pump, I reckon. Needs a new pump. I'm an AA member but unfortunately I haven't got my tow-in vouchers with me. Left the handbook at home.' He pointed to the front of the car. 'The badge is there. Can't

28

you perhaps ask a garage to come out.' As an afterthought he added, 'Where are you heading for?'

'Hermanus,' Goddy lied again. Hermanus was well off the route he planned to take. 'Give me your name, car make and number, and I'll see what I can do.' He looked at the clock. 'I'll be in Hermanus about six. Doubt if any garage will be open so early in the morning.'

The stranger – his name turned out to be Bezuidenhout – wrote the necessary details on a slip of paper and Goddy drove off with the man's 'Thank you very much, sir' ringing in his ears.

Goddy wouldn't be delivering the message, but Bezuidenhout had his wife with him, and daylight was not far away.

For most of the journey he'd been thinking about the steps the Security Police would already be taking. They'd assume he was making for a neighbouring black state; Botswana rather than Lesotho he imagined, since the former had a common border with Zambia – which in turn shared one with Angola – whereas Lesotho was an enclave within the Republic. But they'd not discount the possibility that he was making for Mozambique or Zimbabwe. They'd have alerted the police everywhere – airports, seaports, frontier posts; and Defence HQ in Pretoria, which in turn would alert military commanders in border areas. It was a formidable net which the Security Police could throw around a man on the run. But most probably they'd be concentrating on the route to Botswana, the road north through Beaufort West and Kimberley on the western side of the Republic, for that was the logical escape route. The route he was taking was on the south-east coast, far removed from the western route.

They would now have searched his office, interrogated Mrs Muller, sole member of his staff, a divorcée who worked mornings only. They wouldn't have found anything incriminating in the office nor would Mrs Muller have been able to help. She knew nothing of his clandestine activities.

What they *would* be looking for he had with him. Thank God for that. He'd like to have posted it but that was out of the question. The destination address was far too sensitive. He could of course have used one or other of the safe-house addresses in Western Germany but South Africa's random censorship system made that dangerous. If ever there was a case for delivery by courier this was it. It had been his intention to fly to Europe in mid-July to attend a sales conference in Dusseldorf and make a safe-drop there. As it was, the Security Police would have found his passport and air ticket in the office safe. That bitch Marion certainly had a lot to answer for. Must be her, couldn't have been anyone else.

He was worrying about that when the bridge at Die Mond showed up in his headlights. Soon afterwards he turned off the main road on to a track which led to the deserted camp site. He noticed with relief that the track was overgrown with grass and heather; it showed no signs of recent use. He reached the camp site, parked the car in a gap in the brushwood and locked the doors. It was twenty minutes past five on a cold wet morning.

He drank coffee from Stefan's Thermos, ate some bread and cheese sandwiches, and set his wristwatch alarm for noon, after which he stretched out on the front seat and was soon asleep.

FOUR

Mr Bretsmar had spent most of the day at the Mount Nelson settling with Jan a host of details in connection with *Southwind's* coming voyage. Jan's tendency to rashness and over-enthusiasm was balanced by his father's calculating mind, fertile imagination and wide business experience.

That evening Jan drove him out to the D. F. Malan

Airport to board the South African Boeing 737 for the flight to Johannesburg. It had been agreed that his father would fly down again on the 28th of June, the date on which *Southwind* was due to leave Cape Town bound ostensibly for Mossel Bay.

Soon after take-off Mr Bretsmar opened his briefcase, took out a pocket calculator and was soon engrossed in figures. He was interrupted by the pleasant voice of the first-class stewardess. Was he comfortable, would he care for some refreshment? He looked up, saw that she was attractive, smiled and said, 'Scotch and soda. With ice, please.' When she came back he told her he would not be taking the flight supper. 'I'll be having dinner at home,' he explained with another friendly smile. The last thing he wanted was the interruption of a meal. Back in the pantry she confided to her friend Katrina, 'I fancy the old guy with greying hair. He's really nice. Such a sweet smile.'

Mr Bretsmar had folded the print-outs from his calculator and slipped them into his wallet shortly before the Boeing touched down at Jan Smuts Airport. The answers given by the maze of figures, unintelligible to anyone but him, had lifted his spirits and whereas he'd boarded the plane in Cape Town in a sombre mood, he left it in Johannesburg in a remarkably good one.

Like many wealthy South Africans one of the nagging problems which often engaged his mind was how to get money out of the country. It was during his discussion with Jan that morning at the Mount Nelson that the shadow of an idea had emerged; if *Southwind* were used for André and Pippa's escape there *could* be an advantageous spin-off. It was the extent of this spin-off which he'd been busy calculating.

The opportunity to transfer substantial assets abroad in contravention of South Africa's exchange control regulations was too good to be missed, and it was on this complex subject he had concentrated his mind during most of the flight. He justified his decision to contravene the regulations on three grounds: first, that since he was forced by circumstance to use *Southwind* to get André and Pippa out of the country he was entitled to some recompense; second, the risks involved were in his view minimal; and third and finally, getting money out of the country was something a lot of other people were doing.

Mr Bretsmar was a man whose decisions were determined more by his estimate of the risks involved than by any moral considerations.

Goddy had spent an uneventful day hiding out in the disused camp site. Most of the morning he slept. In the afternoon he'd listened to the car radio with the windows closed and the volume turned well down. There was no mention of him in either of the news bulletins he'd heard. The Security Police must have been puzzled by his failure to return to the flat. They'd probably put it down to a tip-off by someone in the building who'd seen them making their discreet though forced entry into his flat, presumably with master keys. Several times in the afternoon he'd got out of the car and stretched his legs, walked round the clearing, done some elementary PT exercises. He never ceased to be alert, his senses always keyed to danger. Later in the afternoon he shaved and cleaned himself as best he could.

The sun set at five o'clock. By six it was dark but the moon, shining at times through breaks in the cloud, was still uncomfortably high. The rain had stopped. In some ways he was sorry; rain was preferable to moonlight. He finished the coffee and bread and cheese, put the Thermos and sandwich box back in the boot, stretched his arms and yawned. He felt fit and refreshed, ready for the night which lay ahead.

At six-thirty he got into the Volkswagen, started the engine and drove slowly down to the main road. There he turned left and headed for Botrivier where he joined the National Road and headed east for Port Elizabeth. He drove at a moderate speed. Fast driving, like slow driving, attracted attention.

At four o'clock that morning he had passed Humansdorp, less than sixty-five kilometres from Port Elizabeth. The journey had been uneventful, the traffic thin during the later hours of darkness, and there had been little rain. He had stopped on three occasions; twice to relieve himself and once, beyond Plettenburg Bay, to fill the Volkswagen's tank from the jerry cans. He'd stowed the empty cans in the boot. They would be needed again.

Making the descent towards the Gamtoos River Bridge he had rounded a curve and come clear of a cutting when he saw flashing lights on the road ahead. He slowed down at once, his body tense, his senses alert. What was it? Police roadblock? He was too close now to stop and turn without arousing suspicion. As he drew closer the scene ahead took shape, a large articulated truck lay on its side half way across the road. It was illuminated by the arc-light of a breakdown truck, its revolving rooflights still flashing. A police car and an ambulance, both with flashing lights, were parked close to the accident and warning signs, flashing red, had been placed on the approaches. Goddy was about to stop when a policeman standing in the roadway waved him on. He drove past slowly, turning out to avoid the damaged truck where a man with an acetylene torch was cutting into the side of the driver's cab and someone was shouting instructions. The pungent smell of diesel fuel came in through the Volkswagen's window. Some poor bastard trapped in there, thought Goddy, drawing clear and gathering speed.

The incident had shaken him, brought home how highly vulnerable he was. The temptation to turn the Volkswagen and make a run for it had been strong. Flashing lights ahead don't necessarily mean police roadblocks, he admonished himself.

He entered Port Elizabeth by way of the Baakens Parkway,

turned off it at River Road and drove past St George's Park towards Brickmakers Kloof. It was just after five-thirty – an hour and a half before sunrise – when he turned the Volkswagen into a side road and travelled a short distance up it before turning into the drive of Helga's house. The tip-up door of one side of the double garage was open. He drove in and shut the door. Helga's white Opel was in the adjoining bay. Good for her, he thought; she thinks of everything.

He took his bag from the boot, put the Walther pistol in it and made for the front door. It was cold and windy and as he walked towards the house a dog began to bark.

The door was ajar on its safety chain. 'Who's that?' It was Helga's voice.

'Goddy,' he said.

'Oh, Goddy. I thought so.'

There was the rattle of the chain disengaging, the door opened and he went in, closing it behind him and replacing the chain. There were no lights in the little hall but she was soon in his arms. '*Liebchen* – darling Goddy,' she said. 'How marvellous to see you. Stefan told me you were coming. Top secret, he said. All from a public call-box. What's the secrecy? You wicked man. Afraid your wife will know?' She babbled happily on, hugged him tightly, kissed him again. 'And for goodness sake – where's your beard. You've taken it off. You look quite different, darling.'

'I'll tell you everything later, Helga. But first things first. Anyone else here?'

'No-one.'

'Hendrina?' Hendrina was Helga's coloured maid.

'Yesterday I told her to take ten days off. Said I was going up to Jo'burg.'

'Can you trust her not to come back?'

'Absolutely. I paid her for the ten days. She's going to see her mother in Addo. Anything else, Goddy?'

'Yes. Must shave and have a shower. I'm lousy. And I'm as hungry as hell.'

34

She hugged him again. 'Goddy, *mein Liebchen*. Of course. How thoughtless of me. You shave etcetera while I get breakfast ready.' Helga's parents were of German origin. She couldn't speak German but liked occasionally to throw in one or two words she knew. Goddy, as it happened, spoke it fluently.

'Good, I'll do that. Forgotten what soap and water feel like. When I've had something to eat I'll tell you about my problems. They're pretty serious.'

'Yes, tell me afterwards.' She hesitated, laughed mischievously. 'In bed – that's quite the best place to tell me.'

'Yes.' He kissed her again. 'I've been looking forward to that.' They laughed understandingly as lovers do.

Emil Lutgarten was sceptical at first, didn't like the risks. He eyed Otto Bretsmar keenly. 'Who is this one hundred per cent courier you talk of?'

'A close member of our family. I can't say more. But absolutely reliable.'

'What guarantee have I that my money's safe?'

'My personal guarantee, Emil. I'll lodge five hundred thousand worth of scrip with you. That will cover your share. If the diamonds don't arrive you retain the scrip. Fair enough?'

That had convinced Emil. He and Bretsmar had not only been business partners for twenty years but close friends. Bretsmar had not told him of *Southwind's* coming voyage to Europe, nor the reasons for it. He'd simply said that an excellent and wholly safe opportunity had presented itself to get diamonds out of the country free of excise duty and sales tax and without the knowledge of the exchange control authorities.

As it happened he would not have brought the Lutgartens into the project had they not been essential. Emil's brother, Simon, was head of the family diamond business in Antwerp, Europe's great freeport for diamonds. Emil had for years been in contact with various diamond dealers in

South Africa on behalf of his brother. Some of the smaller ones, dubious characters on the fringe of the diamond business, were not too conscientious about recording and reporting export sales to the authorities who collected excise duty and sales tax. These were the dealers through whom Emil Lutgarten would buy the million rands worth of diamonds in the short time available.

It so happened that it was an excellent time to buy. The diamond market was in disarray, prices having fallen heavily during the year. Emil Lutgarten, though not himself a diamond dealer, was sufficiently knowledgeable to ensure that the quality of the stones bought would be good, so there was no problem there. Indeed the whole project fitted together rather neatly: Emil Lutgarten would see to the buying of the stones, Otto Bretsmar would arrange for their despatch, and Simon Lutgarten would attend to their sale in Antwerp, holding them if necessary until the market improved. Emil assured Bretsmar that there would be no difficulty in securing his brother's consent to handling the Antwerp end since he would be paid handsomely for services which, as far as he was concerned, would involve no risks whatever.

Thus it had been agreed that the deal should go ahead. There would be a syndicate of three: Otto Bretsmar and Emil Lutgarten with half shares in the diamonds; Simon Lutgarten, the third member to receive commission on their sale in Antwerp.

FIVE

For several reasons Goddy found making love to Helga that morning more than usually exciting. He had not seen her for some time, she was as always enormously responsive – almost explosively so, as if her sexuality must burst from her body — and somehow the spice of danger lent excitement to the love-making.

Afterwards they lay on her bed in a loose embrace, talking in low tones. 'Now tell me, Goddy,' she said. 'What has happened?'

'The Security Police are after me. I'm on the run. It must not be known I'm here. That's what all the secrecy is about.' Fired like shots from a gun, the short sentences were intended to shock her.

She jerked her head sideways, looked at him with frightened eyes. 'You don't mean it? You're teasing.'

'I'm not. Wish I were. You know I represent Adgarf of Dusseldorf. That job is to some extent a cover.' He raised himself on an elbow, bent over her, looked into her eyes. 'Listen, Helga. Before I go any further I must swear you to secrecy. You understand?'

'Yes, of course. I swear I won't tell a soul. I'd do anything for you. You know that.'

'Well, apart from my job with Adgarf I do certain work, highly sensitive work, for BND — that's West German Intelligence. The work has necessitated my penetrating the anti-apartheid movement in the Republic.' He spoke quickly, as if determined to prevent interruption.

She gave a little squeak of surprise. 'The anti-apartheid movement, why?'

He went on. 'My mission has been to find out to what extent the US is into it. BND suspects that a deep-cover CIA man is closely involved at a high level.'

She half sat up, turned towards him, 'A CIA man? Doing what?'

'Conducting a clandestine operation. Fostering the movement with the object of creating a climate in which the South African Government will be obliged to make substantial concessions in regard to apartheid.'

'But why does that put you on the run? I don't follow.'

'Because someone has tipped off the Security Police

37

about my anti-apartheid activities. In other words I've acted the part too well.' He finished with a mirthless laugh.

'Can't you tell the Security Police the truth? That you're working for the West German Government? Doing something that is in the interests of South Africa.'

Goddy touched her cheek affectionately, ran his fingers gently along her naked thigh. 'It's not as easy as that. If the truth were known to the South African Government it could create a major diplomatic incident. Imagine – a member of the BND actively participating in the anti-apartheid movement in South Africa – furthering terrorist activities in order to check up on the CIA? The South African Government would never accept that situation. Even if they believed the story, which I doubt. And Bonn would have to repudiate me, deny my explanations. Rule one of the intelligence service – governments don't, cannot, protect their secret agents.'

Helga sighed. 'It's a strange story, I must say.'

'You don't believe me?'

'Of course I believe you.' She touched him reassuringly. 'What are you going to do, *Liebchen*?'

He told her then that he must get out of the country. But in order to let the dust settle he wanted to remain in hiding in her house until the 28th of June when he would leave for Lesotho. Once there, Bonn would take over; arrange a clandestine flight for him to Botswana, whence he would return to West Germany via Zambia.

At that she sat up in bed, looked down at him, her eyes wet with tears. 'That's awful, Goddy. You mean you're going to leave South Africa, leave me? I hate that. It's really awful. We'll never see each other again.'

He pulled her down beside him, brushed the tears from her eyes, kissed her. 'Of course we'll see each other again, Helga. You must come and join me in Germany.'

She shook her head. 'You don't mean that. You know you've never belonged to me. You've got a wife.'

'No,' he said perfunctorily. 'I have not. We were divorced years ago. She's in Switzerland.'

Helga sat up in bed again. 'Then why did you never give me your address or phone number in Cape Town — forbid me to write — say that it might create difficulties? Why did *you* never write to me?' She pointed an accusing finger. 'Just those phone calls from public call-boxes. That's the only way I ever heard from you. Why all this secrecy if you haven't got a wife — or mistress?' she added quickly. 'Why, why, why?'

'Because of my work, Helga.' He said it wearily. 'Secrecy is a way of life for me. It's not easy. You see, the less you know about me the safer for both of us.' He kissed her lips. 'The Security Police have just raided my flat. If they'd found letters from you, you'd be under interrogation by now.' He hesitated. 'And I would certainly not have been able to come here for sanctuary.'

'I see,' she said doubtfully, lying back on the bed, her head on the pillow next to him. 'Did you find out what you wanted to about the CIA?'

'To some extent, yes. But not altogether. I was close to obtaining hard evidence when the Security Police raided.'

'Oh God. What a rotten world.' She sighed, moved closer to him. There was a long silence after that until she whispered, 'Love me again, darling. I need reassurance.'

Outside the day was beginning, the light had come and there was the distant sound of traffic.

SIX

Away to port rain and low cloud blown by the south-easter shrouded the land, but when darkness came he picked up the light at Slangkop, checked the position by radio bearings, switched off the navigation lights, shortened sail and closed the land. It would have been easier and safer to use the engine but silence was important so he settled for a jib and mizzen and a cautious approach.

It was some time later that André shouted from the bows, 'Breakers ahead and to port.'

Jan spun the wheel to starboard. Soon white water showed faintly in the darkness where the seas were breaking on Middelmas. Before long they had passed between Oude Schip and Duiker Point and entered the sheltered waters of the bay. When he judged the shore to be close enough, sails were taken in, the anchor lowered and *Southwind* swung to it in the lee of Karbonkelberg. Close ahead the rocky buttresses of the mountain, hidden by rain and darkness, rose steeply from the sea; too steeply for human habitation so that it was a deserted place but for occasional crayfish poachers who made precarious journeys along the footpath beneath the cliffs.

The rocks offshore and uncertain currents made its approaches hazardous and seamen avoided the bay; but Jan had been there before, always with Boesman in his boat, silently and at night, without navigation lights, for they too had been poaching; Boesman for the money, Jan for the adventure.

But it was not to poach that the ketch had crept into the bay this night; a bay so unimportant, so small and poorly situated, that the chartmakers had not thought it worthy of a name. Not that it hadn't one, for it was known to local fishermen as Maori Bay, though there could be few if any old enough to recall the wreck there of the *Maori* many years before.

When the ketch had swung to her anchor and settled, Jan sent his crew of two below. 'Close the companion hatch behind you,' he called to André. 'Mustn't show any light.' Later, when he was satisfied that *Southwind's* anchor was not dragging, he too went below. It was late in the evening of the 28th of June.

The port light screens were drawn and the companion hatch shut so that no lights showed on deck. Down below the saloon with its heater on was a snug retreat from the cold rain-sodden night. On his way through to the after cabin Jan saw that the girl was at the stove making coffee. Old man of the crew because of his twenty-four years, he was not sure of the girl. She was André's friend – or girl-friend; Jan wasn't sure which and didn't really care. Didn't know her all that well. Only met her on odd occasions in the last two years. What he did know was that she knew damn all about sailing and had been seasick for most of the six hours since they'd left Table Bay. Not that she'd complained; just sat huddled in the cockpit, too sick and cold and scared to lend a hand. Pippa – that was her name – was in the same sort of political trouble as his brother and that didn't recommend her to him because he just didn't feel like they did about apartheid, and wasn't likely to either. With these thoughts in his mind he took off his oilskins and neck towel and hung them in the after heads. He dried his face and hands, looked perfunctorily at the weathered face staring from the mirror, ran a hand through thick matted hair and made his way back to the saloon.

André was sitting at the table, chin in hand, the day's *Cape Times* spread in front of him. He looked up. 'Okay, Jan?' His face was tense and strained.

'Depends what you mean?'

'This place. Think anybody saw us come in?'

Jan went to the drinks locker, took out a can of beer, snapped it open, crossed over to the settee and sat down. He held the can poised, ready to drink. 'I wouldn't think so, except the seals. Maybe they did. Anyway it's not a crime. Get yourself a beer, steady your nerves.'

André shook his head. 'Pippa's making coffee.'

'I know. I can see.' He drank from the can.

André looked at his watch. 'Seven-forty-five. What time is he coming?'

'Same as I told you last time. Midnight plus or minus half an hour.'

Pippa said, 'It's ready. Shall I pour three mugs?'

'Yah. Three mugs for three mugs.' Jan laughed cheerfully, raised the beer can and drained it.

Pippa brought over the coffee. 'I feel better.' She looked at Jan uncertainly. 'Those seasick pills are good.'

'Great,' he said. 'A few days at sea and you won't need them.'

'Hope you're right.' The pale face and bloodshot eyes seemed to bely the suggestion that she was better.

For supper they had mugs of soup and sandwiches – thick hunks of bread and butter with corned beef. Pippa had told them she couldn't face cooking a hot meal. 'I suppose I'll be able to soon.' She was apologetic.

There was little conversation during the meal but afterwards, when the washing-up was finished and things had been put away, Jan said, 'Better settle the accommodation problem now.'

'Pippa should sleep here.' André pointed to the starboard bunk. 'Less movement than for'ard or aft.'

'Okay. But when she's got her sea-legs she can move into the stern cabin. Have her own loo and shower.'

'Oh no,' Pippa protested. 'That's yours. You're the skipper.'

'When we're at sea I sleep there.' He nodded towards the navigator's bunk immediately aft of the chart-table. 'André'll have the for'ard cabin. For the time being at any rate.'

André and the girl exchanged glances. The younger man shrugged his shoulders. 'Anywhere'll do.' He switched the subject. 'Reckon we've enough stores, food, water and the rest?'

'If we're careful. Bound to collect some rainwater. Maybe fish, too.'

Pippa pushed her hair from her eyes. 'Could the storing have been noticed?'

Jan looked at her speculatively, wondering about her nerve. He shook his head. 'We've spread it over a week. Cape Town, Kalk Bay, Hout Bay, Gordon's Bay. Small loads each time. Never more than enough for the trip to Mossel Bay.' He ran a large sunburnt hand through his hair. 'We've got everything we're likely to need. Except the charts and radio spares.'

André said, 'Do we really need them all that much?'

'Need them! You must be crazy if you think I'd attempt this voyage without them.'

'Pity Dad didn't get them earlier. Would have avoided all this hassle.'

'What hassle?' Jan's chin jutted aggressively.

'Coming in here. On a night like this. Involving Boesman. Unnecessary risks.'

'Christ! I like that. Coming from you. *Southwind* wouldn't have to be here if you two hadn't ...' He stopped, his eyes unforgiving. 'Don't blame Dad. He's been super. Not his fault the Security Police are breathing down your necks. The old man always told you to leave well alone. But you wouldn't listen. Now you and your friend Goddy have got us all involved. The whole bloody family.'

The girl stood up. 'For heaven's sake don't let's go over that again. It can't help in any way. We know your views, Jan. You know ours. Can't we leave it at that?'

'Not if André starts blaming the old man. I won't stand for that.'

She looked from one to the other. 'Please don't quarrel. We're in a difficult situation now. We've got to get out. I just pray that Goddy will make the rendezvous.'

'Too bad if he doesn't. I'm not waiting for him.' Jan glared balefully. 'Don't forget I'm in this, too. *And* through no fault of my own.'

Pippa said, 'We're very grateful, Jan. We really are.'

'You didn't *have* to come,' said André. 'I could have managed.'

'Damn sure you couldn't. Anyway, the old man wouldn't have let you take *Southwind* without me.'

André sighed. 'I know. That's right. We *are* grateful. But you wouldn't have come unless you'd wanted to.'

Jan thought about that. 'Yes. That's true. It does suit me. Have to be honest.' There was the hint of a smile in his blue eyes. 'Haven't done a long voyage since the South Atlantic race. Looking forward to this one. Should be really good. Helluva lot more fun than shuffling trust deeds.' He went over to André, patted his shoulder. 'Sorry, man, I know things aren't good for you.'

There was an awkward silence. André sat down again. Pippa took her bag from the starboard locker, began rummaging through it. Eventually André switched on the radio. A male voice with back-up singers chunted and wailed *Making up Your Mind*, and the saloon vibrated to the booming, twanging accompaniment.

Jan glared. 'Must we have that crummy row?'

André turned down the volume. 'News coming any minute now.'

'Why bother? It's always the same old crap.'

'We have to bother.' André nodded towards the girl. 'We just have to.'

'It's terribly important, Jan.' She turned to him appealingly. 'They may have got him.'

'Who?'

'Goddy, of course.'

'Oh, him.' He said it contemptuously. 'Okay. If you must. I'm going topsides to check the cable. Switch off the light before I open the hatch.'

André switched off the light and Jan went up the companion-ladder.

SEVEN

The 28th June broke fine and clear though the cold wind persisted. It was to be Goddy's last day in Helga's house. That night he would begin the journey back along the route by which he'd come to Port Elizabeth eight days earlier. The return journey of about 750 kilometres would end at Rooiels Bay, the rendezvous where he'd be picked up in the early hours of the 30th June.

Each day Helga's shopping included *The Cape Times* but there'd been no message for him in the personal columns so he concluded that all was well at the Cape Town end. Neither had there been any mention of him or the raid on his flat in newspapers, radio or TV. This was no surprise. The Security Police would do nothing to inform him in any way of what they knew or what they were doing. That was their method. Helga had been marvellous. There was no-one else to whom he could safely have gone. Not only had she given him sanctuary in the most comfortable circumstances, but she'd done much to keep him cheerful and boost his morale. In the mornings she'd gone shopping, leaving him upstairs in the spare room at the back of the house where the curtains were kept drawn. They'd agreed that he should never answer the telephone or a doorbell ring. To all intents and purposes he did not exist.

She'd cancelled whatever appointments she had, including one for dinner and a cinema with a man she'd long known but with whom her friendship was entirely platonic, or so she assured Goddy. Though he assumed he was not the only man in her life, in the three years he'd known her he had found no indication that there was anyone else.

They'd spent the afternoon and nights together, talking endlessly, listening to music and the news, watching TV and sometimes making love. An excellent cook, she had gone out of her way to make meals interesting. Even Goddy, hard as cold steel, had something of a conscience about her. She was, he realized, deeply involved emotionally whereas he, though fond of her and excited by her sensuality, was not. For him there was no emotional involvement. He was, he confessed to himself, unashamedly using her, exposing her to danger. As he had done Marion.

He and Helga had met three years earlier at a dinner party in the home of a Port Elizabeth industrialist, an ex-patriate German. She was forty and a widow of two years' standing. Though not beautiful, she had a pleasant, well-structured face, considerable personal charm and an attractive figure. They had liked each other immediately; she called it 'the correct chemistry'. Before long the relationship had become something more than friendship. It was scarcely an affair, because they saw little of each other, his business interests bringing him to Port Elizabeth only four or five times a year, usually for a few days at a time. He had never permitted letters, nor allowed her to phone him, though he phoned her at times. In whatever words the relationship might be described, its flame had burned brightly now for three years notwithstanding his insistence on the utmost discretion.

Overshadowed by his impending departure, their appetites had been poor and their conversation subdued at the evening meal that night. He'd declined the wine as he had the whisky and soda she offered him at sundown. It was imperative, he told her, that he should be clear-headed for what the night might bring.

While she took the things from the dining-room table, he consulted the AA Road Atlas she'd bought him and made indecipherable notes of time and distance. In case of hitches he'd allowed two nights for the journey, though he could have done it in one in the ten hours of darkness available.

46

Over the last few days he had worried about the Cape Town end, for what was happening there was beyond his control. *Southwind* should have left that afternoon. He wondered how far the ketch had got and what the weather was like? If it was bad they might not make the rendezvous on time.

Helga came back into the drawing-room

He glanced at his watch. 'I'd better pack now. Not that there's much to pack.'

'I'll help you, darling.'

They went up to the spare room together. While she sat in an armchair he changed into warm underwear, blue jeans, woollen jersey, denim jacket and the jogging shoes she'd bought the day before. He put his few spare clothes, the brown leather shoes and shaving gear in the carrier bag, the Walther pistol in the denim jacket. Downstairs she gave him the Thermos refilled with hot coffee, and the sandwich box. 'Brown bread and beef,' she said. 'Keep you strong, *Liebchen*. I've put the jerry cans in the Volkswagen's boot. They're full.'

'Thanks, Helga. That's great.' He smiled sadly. 'It's about time, I'm afraid.'

'Yes.' She faced him, standing close, looking up, her hands on his shoulders. '*Auf wiedersehen, Liebchen*.' Her eyes were misty with tears. 'Take care. I love you so much.'

He held her tightly, kissed her. 'Bye Helga. There's no way I can thank you enough.'

'Promise you'll write from Germany?' There was a break in her voice.

'I promise,' he said. 'Then we'll make plans.' He hoped the lie would help her.

She said, 'When did you say you expected to get to the Lesotho border?' He sensed her desire not to bring the moment to an end.

'Before daylight. I'll leave the car in the bush short of the border. Walk over the mountains.' It was important that she should believe he was going to Lesotho, though every mile of his journey would take him in the opposite direction.

'Don't come out to the car,' he said. 'And don't turn on the garage or gate lights.' He switched off the hall lights, took her in his arms, kissed her once more. 'Goodbye, Helga. Bless you.' He unlocked the door, opened it and went out.

'Oh, Goddy, take care, darling,' were the last words he heard as the door closed behind him.

Once in the Volkswagen he put the Walther pistol in the glove box, the AA Road Atlas on the parcel shelf, and started the engine. Pulling out of the garage he drove slowly down the drive. When he reached the road he switched on the lights. There was still a fair amount of traffic about, enough to make the Volkswagen inconspicuous as he travelled along the boundary of St George's Park and turned into Rink Street, heading for the Cape Road. It lead to the National Road which would take him down the coast.

Soon after entering Rink Street he passed a stationary traffic police car. In his rear-view mirror he saw it pull out and take station behind the Volkswagen. Pure chance, he thought, can't be following me, they'll be looking for CA not TJ number plates. To test his belief he turned right into Havelock Street. The police car followed. More coincidence he decided. He carried on for another two blocks before turning left again. The headlights of the car behind followed him round. He carried on, reached Russel Road, turned left and drove down the well-lit thoroughfare which led to the Cape Road. Ahead of him at a busy intersection a number of cars were waiting at the traffic lights. He joined them in the outer lane. The police car came up immediately behind him as the lights went green. It had made no effort to overtake but there was now little doubt in his mind that he was being tailed. Had he unwittingly committed some traffic offence? Or was it . . .? The red traffic light changed to green, the traffic moved forward and he went with it, increasing speed. A gap showed in the line of cars on his left. He spun the steering wheel left, accelerated and slipped into the gap. A car behind hooted its disapproval. Seconds later he did a sharp turn left into the next side street. As he turned he heard a siren begin to shrill. A quick glance in the driving mirror showed the police car trying vainly to cross the line of traffic on its left in an attempt to reach the street he'd taken; for the first time its blue rooflight was flashing.

Driving fast he made a series of left and right turns, doubling back on his tracks towards the city centre. Before long he'd reached the northern side of Port Elizabeth, close to the sea. He raced down Commercial Road and was soon on the trunk road to Uitenhage, an industrial town less than forty kilometres away. Once there he would turn south, join the National Road near van Staden's Pass and get back on the route down the coast.

The police would still be searching for him in Port Elizabeth. They now had the Volkswagen's number and would be passing it by radio to other police cars in the area. Shortly before Redhouse he left the main road and took the lower, less busy road to Uitenhage. It would be slower but safer. The urgent problem now was the Volkswagen's number plates. He looked at his watch – ten-fifteen.

A middle-aged woman dressed soberly in grey stood in the arrivals hall looking out through tall windows beyond which lay the tarmac and runways of Jan Smuts airport outside Johannesburg. It was the second time in a week that she had been there waiting for him, fearful on each occasion of the news he might bring.

Yet once again she consulted her watch. The evening flight from Cape Town, due at eight-fifteen, was running late. Twelve minutes overdue. Usually so punctual. Why was it late, she asked herself. Couldn't be anything serious or they'd have made an announcement by now. Wouldn't they? Probably had to wait for an important passenger in Cape Town, a cabinet minister perhaps. Whatever it was, it was just another worry to add to many others which chased through her mind. Otto always says I worry too much, she thought. I can't help that. It's me. Perhaps he isn't on the flight. Things may have gone wrong in Cape Town. How can I know? Oh God, please let everything have been all right.

Her thoughts were interrupted by a warning crackle on the loudspeaker, then the announcement, 'Flight SA 332 from Cape Town is now landing.' The disembodied voice conveyed neither relief nor anxiety, just a plain statement of fact.

She moved closer to the windows, stared out on to the tarmac where curiously shaped vehicles fussed round parked aircraft. She saw people looking towards the southern end of the airport, heard the distant sound of an approaching aeroplane. Soon the lights of the Boeing were flashing across the runway, its engines roaring in reverse thrust. It disappeared from sight behind a row of stationary aircraft and she waited for what seemed a long time before it taxied in and stopped not far from where she stood. Passengers began to come down the gangway. She watched them making for the entrance hall until she saw the tall upright figure, briefcase in one hand, newspaper in the other. He looked fit and confident as always, his walk brisk, wasting no time. She sighed with relief. Her husband was a calm, reassuring man; the sort she much needed just now. He'd been away for less than fifteen hours; it seemed like weeks.

He came into the hall, looked round at the waiting crowd. She waved. He smiled, came over and they embraced.

'Oh, Otto,' she said almost tearfully. 'I'm so glad you're back.'

'It's good to *be* back, Kate.' He squeezed her hand.

'Your hand's cold,' she complained.

'It's cold down there. Walking in. Shouldn't be surprised if there's frost tonight.'

He had no luggage to collect so they made for the car park. It was her car and they had their usual friendly argument about who should drive. As always he had his way. 'All right, you drive,' she said.

The car left the airport and joined the stream of traffic on the motorway into Johannesburg. They were silent as if mesmerized by the endless succession of lights flashing by. She knew he didn't like to talk when driving in traffic, particularly at night, but she had to ask the question uppermost in her mind. 'Everything all right, Otto?' In the darkness she gave him an anxious sideways glance.

'Yes. Tell you about it when we get home.' He patted her knee. 'Have to concentrate. Lots of traffic. Too many bright lights.'

So everything *was* all right. Well, thank God for that, she thought.

Thirty-five minutes later he turned the car into the entrance to their drive in Morningside. The gate lights were on but the gates, set in high walls, were locked. He hooted. An African guard came running down the drive with an Alsatian on a leash. He unlocked the gates, swung them open. The car passed through and the African shut and locked the gates behind it, then came to the car window.

Mr Bretsmar said, 'Hullo, Titus. Everything okay?'

'Yes, my baas. Okay.'

The Alsatian was barking a noisy welcome, leaping at the car windows. The African jerked at the leash. '*Tula*, Wolf King.'

Mr Bretsmar said, 'Thanks, Titus.' The car moved on up the drive, the African and the Alsatian following.

EIGHT

It was dark and though the rain had stopped the south-easter was still blowing. Since eleven o'clock Jan and André had done half-hour spells in the cockpit keeping a lookout to seaward, watching the mouth of the bay since it was the only direction from which Boesman's boat could come. Jan's half-hour was almost up when he heard the faint chug of a diesel above the noise of seas breaking on Oude Schip and Duiker Point, but there were no lights to be seen. Typical of Boesman, he thought. Torch in hand he waited, still not certain that the boat was entering the bay though it must have been close for the sound to have carried across the wind. Reassured as the noise of the engine grew stronger he flashed the torch several times. Answering flashes came almost at once. Before long the whites of a wheelhouse and gunwhale showed faintly in the darkness. Jan put fenders over *Southwind's* side. The fishing boat came slowly alongside.

'It's Boesman here, Master Jan,' called a familiar voice.

'Fine. I'll throw you a line.'

The line was passed, Jan made it fast and the two boats drew together. He could see the shadowy images of Boesman's crew – his two elder sons – moving about on the fishing boat's deck from which came the pungent smell of fish. André and the girl appeared from below. There was a warm exchange of greetings between Boesman and the Bretsmar brothers before he asked to be excused. He disappeared into the wheelhouse but was soon back.

'The charts and radio spares, Master Jan. The Ou Baas told me to give them to you. He couldn't wait in Hout Bay any longer. Told me you'd be in Maori Bay.'

Jan took the long tube and parcelled box. 'Thanks, Boesman. That's great. I told Dad that if we couldn't make Hout Bay by ten o'clock we'd anchor here. We were two hours late leaving Cape Town. Could have made it otherwise.'

'That's nothing. Don't worry. No trouble coming in here. Like old times,' he chuckled.

'Why no lights, Boesman?'

'Same reason you got no lights. They can think we're poachers if they see us here.'

'They'd be right about you most of the time, Boesman.'

The coloured man laughed, a high-pitched cackle. 'Me poach? No, sir.'

André said, 'Like to come below for a drink, Boesman? Or coffee. Can't see each other here.'

'No thanks, André. It's late, man. We got to be on the fishing grounds by daylight.'

The younger brother was Boesman's favourite. He'd not called him 'master' since the day, many years before, when André had threatened never to speak to him again if he did.

Jan said, 'Where you heading for, Boesman?'

'Draaipunt Reef. There's fish there. But you must know where to put down your lines.'

'Bet you do.'

'That's right, man.' The spluttering laugh suggested missing teeth.

'How's the family?' asked André. 'Danie got a job yet?'

'Fine, thanks. He's fixed up with the railways. Good pay too. I tell him always he must come fishing like his brothers. But he don't want that.'

'Remember me to him, Boesman.'

'Sure I will. Your Dad tells me *Southwind's* heading for Mossel Bay.'

'That's right,' said Jan. 'Then on to Port Elizabeth if we've time. Depends on the wind.'

'Should be good sailing now. Plenty of south-easter. Later it'll switch to nor-westers.'

'Right. Well, so long, Boesman. Thanks a helluva lot for your trouble, man.'

'That's okay. So long, Master Jan.'

The line was cast off, the fishing boat went astern, turned and headed for the mouth of the bay. When the throb of the diesel had faded *Southwind's* anchor was weighed, a foresail and mizzen set and the ketch made for the open sea; still without lights and with cabin screens drawn.

By two o'clock in the morning a broad reach to the south-west had taken them well off the land. Jan switched on the navigation lights. To round Cape Point, some twenty-five miles to the south-east, was going to involve a lot of windward sailing.

The south-easter was blowing hard and *Southwind*

pounded, lurched and sprayed as she beat into it. Pippa was seasick after leaving Maori Bay. Jan sent her below. It was no weather for a novice in the cockpit at night.

At four o'clock, satisfied with progress, he handed over to André, having drawn attention to the lights of nearby ships and the lighthouses ashore.

Before leaving the cockpit he took bearings of Cape Point and Slangkop lights. Down below he dried his hands and face, went to the chart-table, plotted the bearings and fixed the ketch's position. That done he poured himself a hot drink from a Thermos and ate some wholemeal biscuits. The girl was huddled in a sleeping bag in the starboard bunk, her back to the lee cloth, breathing deeply in her sleep.

He broke the seal and opened the chart tube which Boesman had brought off, took the single chart and the pictures from it and laid them in the bottom drawer of the chart-table beneath the stack of charts already there. Next he put the radio spares parcel in an overhead locker in the stern cabin. That done, he checked below decks fore and aft to see that all was secured. Only then did he go back to the cockpit.

The Bretsmar house, set on high ground facing north with commanding views across to the mountains of the Magaliesberg, deserved its name *Schoongesicht*. Not only was the view beautiful but so was the house, and though Mr Bretsmar's business activities had made possible its purchase, its considerable charm was due largely to Mrs Bretsmar; this the architects, interior decorators and landscape gardeners concerned would readily have conceded.

The splendid garden with its acres of lawn, flower beds, shrubberies, rockeries and ornamental trees, its tennis court, swimming pool and sauna, was entirely surrounded by a high wall. The house, the walls and the gates were protected by an electronic alarm system. *Schoongesicht* stamped Mr Bretsmar as a man of considerable means and his wife as a woman of unusually good taste.

The Bretsmars, however, like so many other people, had problems and it was these they were discussing in the privacy of his study not long after their arrival from the airport. He'd told his wife what had happened during his visit to Cape Town and the discussion had moved on.

Standing with his back to the fireplace in which logs crackled and burned, giving off a faint but pleasant smell of wood smoke, he said, 'Nobody knows what the next few years will bring. Any man who says he does is a fool. Look at Zimbabwe. Go back three or four years. How many Rhodesians thought there would be a black government there now with Mugabe as prime minister? Ian Smith said never in his lifetime. Many believed him.'

Mrs Bretsmar frowned. 'A lot of people think Mugabe is doing a good job.'

'Whatever he's doing he's a Marxist. At the moment he's being comparatively moderate because he wants a stable economy and for that he must keep the whites – at least for the time being. But already he's making plans for a one party system. In the end Zimbabwe will be a communist country. Mark my words.' Mr Bretsmar was a man of decided views.

Little clicking noises of disapproval came from his wife. She disliked political discussion because it involved facing unpleasant realities; above all she feared and resented what politics were doing to her family. If only everybody – and for her that meant the world at large – would mind their own business, keep their noses out of other peoples' affairs – and that for her meant South Africa – if they'd just let things be, all would be well. The Prime Minister and his government were doing their best to improve conditions for the non-whites. After all their wages were . . . her thoughts were interrupted by her husband's gruff challenge. 'You're not listening, Kate. Do you know what I've just said?'

'How uncertain the political situation is?' she suggested.

'I thought you weren't listening. No. What I said was that we must not only learn from the lessons of Zimbabwe but we must understand that there is a real threat of sanctions sooner or later if the Namibian problem is not settled on UN terms. And those terms are not likely to be acceptable to South Africa.'

'I'm sorry, Otto. I was worrying about our sons.'

Mr Bretsmar nodded. 'Don't think I don't worry about them, my dear.' He took a cigar from the silver box on the coffee table and a cigar-lighter from his pocket. 'As long as I can remember we've been kidding ourselves it can't happen in our time.' He worked industriously at the cigar. 'I certainly hope it doesn't. But there are certain things a man must do in case it does. Take precautions. Make provision. God helps those who help themselves.'

Mrs Bretsmar sighed, ran thin hands across a careworn face. 'I get sick with worry about the risks. My boys taking on a voyage like that . . . and . . .' She looked up quickly, lowered her voice, 'and the diamonds. I mean, I think that's terribly risky. You say the boys don't even know. I tell you, Otto, this is doing terrible things to me.'

He put down the cigar, moved over, sat beside her on the leather settee, a reassuring hand on her knee. 'Listen, Kate, I know how you feel but you exaggerate the dangers. It's no worse than any other long voyage for small craft. *Southwind* is a fine boat with first class gear. She did well in the last South Atlantic race. Jan is an excellent seaman. André has done a lot of offshore cruising.'

'The girl, Pippa. What does she know?'

'She'll learn. They'll teach her.'

'I wonder. But the other business, Otto. The diamonds, the pictures, maybe selling *Southwind* in Europe. That's playing with fire.' She shot him a frightened glance.

'Not at all. I wouldn't have taken the risk if I thought that.' He got up, lit the cigar and stood once more with his back to the fireplace. 'Only the Lutgartens know about the diamonds. And they're as involved as we are.'

'What did you tell Jan?'

'I told him that the syndicate's ore samples were in the radio spares box. It was one of several that came with the Marconi Falcon when we bought it; spares were in it then; it has the original labels and it's the right weight. I mean the weight of the diamonds is consistent with the radio spares. We've left nothing to chance, Kate. Simon Lutgarten will go on board in the yacht harbour in Antwerp to collect the box. It's a freeport for diamonds so there's no customs problem. Lutgarten's a man of standing, well known to the customs authorities. I told Jan that the syndicate didn't want the ore samples assayed here in case the big mining groups got word of our find and of the areas we have under option for mineral rights.'

'So Jan knows nothing of the diamonds?' Mrs Bretsmar sounded doubtful.

'I've told you many times, Kate. He does *not* know about them. He does, as I've said, know about the pictures – and he'll see to the sale or profitable employment of *Southwind* over there. André and Pippa don't know anything. Not even about the ore samples. As far as they're concerned the packages are radio spares and charts, nothing more or less.'

'What'll Jan do with the pictures?'

'Hand them to Simon Lutgarten. He'll see to their sale in Antwerp or Amsterdam. On a commission basis.'

She frowned, went on, determined not to let matters rest. 'What about Boesman?'

'All he knows is that he delivered the charts and radio spares to Jan for the trip up the coast. When I saw him this afternoon I said there'd been a slip-up. A delivery failure. So I'd had to pick them up from the chandlers after *Southwind* left Cape Town. I told him I had to catch the plane back to Johannesburg this evening. Asked him to hand the package to Jan when *Southwind* got to Hout Bay. Boesman said he'd be leaving there for the fishing grounds at about eleven tonight. I said that if *Southwind* couldn't make Hout Bay by ten o'clock Jan would be waiting for him in Maori Bay.

That's what Jan and I had agreed. Boesman will be on his way to Maori Bay tonight.'

'You didn't tell me.'

'How would it have helped?'

'I suppose you're right.' Mrs Bretsmar sighed, looked into the fire. 'But I don't like it. Using Boesman, I mean. Not that I like the other things either.'

Mr Bretsmar pointed his cigar at her. 'But that's the whole point. He's been close to the family for thirty years. Worked for us for twenty. I set him up in the fishing business. Lent him the money to buy the boat – on very favourable terms too. Jan and André are like sons to him. He couldn't be more trustworthy. And his sons are his crew. I'd trust him with my life. Anyway, why should he be suspicious?'

'I don't know. I just worry.' She shook her head, her forehead deeply creased. 'What if Boesman's caught . . .' She hesitated. 'You know what I mean.'

Mr Bretsmar took the cigar from his mouth, his eyes smiling. 'Better him than me.' His tone was jocular. 'No, I don't mean that. But seriously, Kate, why should he be caught? He's a Hout Bay fisherman. Normally puts to sea round midnight to reach the fishing grounds by daylight. He goes alongside *Southwind* in the dark and hands over the charts and radio spares. What's so strange about that?' He laughed again, less spontaneously this time. 'If anyone sees him, maybe he's handing over crayfish. It's after midnight. Dark. No moon.' He caressed the back of her neck with practiced fingers. 'Want to know something, Kate?'

'What's that?'

'Your husband didn't come down in the last shower of rain. I've spent hours planning this. Every detail. For example, the decision to use Boesman. If I'd tried to take the diamonds and pictures on board *Southwind* in Cape Town it would have meant going in through the dock gates under the eyes of the police and customs and immigration officials there. That would have been crazy. Much too risky. Look –

the main thing is we're getting André and the girl out of the country. If the Security Police catch up with that man Godeska it's tickets for André and Pippa and their anti-apartheid *boeties*. Then you'll really have something to worry about.'

'Oh my God, Otto. Don't say that.' She sat bolt upright, watching him with alert, frightened eyes. 'You don't think . . . I mean André's not *really* done anything bad? It's just young idealism isn't it? You know what these university kids are like.' She clutched his arm. 'Tell me, Otto. You don't think André has got badly involved? I mean he's such a gentle boy. He wouldn't do anything . . . you know what I mean, don't you?'

Bretsmar pursed his lips, blew smoke rings, watched them climb to the ceiling. He had no wish to add to his wife's burdens so he did not tell her all that he knew. Moving his head in a slow non-committal gesture he said, 'Who can say? Who knows what goes on in the minds of these young people? He's been close to Godeska. The important things is to get André out of the country before he *is* involved.'

'Well, I suppose I should be grateful for that. But Heaven knows where it will all end, when I'll next see my boys.' She took a tissue from her handbag, blew her nose and dabbed the corners of her eyes. Kate Bretsmar was a kind, God-fearing woman brought up on a Free State farm by Calvinist parents. She loved her sons and husband dearly, and with that instinct peculiar to her sex she sensed that her family was in greater danger than her husband would admit.

'What are they going to do for money over there?' she asked.

'That's been looked after, Kate. I've told Jan that there's twelve hundred pounds in sterling in an envelope in the same parcel as the radio spares box. Sixty £20 notes. When that's finished they can get more from Harry Morris in London – *if* they need it.'

'Poor kids,' she said. 'Fancy being forced to run away from their own lovely country.'

'That man Godeska has a lot on his conscience,' said Mr Bretsmar with unusual bitterness.

NINE

Goddy left the main road as he entered Uitenhage. Screened by darkness he drove through the south-western fringe of the town using minor roads and streets until he reached the main road to the coast. There he turned, crossed the bridge over the Swartkops and headed south.

Some distance down the road he saw a closed filling station, a large one with garage premises behind the lighted forecourt and a used car-lot. There was no-one about but in the space between the garage and the car-lot a brazier glowed; that meant a night watchman.

He drove on, turning right soon afterwards on to a farm road. A short distance along it he parked the Volkswagen behind thorn bushes. With the Walther pistol, pliers, a screw-driver and file in his pockets he left the car.

It was dark, the moon had not yet risen, and the night air was cold. The only sounds were those of cars passing on the main road and the croaking of frogs in a nearby stream.

The lights of the filling station showed faintly in the distance as he made his way across bush-covered veld towards the car-lot. When he got close he knelt, watching and waiting, his senses alert. The brazier was hidden but he thought it must be some thirty metres on his left. Inside the lot there were five rows of cars, about fifty in all. It was surrounded by a high wiremesh fence and lit dimly by a light on the garage wall. Driving past earlier he'd noticed that the entrance gates gave on to the main road. He'd little doubt they were locked.

Crawling towards the fence he took care not to snap dry twigs. On reaching the nearest corner he cut a hole, mesh by mesh, until it was large enough to crawl through. Once through it he went on, crouching, until he was near the centre of the lot, screened on all sides by cars. He selected a big sedan, in the dark ran his fingers across the registration letters on the rear number plate. OB – an Orange Free State car registered in Bloemfontein. Couldn't have been better for his purposes.

Working largely by feel, stopping at intervals to listen, he removed the number plates, put the tools back in his pockets and crawled towards the hole in the fence. Pushing the number plates through ahead of him, he lay at full length and began to wriggle after them. His head and shoulders were clear when he was blinded by a torch beam.

'*Wat maak jy?* – what are you doing?' It was a loud, rough challenge.

He knew from the voice that the threatening shape above him was an African. The man would be armed with an assegai and knobkerrie, standard equipment for night watchmen. The situation was hopeless, so hopeless that for a moment his mind numbed. But it soon cleared. *Southwind* would be waiting for him at Rooiels Bay within the next thirty-six hours. Only the African stood between him and freedom.

'All right, okay.' He spoke in a humble, subdued voice. 'You've got me.' He pushed the number plates towards the man's feet. 'Here, take them. They're no good to me now.'

The African said something but his words were drowned by the rattle of a passing truck.

As the torch beam switched momentarily to the number plates Goddy rolled on to his side and shot the African twice in the stomach at point blank range. The man sagged, groaning, then slumped forward.

Goddy dragged himself clear of the fence, dusted down his clothing, pocketed the Walther pistol and made off through the bush with the number plates. Half an hour later he had taken off the Volkswagen's plates and bolted on the stolen ones. He put the tools and old number plates in the boot, got into the car, backed it clear of the bushes and headed for the main road. Once there he turned right and made for the coast.

Somewhere in the distance the siren of a train sounded.

Driving towards the coast road he made a cool assessment of his situation. The killing of the night watchman had been regrettable but unavoidable; not too high a price to pay for freedom and completion of his mission. The two issues were inseparable.

When would the body be found? Certainly not before daylight, quite possibly later. It was already after midnight, the day just beginning was a Saturday, and the filling station would remain closed over the weekend.

If they did find the body at daylight, what then? Before dawn that morning he would have reached the Tsitsikamma Forest where he would hide the car and lie up throughout the day. Another point in his favour: once they found the body and the hole in the fence, it might well be some time before they discovered that number plates had been stolen from one of the fifty or so cars parked in the lot? Would they attribute the killing to that, and at what stage, if ever, would the police connect the stolen number plates with the Volkswagen which they'd pursued in Port Elizabeth? And if they did, on what evidence would they conclude that it was now heading for Cape Town via the coast road? From Uitenhage he could have gone in any direction – to Natal, the Eastern Cape, the Orange Free State, the Transvaal.

Cautious by nature and training, he did not exclude the possibility that the police might, sometime during the next thirty-six hours, broadcast details of the stolen number plates. But he believed the odds to be in his favour.

What really worried him was the licence disc on the windscreen for it no longer matched the number plates. If for any reason the police stopped him the situation would be dangerous.

After Humansdorp he left the National Road and took the upper road which led through Joubertina, Harlem and Avontuur. It would have far less traffic than the National Road and though it made the journey appreciably longer he had time to spare: six hours of darkness left and no more than 250 kilometres to go to the Tsitsikamma hide-out. His judgement proved correct. For the greater part of that night he seemed to have the road to himself. At long intervals a car or truck would pass, and on a few occasions one would overtake. It was then, seeing head-lights coming up behind, that his muscles would stiffen, his pulse rate quicken and his mind pose the inevitable question – was it a police car?

About three-thirty that morning he reached Avontuur, turned left and began the long descent by way of Prince Alfred's Pass, the winding mountain road which led down to the Tsitsikamma Forest and Knysna. An hour later, and still some twenty kilometres from Knysna, he turned the Volkswagen off the road into a forest fire-break and drove up it, stopping when he was some distance from the main road. Leaving the fire-break, he parked the car in a dense thicket. Though it was well hidden he left it before daylight to walk deeper into the forest. With him he took the Thermos, sandwiches, his pencil torch, battery shaver, the AA Road Atlas and the Walther pistol. There, in a secure hiding place and well out of sight of the Volkswagen, he spent the day. The gloom of the forest was relieved by occasional shafts of sunlight but it was cold and he wore the jersey Helga had bought him. A mountain stream trickled and babbled somewhere nearby but much as he would have liked to wash and freshen himself he did not leave the hide-out, for movement was dangerous. He slept for a few hours in the morning. At midday he had a modest meal of coffee and sandwiches. Eating them he thought of

Helga. What a wonderful help she'd been. If he'd led a different life she was the kind of woman he'd liked to have married.

After he'd eaten he cleaned the Walther pistol as best he could, took out the ammunition clip, pulled a handful of grass stalks through the barrel to loosen the powder and blew it out.

Some of the time he spent consulting the Road Atlas, planning with military precision the remaining stages of his journey. To reach Rooiels he still had some 500 kilometres to go. He was due at the rendezvous not later than five o'clock in the morning. To arrive earlier was acceptable, but he could not afford to be late. Driving at moderate speed and allowing a couple of hours for unforseen delays would entail a journey of about nine hours. With this in mind he decided to leave the hide-out at seven o'clock that night. Flanked by mountains, daylight went early in the forest and by six-thirty darkness was well established. Only then did he return to the Volkswagen and fill its tank from the jerry cans.

Daylight came at seven with no sign of the sky clearing. The rain had stopped but not the wind which blew with unremitting vigour as *Southwind* drove to the south-east, crashing into head seas, sluicing spray over the deck, the cockpit wet and miserably cold. Away to port the coastline showed dark and rugged against the rising sun.

Jan kept the ketch well offshore, the distance from the land opening steadily as the morning wore on. At noon they were seventeen miles SSW of Cape Point and he put her on a long beat to the south, shortening sail because they had time to spare.

In the afternoon Pippa came up, pale and timorous, looking smaller than she really was in the oversize oilskins André had given her.

'We'll be anchoring in sheltered water tonight,' he'd said,

when she put them on below. 'That'll help you. Takes a few days to get used to this.'

'I'm all right, André.' She was struggling to get the jacket over her head. 'Really I am. Ow! My hair. Just hope I'm not a nuisance.'

'Of course you're not.' He put an arm round her, hugged her affectionately. 'Don't worry. We're going to be glad to have you around. Cooking, and other things.'

She smiled at him. 'There're not going to be any other things, if you mean what I think you do.'

By two-thirty they were twenty-five miles south of Cape Point. Some time afterwards, having rounded it, course was altered to the north-east. This brought wind and sea on to the starboard beam. No longer pounding into head seas, *Southwind's* motion settled into a more comfortable rythm.

With mizzen and foresail set they were making five knots which was about what Jan wanted. But it didn't last; the wind slackened later and they saw two frigates far away to starboard, steaming in company several miles apart.

For some time Jan watched them through binoculars. 'Making for Simonstown,' he said. Two aircraft came in from the north-west, flying low over the water, heading for the frigates.

'Buccaneers, maritime reconnaisance.' He spoke with authority. 'Anti-submarine exercise, I reckon.' A lieutenant on the reserve, he'd done his national service in the South African Navy.

Before long the frigates had passed, one ahead, the other a few cables astern of *Southwind*.

André looked worried. 'Reckon they'll know who we are?'

'A signalman or some other bod on the bridge will probably have checked the name on our transom. Good thing too. Evidence that they sighted *Southwind* heading north-east – that's a fair enough course for Mossel Bay in this wind. Fits in with my entry in the yacht club register yesterday. I gave our ETA at Mossel Bay as Wednesday morning.'

A few minutes later they again heard the distant sound of jets, this time coming from seaward. It grew to a roar, then a high-pitched scream as the Buccaneers passed overhead in line astern.

'Great life,' said Jan. 'Long as no-one's throwing flak at you.'

After sunset they picked up the light at Cape Hangklip, the western extremity of False Bay, a bay so named because in earlier days mariners had mistaken it for Table Bay. Jan kept the ketch heading for the light until it was a few miles to the north-east. Then he altered to a northerly course and they ran with the wind on the starboard quarter, a good point of sailing and a comfortable one. Once they were in the lee of the land Pippa arrived in the cockpit to announce that she felt better.

'Good,' said Jan. 'Reckon you'll be able to cook?'

'Yes. Sure I will.'

'André'll give you a hand with the stove. It's a bit temperamental.'

'What'll I cook?'

'How about a nice stew and veg?'

'Yes but . . .' She hesitated.

'André will show you where everything is, how the tins are marked, etcetera. No problem.'

By seven o'clock *Southwind* was running parallel to the land, no more than a couple of miles off it. Her navigation lights had not been switched on. Later they passed Pringle Bay, rounded a promontory and reached the sheltered waters of Rooiels Bay where they anchored a few cables offshore. To avoid the sound of chain running the anchor was lowered, not dropped. There was no reason why a yacht should not anchor there for the night but Jan preferred not to advertise their presence.

It was mid-winter and there was little to be seen ashore save a light or two from cottages occupied out of season, and the headlights of cars moving along the coast road at long intervals.

Once again the portlight screens in the saloon were drawn and the companion hatch shut. With the cabin heater on, it was snug and warm. The men had got rid of their foul-weather gear and seaboots and were sitting round the table drinking beer and listening to the SABC news. They hadn't shaved, stubble was beginning to show on their faces and their hair was tousled. Pippa, in jeans and a T-shirt, had made a horsetail of hers and tied it with a blue ribbon. She appeared to have gone to some trouble to make herself spruce. While busy at the stove she joined in the conversation at times. When eventually she put the food on the table it was attacked ravenously. André poked his fork into the air between mouthfuls. 'It's great,' he mumbled.

'Don't speak with your mouth full, André. And keep your fork down,' she admonished.

'It's really good.' Jan looked up approvingly.

She helped herself and sat down. 'Anyone would think you two were hungry hyenas.'

André nodded. 'We are.'

'What d'you expect,' grumbled Jan. 'First proper meal for thirty-six hours.'

'Never thought I'd face food again.' Pippa wrinkled her nose. 'Must say, though, this tastes rather good.'

André gave her a proprietorial smile. 'Of course. You're a great cook.'

'Me, cook? Heating what comes out of tins?'

'Takes skill. Must be your biology and physics.'

Tinned apricots and cream followed the stew, then biscuits and cheese, after which she produced mugs of coffee.

Jan looked at the bulkhead clock. 'Nearly eight-thirty,' he said. 'Now listen. Drill for tonight. André and I will keep

67

one hour anchor watches until midnight. We must get what sleep we can between now and then. The sun rises at about seven. We've got to be out of here well before that. Say at a quarter to six. That gives us about five and a half hours after midnight in which to complete the job. Should be just about right.' He slid out from between the settee and the saloon table. 'I'll go up now for the first anchor watch. You two wash up, stow away, then get your heads down.'

'Aye, aye, sir.' Pippa saluted. 'Anything you say goes.'

'That's right,' said Jan. 'Remember it.'

'Fancies himself, doesn't he?' André gave his brother a dark but affectionate look.

TEN

By ten o'clock Goddy had passed Mossel Bay having driven down the Garden Route by way of Knysna, the Wilderness and George. The journey had been uneventful and Rooiels now lay some two hundred kilometres ahead. The traffic was as sparse as he'd expected on a Saturday night in winter, the filling stations were closed and the kilometres slid smoothly by. Reception on the car radio was poor and none of the odd patches of news he heard were in any way relevant to him. He put on a cassette – Beethoven's Fifth – and relaxed.

After by-passing Mossel Bay the road turned inland again. Later, near Albertinia, his headlights picked up a sign, *The Fisheries*, pointing down a side road which led to the sea. It made him think of Stefan. Dear old H for Hubert – what an oddly Victorian code name! Stefan would do what had to be done and do it well. Unless? – Goddy shied away from the thought that events might have caught up with Stefan.

It was getting on for eleven o'clock. Unless there were delays he'd be there in a few hours. Darkness wore on, the country towns slipped by, and once when he felt his attention wandering he stopped and drank coffee. After that, cold as it was, he drove with an open window.

Between Heidelberg and Riversdale he was almost involved in an accident with a car which pulled out suddenly from a side road just ahead of him. To avoid it he had to brake violently and swerve left, almost hitting the rocky wall of a cutting. As he corrected the swerve and brought the Volkswagen back on the road he heard the screech of tyres followed by a crash. The other car had hit the far side of the cutting. The last thing he could afford was involvement in an accident so he accelerated away. Fortunately there was no traffic in sight, his own car was unmarked and he doubted if anyone in the crashed car would still be conscious, if indeed alive. The incident had given him a bad scare. After it he drove with increasing vigilance.

In the early hours of morning, approaching Caledon, he pulled off the road, got out and relieved himself. He'd just got back into the Volkswagen when a car coming from the Caledon direction pulled up opposite. The driver came over. 'Good day, sir,' he said. 'I'm looking for the turn-off to Greyton. It's a small road, you understand. Not much used. We've got friends up there – farming friends. We should have reached them yesterday afternoon, but we had clutch trouble. Okay now, but it took time to fix. These country garages, you understand. I've got the wife and kids in the car. Tough on them. They had to sleep in it.' He stopped to clear his throat. 'Reckon I should have seen the sign for the turn-off to Greyton by now. Have you perhaps passed it?'

It was too dark to see the stranger's face but Goddy realized he was a talker, the sort who could go on for a long time. He hadn't seen the Greyton sign but it was important to get rid of the man as quickly as possible so he said, 'Yes. I passed it about five kilometres back.'

'Fine. Thanks a lot.' The stranger peered in through the open car window. 'Tell me, how d'you find the VW Golf? I hear that . . .'

Goddy released the clutch, the car moved forward almost taking the man's head with it. 'You can't miss it,' he shouted to the stranger. 'About five kilometres back.'

The Volkswagen's headlights picked up the advance sign for the Botrivier road junction – straight ahead to Cape Town, left to Hermanus and Kleinmond. Goddy breathed a sigh of relief. He'd be taking the Kleinmond road. Only another sixty kilometres to the rendezvous at Rooiels.

Just beyond the signboard his headlights lit on a uniformed figure standing next to a BMW motorcycle. Goddy's heart pounded – a provincial traffic officer! As he passed he had a momentary picture of the man staring at the Volkswagen. Shortly afterwards the rearview mirror showed a single headlight flash on. It pulled away from the roadside, came swiftly after him.

Obeying his first instinct Goddy accelerated. There was no doubt in his mind that this was pursuit. The Volkswagen gathered speed and so did his thought processes. The powerful BMW would soon overtake him. He decided in that instant not to turn into the Kleinmond road but to carry straight on for the Houwhoek Pass, the direct route to Cape Town. Less than a minute later the Volkswagen, doing rather more than 120 kph, was overtaken. With siren screaming and lights flashing the BMW drew alongside the driving window. An imperious, leather gauntleted hand signalled the Volkswagen to draw over to the side of the road. Goddy reduced speed, moved left and the traffic officer drew ahead. There was no other traffic in sight. Accelerating suddenly, Goddy drew level with the BMW and swerved into it, the Volkswagen's off-side front wing striking the big motorcycle a glancing blow. The BMW wobbled erratically, then somersaulted off the road, the body of the traffic officer cartwheeling ahead of it. Goddy went on for a short distance, stopped and turned. He drove back past the scene of the crash but didn't slow down. The BMW had finished up against the trunk of a tree. Some ten feet from it, and about the same distance from the road, lay the leather jacketed body of the traffic officer, a huddled heap with one leg bent back at a curious angle. His crash helmet, solitary and forlorn, lay at the side of the road.

Driving fast Goddy reached the Botrivier road junction and turned off for Kleinmond. He was sorry about what had happened. For the few seconds that the traffic officer had been riding ahead in the Volkswagen's lights he'd looked a decent enough young fellow. If he was as efficient as he looked, the last radio message to control would have reported that he was in pursuit of a grey Volkswagen Golf, registration OB so-and-so (Goddy had forgotten the numbers), heading for Houwhoek Pass. That could only mean the direct road to Cape Town. After that they wouldn't be looking for a Volkswagen on the Kleinmond road, the long diversionary loop which hugged the sea all the way round to Gordon's Bay.

A rhythmic, scraping noise came from the Volkswagen's offside front wheel. He assumed that the impact had buckled the wing, pushed it in on the wheel, but it hadn't affected the car's performance, so all was well. Lucky, he reflected, that the Volkswagen hadn't burst a tyre. That would have been awkward. He looked at his watch – three-twenty-seven. The timing was good. Couldn't really have been better.

With ten minutes to go to midnight Jan went below and switched on the saloon lights. They were both asleep; André on the settee and Pippa in the starboard bunk. 'Wakey, wakey,' he called. 'Show a leg.'

'Oh no.' Pippa sat up, rubbing her eyes. 'Surely not yet.'

André turned on his side, groaned. 'For God's sake. I've hardly had any kip.'

'Come on. Make it snappy. Rain's stopped. Very cold. You'll need warm gear and seaboots.' He stubbed a finger at his brother. 'You – André – inflate the dinghy and get it over the side. Then put the spare anchor and line in it.' He switched to Pippa. 'Up top for you, Pippa. Stand by the after hatch and I'll pass up the drums and other gear.'

Leaving them pulling on jerseys and seaboots and grumbling about his dictatorial manner, Jan went through to the stern cabin. His mood was buoyant. This was adventure, something real, a job worth doing.

They worked on deck without lights of any sort and that complicated things so that the preliminaries took longer than he'd expected. The rubber dinghy had been inflated, lowered into the sea and secured alongside with the spare anchor and anchor rope in its stern sheets. Strips of canvas had been laid to protect the decks where drums of paint, brushes, rollers and other gear stood ready for use.

'Remember,' Jan had warned when they were placing the drums. 'Green on the starboard side, beige on the port. For God's sake don't get them mixed.'

The preliminaries completed, they got on with laying out the stern anchor. Jan cast off the painter, André paddled the dinghy into the darkness astern and was soon lost to sight. Twenty fathoms of anchor rope had been coiled in the dinghy's stern, its inboard end made fast to the foot of the ketch's mizzenmast.

Before long André and the dinghy were back alongside. 'Okay,' he said. 'Stern anchor's down.'

Jan made fast the dinghy's painter and André climbed aboard. The anchor rope was hauled taut and when they felt the anchor hold, the rope's end was made fast inboard.

It was decided to start painting on the starboard side but before this could be done the ketch had to be heeled over to port. Main and mizzen booms and the spinnaker pole were made ready for turning out, guys were rigged and topping lifts shortened. Eight drums of diesel fuel were brought up on deck and stowed on the canvas strips.

'Helluva weight,' complained a breathless André when he'd hauled the last of them out of the hatch.

'Strong sod like you shouldn't complain,' said Jan. 'Ten gallons of diesel per drum. No more than fifty kilos each. Keeps you fit, man.'

'I can do without that sort of fitness.'

'You're going to need it. We've got to handle them a lot more yet.'

'Don't sound so effing cheerful. It's too early in the morning.'

'Right. Let's get on with it.'

They tackled the drums one by one, lifting and securing them by their handles to the extremities of the booms and spinnaker pole: four on the main boom, two on the spinnaker pole and two on the mizzen boom. The booms and poles were turned outboard and *Southwind* heeled to port as the weight of the drums began to exert leverage. When the angle of heel was sufficient the guys were made fast, the drums hanging just clear of the water. The ketch's starboard side was now high enough to enabled painting well below the normal waterline.

Jan and André got down into the dinghy and began painting from the bows aft. Pippa acted as general help, refilling paint buckets, passing brushes and rollers, tending the dinghy's painter and sternline, and providing mugs of coffee as the night wore on.

The work went steadily, the white hull slowly but surely turning to green. For the most part they worked in silence, speaking only occasionally and then in low tones. There were minor disasters – spilt paint, a brush or roller lost over the side, the dinghy listing too heavily at times when they forgot about weight distribution. Sometimes these incidents were treated with restrained hilarity, at others with annoyance and recrimination.

Using a quick-drying marine paint they finished the starboard side in less than two hours.

Then they had to go through the whole business of re-rigging the booms, spinnaker pole and drums on the starboard side. That done – with some difficulty and much exertion – they painted the port side. André had already unscrewed and removed the name-plate from the transom. When the transom had been repainted he screwed a new name-plate on it. *Southwind* had become *Sundance*, port of registration Hong Kong.

By four-thirty they'd finished painting, the last parts of the ketch to receive attention being the coachroofs and cockpit coaming. Formerly blue, all of these they'd painted beige.

'Now we clear up,' said Jan. 'Re-stow everything and get her shipshape.'

ELEVEN

During the drive from Botrivier to Kleinmond, Goddy's mood swung between elation and depression. Elation when he thought of the difficulties and dangers he'd overcome in executing his mission; depression when he realized that unless *Southwind* was waiting for him at Rooiels Bay he would be in considerably greater danger than he already was. The police were now fully alerted. The trail of disaster he'd left behind ensured what his fate would be if he were caught. In the Republic of South Africa the penalty for murder was hanging.

While he regretted the deaths for which he'd been responsible he did not think of them as murder. They were to him no more than casualties in an undeclared war — operational necessities to which he had been driven in order to complete his mission.

Absorbed in these thoughts he reached the bridge at Die Mond before realizing that he'd already passed the turn-off to the old camp site: the hide-out he'd used on that first night ten days ago. He thought of André and Pippa. Good to be seeing them again. Decent sincere young people. Absurdly idealistic of course but indispensable for his purposes, of which they knew nothing. He was not sure about Jan. He'd only met him a couple of times, but that had been enough to sense the mutual dislike. Jan, reflected Goddy, was one of those tough, thick-headed young South Africans who thought they knew all the answers because they had rich fathers. Still it was important to make the best of things. Somehow or other they would have to get on during the long voyage which lay ahead. *Southwind* was essential to his escape plans: without Jan there'd have been no *Southwind*.

Betty's Bay and Silversands passed in quick succession after which the road swung to the north. Here and there lights showed among the scatter of houses but there were no other signs of life for these were remote seaside resorts, it was mid-winter and close to four o'clock in the morning.

When Pringle Bay showed up, his excitement grew and he held the wheel more tightly. Not long now. Minutes later he'd crossed the causeway over the river mouth at Rooiels Bay. It was a cold dark night and the ketch would not, he knew, be showing lights but nevertheless he stared seawards. *Southwind* should be somewhere out there, hiding under the blanket of darkness.

After the causeway the road climbed, cutting into the mountainside, running along cliffs which dropped precipitously to the sea. He drove on for a few kilometres before reaching the lay-by he'd selected on the outward journey ten days earlier. He parked the Volkswagen facing the sea, took his bag from the boot and put it down beside the car. Back in the driving seat he started the engine, released the handbrake, engaged bottom gear, opened the driving door, released the clutch and jumped out as the car moved forward. It travelled about fifteen feet before plunging over the edge of the lay-by.

From far below him in the darkness there came a harsh banging and clattering. It ended suddenly and he realized that the car must have reached the cliff edge and become airborne. A few seconds later it hit the sea and the sound of the impact was amplified by the cliff face. The water there was deep. It could be weeks, perhaps months before an angler spotted it lying on the bottom.

It was almost half past four. It had been agreed that André would wait at the rendezvous from five to five-thirty. Goddy slung the strap of the carrier bag over his shoulder, for reassurance checked that the Walther pistol was in his pocket, and began the walk back towards the causeway. On two occasions he saw the distant headlights of cars moving along the coast road but long before they'd passed he had left the road and taken cover.

On board *Sundance*, alias *Southwind*, cleaning up and re-stowing after the painting took almost an hour. When it was finished they went down to the saloon. They had paint on their faces, hands and clothing and had to clean themselves as best they could with cotton waste dabbed in spirits. Jan suggested a celebratory tot of rum. He poured it, held up his mug. 'Phew. That was some job,' he said. 'Here's to the voyage of the *Sundance* and all who sail in her. May it be a successful one.' He swallowed the rum at a single gulp.

André and Pippa repeated the toast but Pippa, trying to emulate Jan, choked. 'It's fire-water,' she gasped, her eyes streaming. 'Only had it with Coke before.'

'Right.' Jan put his mug in the sink. 'That's it.' He looked at the clock over the chart-table. 'You'd better take the dinghy now, André, and pick up that guy – if he's there, which I doubt.'

'You wouldn't,' said André, 'if you knew him.'

'If he's not shown up by five-thirty you come back. Don't give him a minute more. Understand?'

'Yes.' André's eyes were sullen. 'Of course I do.'

The wind was freshening as Goddy crossed the causeway. He came to the beach, found the granite outcrop, and began

76

pacing off the distance. Before he'd finished a voice in the darkness called softly. 'Mind the water. It's very cold.' It was André's voice giving the coded challenge.

'In mid-winter, friend, this must be.' Goddy's slight but unmistakable accent lent a poetic quality to the coded reply.

They felt for each other, touched, shook hands warmly. André spoke in a whisper. 'Marvellous. I knew you'd make it, Goddy. How've things gone?'

'Not too bad.' Goddy's whisper exaggerated his hoarseness. 'At least I'm here.'

André took his arm. 'Come on. Not far to the dinghy.'

They moved towards the sound of wavelets lapping the beach. André stopped. 'Better take off your shoes. Roll up your pants.' He groped in the sand, found the dinghy's painter where it was staked clear of the water. They followed the painter down to the rubber dinghy, pushed it out and climbed on board; André put the paddles in the rowlocks and began rowing.

'Is she far out?' Goddy whispered.

'No. We'll soon be there. The wind's offshore, helping us along. Tell me, any problems?'

'Not really.'

'Where were you most of the time?'

'On a farm near Beaufort West.'

'Could you trust the people?' André's tone suggested surprise.

'Absolutely. There was only one person. Tell you about him later.'

For some time André rowed in silence. Occasionally he looked over his shoulder. 'Should be seeing the ketch any minute now.' He laughed. 'This inflatable can do eighteen knots when we ship the outboard. It's a Mercury 20. And here I am rowing my heart out.'

A low whistle came from their right.

'That's Jan,' said André. 'Must have heard us. We're too far left. Nearly overshot.' He stopped rowing, listened intently until he heard the faint *plop-plop* of water against a

77

hull. He rowed towards the sound. Quite soon the ketch loomed up in the darkness. They went alongside.

A voice whispered, 'Mind the wet paint.' It was Jan. He and Pippa helped them on board and the dinghy was hoisted.

'Oh, Goddy. How super to see you again.' There was a break in Pippa's voice. 'Isn't it marvellous? Everything's working according to plan.'

Goddy put an arm round her, kissed her. 'You're right, Pips. It is a miracle. Can't tell you what it's like to be here.'

'Pipe down for Christ's sake,' Jan whispered gruffly. 'Cut out the chat. Deflate the dinghy and stow it in the canister and shove the Mercury down below.'

There was an embarrassed silence. 'Get the anchor up, André,' he added. 'Time we got under way.'

Once clear of the bay, Jan put the ketch on a broad reach to the south-west. Anxious to open the distance from the land and clear the shipping lanes he held her on this course until daylight when he altered to W-by-S. Once again they were beating to windward, pounding into head seas, the cockpit wet, cold and miserable.

They were short of sleep, Goddy more so than the others, and tempers frayed as the morning wore on. By mid-morning Pippa had taken to her bunk again, troubled by seasickness. Not long afterwards the Pole succumbed. This pleased Jan. He had taken an instinctive dislike to the newcomer, the man who'd led André and Pippa astray. To Jan he was one of those dangerous communist agitators but for whom the Africans would have been happy with their lot. He realized, however, that he'd have to conceal his feelings. A long voyage lay ahead. Somehow he'd have to get on with the man.

The brothers were standing three hour watches and while André was in the cockpit for most of that forenoon, Jan spent his watch below charging batteries, pumping the bilge and removing the name *Southwind* wherever it appeared; as in the reference books in the rack over the chart-table, and in the logbook which he stowed away having put a new one in its place. This already contained a record of *Sundance's* voyage from Hong Kong to the noon position that day – a fictitious voyage meticulously compiled and logged by André over the last five days. The two horseshoe lifebuoys with *Southwind* painted on them had during the night been taken from their racks on the stern guardrail and stowed away below. Yellow and red lifebuoys, bearing the name *Sundance* had taken their place. The old *Southwind* nameplate from the transom had been stowed away under a mattress in the stern cabin. It might be needed later.

Jan took over from André soon after midday, having first fixed the ketch's position by radio bearings.

'She's on auto-steering,' André said. 'Course south-by-west.' He pointed to the row of instrument dials beneath the cockpit coaming. 'Logging just on six knots. Seems to like this rig.'

Jan looked at the wind burgee on the mainmast, checked the set of the sails with an experienced eye. 'Yes. You're right. Our noon position put us about twenty-five miles south of Cape Point. She's making good seven. Current's with us. Your pal Goddy's not going to be much use. He's out.'

André frowned. 'Give him a chance. He's had a helluva time. Can't be much fun being on the run like that. And he's had no sailing experience.'

'I don't think I like the guy.' Jan spoke with quiet conviction.

'You will when you get to know him. He's full of guts.'

For the twelfth time in a minute the bows pitched into a head sea throwing a sheet of spray over the cockpit, drenching their oilskins which shone wetly in the sunlight. André stretched and yawned. 'When are we altering to the west?'

'Right now,' said Jan. 'Before you go below. You can give me a hand.' He took the wheel, over-rode the auto-steering and with André's help eased the sheets and brought the ketch round to a westerly course leaving the wind on the port quarter. When *Sundance* was settled on the new course André did another noisy, arm-stretching yawn. 'Well, I'm off below. Can't wait to get some kip.'

'Okay. See you. Tell Pippa I wouldn't mind something to eat about two o'clock.'

'You must be joking. She's dead beat, Jan.'

'She'd better leave that bunk. Come up here for some fresh air. She won't get any better down below.'

André shook his head. 'Not just seasick. She's totally out. Worked like a mad thing last night.'

'So what?' said Jan. 'We all worked like blacks.'

'Do you have to say it that way?' André's irritation showed in his face and voice.

'Like what?'

'You know what I mean. Why *blacks*?'

Feeling weak and wretched, Goddy staggered back to his bunk from one of his many visits forward to the WC to vomit. Not that there was anything to bring up other than froth and mucus, for his stomach had long since emptied.

He'd clambered back into the bunk and adjusted the lee cloth as André came down to the saloon and switched on the radio. A man was speaking. Goddy realized it was the SABC news service but, sick and drowsy, he made no attempt to listen until somewhere in his consciousness what the unseen voice was saying began to register.

'. . . the dead traffic officer is presumed to have been a victim of a hit-and-run incident. It is some time since motor-cycles have been used for patrol duties by officers of the Provincial Traffic Department but recently several makes of machines have been undergoing tests with a view to their possible reintroduction. Traffic officer Marais was one of a number of men selected for these duties. He was riding a powerful BMW when he was killed. He leaves a widow and two young children . . .'

The newsreader switched to another item and Goddy lost interest.

So the man was dead. Not surprising after that impact. A vivid picture formed in his mind of the traffic officer's body cartwheeling through the air.

TWELVE

Towards evening the wind fell away and sail was taken in. Jan started the diesel and they continued to the west under power. It was important to get as far from the South African coast as possible. During the day they sighted a number of ships, mostly tankers and bulk carriers, almost all of them closer to the land than the ketch.

For some time the motion had been more comfortable and this brought Pippa to the cockpit where André was on watch.

'Feeling better?' he asked.

'I think so. The wind's gone, hasn't it?'

'Yes. Very cold still. Got on your warm gear?'

'Yes. It's super.'

It was a dark night, the clouds shutting out the stars. He could scarcely see her.

'How far are we now, André?'

'About thirty-five miles south-west of Cape Point. When Jan takes over at eight we'll alter to the north-west. Know what that means?'

'Not really. Been feeling too sick. The whole thing seems unreal. I can't believe it's actually happening.'

'It means "Europe here we come".' There was a boyish note of enthusiasm.

'How marvellous. D'you think we're safe now? It's difficult to believe after all the trauma.'

'I know what you mean. But it *has* actually happened. We've got away and Goddy's with us. By daylight we'll be well to the north-west.'

'Poor Goddy. He looks so tired.' She paused. 'What will the authorities think when *Southwind* doesn't arrive in Mossel Bay?'

'Simply that she's failed to arrive, I suppose. Lost at sea.'

The shape in the darkness sitting near him sighed deeply. 'What's the trouble?' he asked her.

'If the Security Police catch up with Stefan they're bound to find out we were involved.'

'It'll be too late for them then.'

'Yes. But they'll – well you know. They'll make him talk.'

'So what?'

'They'll know we never intended to take *Southwind* to Mossel Bay. That we've cleared off in her.'

The only sounds then in the cold night were the slap of water against the bow and the throb of the diesel.

At last he broke the embarrassment of their silence. 'How will that help them? The sea's a big place. We could have gone to Mozambique or Angola or the Seychelles or South America or the West Indies, almost anywhere. They can't do anything about that. There are lots of places where we couldn't be extradited for a political offence.'

'Awful for your parents, André. They'll think you and Jan have drowned at sea.'

André hadn't told her all he knew. It wasn't that he lacked confidence in her but it was important for his father's sake that she shouldn't know too much. 'Anyway, what about *your* father?' he countered. 'He doesn't even know you're on board *Southwind*. What's he going to think when he hears you've disappeared? *And* your step-ma?'

'I don't think he'll be too surprised. He knows my political philosophy. Calls me an anti-apartheid nut-case. Often lectures me on the subject. Linda, too. They'll think

I've cleared off to Botswana or Lesotho. Something like that. Of course Dad'll worry, but not for long. He's too besotted with Linda. They'll know I'm okay when we get to England.'

The silence of private thought was broken by Pippa. 'Doesn't Goddy look awful? As if he'd seen a ghost.'

'He must be exhausted.'

'Says he'll tell us what happened when he's caught up on sleep.'

'Seen anything, André?' Jan's voice came from the companion hatch where his head and shoulders were silhouetted against the faint light from below.

'Three tankers early on in the watch. We're too far to the west now. Shore lights all gone. Had a good sleep?'

'Not bad.' Jan yawned noisily. 'Nearly two hours. You okay, Pippa?'

'Yes. Much better, thanks.'

'There's stew and veg on the stove. Like to come and sample it?'

'Oh super, Jan. I should have done that, not you.'

'Glass is falling. What's the weather look like up there, André?'

'Still overcast. Light breeze from the west.'

'Good. I've been listening to Cape Town's bulletin. Forecast nor-westerly, force six to seven, with rain. Join you in a few minutes. When I've had some grub. We'll put up sail then.'

While they spoke Pippa was thinking how different they were. André tense, thoughtful, the academic drawn by his social conscience to do things out of character for a man so gentle and considerate. Jan the antithesis – rugged, arrogant, conservative to a degree, supporting apartheid on the grounds that it was the only workable system for a South Africa whose problems were unique and whose principal critics had themselves practised apartheid in the colonial era. Its dismantling, he'd said, would lead to despotic systems, Soviet orientated. Under his new masters the black man would be worse off than before.

To Pippa his views were absurd but typical, she thought, of the myopic society in which he'd grown up. 'His mind is a strait-jacket,' André had once explained. 'He can't begin to understand the moral issues involved. I doubt if he knows what a moral issue is.' It was sad, she thought, that an otherwise decent man could be so blind to injustice and suffering. But she realized that but for Jan they couldn't have got away in *Southwind*, so she forgave him much.

The night was cold, dark and wet, the wind bringing rain from the north-west, when Stefan Carralin left his flat in Claremont and drove out via Mowbray to the N2 freeway. By nine-thirty he was on the freeway, heading for Sir Lowry's Pass.

A conscientious man, anxious always to perform well, he had rested during the afternoon. Later that evening he'd eaten a light meal and listened afterwards to a Debussy prelude. These precautions had, he felt, prepared him psychologically for the mission to be accomplished in the long night ahead.

Near midnight he pulled into a lay-by, stretched his legs, lit a cigarette, drank hot coffee from a Thermos and emptied the car's ashtray. Ten minutes later he was back on the road. It was not long before the Capri had passed Swellendam, close on 250 kilometres from Cape Town.

For the fourth time that night he reached the letter H:

Heyman's law: The principle, with respect to visual stimuli, that the threshold value of a visual stimulus is increased in proportion to an inhibiting stimulus simultaneously operating.*

It was his custom during a long journey to occupy his mind by reciting psychological definitions, one for each letter of the alphabet. Having got to Z he would begin again at A. The recitation was done in an undertone, slowly and methodically, usually interrupted only by spasms of coughing. They were not infrequent for he was a chain-smoker.

* The psychological definitions quoted on pages 84, 86 and 87 are taken from James Driver's *A Dictionary of Psychology* published by Penguin.

In these early hours of morning there was little traffic and the kilometres slipped smoothly by, the Capri rolling on through the night, its engine purring contentedly, never extended by the moderate speed at which he drove. Heidelberg and Riversdale were passed, then, near Albertinia, the rain came again, blustering sheets of it, and he put the windscreen wipers on 'fast'. Soon afterwards he saw the sign he was looking for, *The Fisheries*. Turning right he followed the side road down to the sea. When he reached the coast he swung east, following the shore line towards Mossel Bay. Half an hour later he pulled off the road on a deserted stretch near Ystervarkpunt.

It was blowing hard but the rain had stopped. With jerry cans from the boot he topped up the Capri's tank. In a corner of the boot there was a black leather box. From it he took a Marconi marine radiophone and extended the aerial. He switch on the transmitter, checked the frequency setting and signal strength. 'MAYDAY – MAYDAY – MAYDAY,' he called into the mike. 'Ketch *Southwind*, position twenty-five miles sou-sou-west of Bull Point. Have struck floating wreckage and am sinking, repeat sinking. Weather bad. Require immediate . . .' He lowered his voice, mumbled a few unintelligible syllables and switched off.

Almost at once the harbour radio station at Mossel Bay and two tankers acknowledged. Mossel Bay, having promised immediate assistance, asked, 'How many persons aboard *Southwind*, and what life-saving equipment have you?'

Stefan switched off the receiver, returned the set to its leather box and put it in the boot. Back in the car he opened a new packet of cigarettes, took one out and lit it. A spasm of coughing followed. It subsided and he wiped his eyes, switched on the engine, reversed the Capri and began the return journey to Cape Town. He was back on the National Road near Albertinia by a quarter to four. He should, he reflected, reach his flat in Claremont before nine o'clock that morning.

The first signs of daylight came as he passed Caledon and faint though the light was his spirits lifted. He'd been driving since nine o'clock on the previous night – ten solid hours broken only by the coffee stop on the outward journey and the fifteen minutes near Ystervarkpunt. He stubbed out a cigarette.

Next letter? K – K, fifth time round.

Kalotropic: relating or referring to the influence of an individual's own aesthetic tastes on the context of his imagery.

Kalotropic. Nice word. To what extent, he wondered, had Goddy's aesthetic tastes influenced the context of his imagery? Come to think of it, he knew little of Goddy's aesthetic tastes. The Pole was a very private person. One knew little about him or what was going on in his mind other than his determination to fight apartheid. He recalled their discussion at Swartklip that first night when the Pole had been on the run.

'You commit the MAYDAY to memory, Stefan. It's simple enough. Not a word to be recorded, understand? The only variation will be the state of the weather. Good, bad, whatever it may be. Short and simple. Got that? Patrick will lend you the VHF set. He'll ask no questions.' Patrick was the code name of a salesman in an electronics firm in Cape Town. Stefan had met him on several occasions.

'You send the MAYDAY at 0300 on Thursday, fourth of July – Independence Day,' Goddy added with a chuckle. 'You'll see a sign, *The Fisheries*, near the Albertinia turn-off. Go down that road, turn left when you reach the sea. Pick a suitable spot near Ystervarkpunt, say forty to forty-five kilometres from Mossel Bay. Transmit the MAYDAY on the international distress frequency – 2182 kiloHertz. Patrick will show you the setting. Okay?'

Stefan had said yes, there were no problems. Then he'd asked Goddy if he was going to Mozambique.

'Yes,' Goddy had said very quietly. 'To Maputo. But forget I ever told you.'

'Sorry. Shouldn't have asked.'

'That MAYDAY's vital, Stefan. Lives may depend on it.'

And so they had parted without Goddy giving any indication of how he proposed to get to Mozambique. But Stefan had his own ideas. Sometime back André Bretsmar had told him that he and his brother were taking *Southwind* to Mossel Bay during the winter vac. André and Pippa were Goddy's cell mates so they were now at risk. With Goddy on board – he'd probably joined the ketch at night somewhere on the coast near Port Elizabeth – they'd be making for Maputo, the nearest port in Mozambique. Once there they'd be sure of sanctuary and safe passage to Europe. The ketch would already be well up the coast, several days ahead of the MAYDAY position. The sea rescue service, lifeboats and helicopters, would be searching for her in the position given. They'd find nothing, recall that the MAYDAY signal had petered out and conclude that *Southwind* had sunk. Clever idea, Goddy. Really clever.

Early morning continued dark and wet under scudding clouds, and headlights were still necessary. Before long the Capri had done the long climb up the Houwhoek Pass and on past the Grabow turn-off. When the summit of the Hottentots Holland mountains was reached he pulled off the road, drank some coffee and lit a cigarette. He was very tired.

He started the engine, got back on to the National Road and began the descent by way of Sir Lowry's Pass. Though close to eight o'clock it was still dark and wet and cars coming from the Cape Town side were using their lights.

Back to A – sixth time round. *Asthenic: used of depressive feelings or emotions, or of a type of human physique with small trunk and long limbs, claimed by Kretschmer to be associated with schizoid characteristics.*

Kretschmer, German – much the same as Bretsmar.

André, he recalled, had said that his family was Swiss by origin; his grandfather had come to South Africa as a boy.

The road ahead began a long looping turn to the left. The Capril took the turn and the rain came in swathes, hissing, pounding the car roof, obscuring the windscreen. He put the wipers on 'fast', concentrated on the white line which marked the verge. Bright lights came sweeping round the bend towards him. Christ! Why didn't the bastard dim? He flicked the Capri's lights on to bright and a spasm of coughing assailed him. Spitting out the cigarette he gripped the wheel, staring, trying to see ahead through tear-filled eyes and the curtain of rain. His last recollection was of bright lights high above him, frighteningly close.

THIRTEEN

The panelled office of the Chief of Security Police in Pretoria was as large, impressive and intimidating as the man who occupied it. Though wearing civilian clothes the gaunt muscular figure behind the African mahogany desk held the rank of a lieutenant-general in the South African Police. The grey eyes, set deep in a lined face, were cold and penetrating.

Four men faced him across the desk: Badenhorst, his deputy, Muller from the Cape Western Division, Engelbrecht from the Ministry of Foreign Affairs, and Henning from Intelligence. The discussion which was taking place was conducted in Afrikaans.

'Right,' said the gaunt man, 'Let's have your latest summary, Muller.'

Muller, sombre, balding, sad eyes behind steel-rimmed glasses, consulted his notes. 'I regret to say, General, that we still have not found Godeska or the Volkswagen. We know from the radio report made by Traffic Officer Marais shortly before he was killed that he was pursuing a grey

Volkswagen Golf – one with a rear bumper heavily dented on the left hand side.' He looked up through his glasses at the General. 'Its OB registration numbers were identical with those on the plates stolen from the used car-lot outside Uitenhage.'

'Do we positively know that Godeska was in the Volkswagen?'

'The available evidence suggests that he was, General.' Muller adjusted his glasses with a bony forefinger before returning to his notes. 'The traffic officer driving the car which pursued the grey Volkswagen Golf in Port Elizabeth – '

'And lost him,' interrupted the General abruptly.

'Yes, unfortunately so.' Muller nodded concurrence. 'The traffic officer reported that the Volkswagen's rear bumper was heavily dented on the left hand side. As you know the description of the vehicle which we circulated immediately after Godeska's evasion of arrest in Cape Town drew particular attention to the dented bumper. We assumed, correctly it seems, that Godeska might have changed his number plates in order to get away.'

The General's head went up and down in a slow movement of acquiescence. 'The TJ plates that the Volkswagen was using during the chase in Port Elizabeth? Have you checked that registration number, Badenhorst?'

The dark, sleek man nodded. 'Yes, General. It belongs to a house surgeon in the Johannesburg General Hospital. We have checked his movements. For the last three weeks he has been attending a medical seminar in San Francisco. He is still there. We have cleared him completely. The number plates used by the Volkswagen must have been made illicitly. Probably in Cape Town.'

'That is opinion not evidence,' said the General. 'They could have been made anywhere. You say the evidence suggests Godeska was in the car. What evidence?'

'Circumstantial evidence, sir. A man in a grey VW Golf matching the description of Godeska's car is chased in Port

Elizabeth; he is using false number plates. A couple of days later a grey VW Golf which matches the wanted car is chased near Botrivier. It is using the same registration numbers as those stolen from the used car-lot near Uitenhage. The man is desperate. He killed a night watchman to get those plates. About thirty hours later he runs down and kills the traffic officer near Botrivier. In my opinion . . .'

The General held up a hand. 'I accept your conclusion. We must presume the driver was Godeska. Having got as far as Port Elizabeth, why was he returning to Cape Town?'

'He *may* have assumed,' Henning spoke with his customary caution, 'that the safest thing to do was the most unlikely. That was to return to the place from which he was escaping. If, as we suspected originally, he was making for Maputo his plans must have been badly upset by the police chase in Port Elizabeth. He knew then that his car had been identified. So he reverses direction, steals new number plates, and heads for Cape Town.'

The General leant back in the swivel chair, looked with narrowed eyes at each of the men opposite him. 'I accept the likelihood of your proposition, Henning. But until we find Godeska or his car I cannot accept its certainty. My view that he would make for Mozambique or Botswana still holds. We must not relax our surveillance. Every possible escape route must be watched. Control in the Cape Town docks is to be tightened up. If Godeska was in that Volkswagen he's probably in the Cape Town area now. He may try to get on board a ship bound for Maputo or Luanda. Gangway control on any ships scheduled to sail to either of those ports must be rigid.' He looked round the table again. 'Anything more to report, gentlemen?'

The fair-haired, blue-eyed man from the Ministry of Foreign Affairs who had not so far spoken, put down the cheroot he had just taken from his pocket. 'My Minister is greatly concerned, General, that there has been this delay in finding Godeska. As you know, the Prime Minister himself attaches the greatest importance to preventing him from leaving the country. We know he is in possession of material which is highly dangerous to the security of the Republic. That fact alone justifies taking every conceivable step necessary to apprehend him.'

The General's mouth twitched in a manner which his deputy knew indicated irritation. 'Every conceivable step is already being taken, Engelbrecht. I am well aware that the apprehension of Godeska takes precedence over all other matters we have in hand at present. We are acting accordingly. If it is humanly possible we shall get him. I can assure you of that. You will please convey what I have said to your Minister.'

Engelbrecht tidied his moustache with a forefinger. 'I will do that, General.'

Badenhorst said, 'One more point, General. The media. Do we release anything yet?'

'Nothing as from us.' The General was emphatic. 'It must not be known that the Security Branch is interested in the killing of the night watchman or the traffic officer. The district commandants concerned have already been instructed to inform the Press that these are routine matters under investigation by their CIDs. One a case of murder, the other a hit-and-run incident.'

Engelbrecht stopped in the act of lighting the cheroot. 'Might it not help if the public were told more? That Godeska is the wanted man, for example?'

The General looked up from the notepad on which he was fashioning an abstract design with a gold ballpoint. 'The only person who that would help would be Godeska. It is important – vital – that he should not know what we know at this time.' His penetrating stare caused Englebrecht to look away.

Henning, slight, courteous, myopic, nodded approval. 'I would very much like to support that view, General.'

There were no more questions and the General declared the meeting closed. Badenhorst collected the briefing sheets from Muller, Henning and Engelbrecht and was about to pick up the General's copy. 'Leave it.' The General waved him away. 'I'll put it in my safe.'

During *Sundance's* first night at sea after rounding the Cape the weather steadily deteriorated. With the ketch on auto-steering Jan and André had spent most of the afternoon securing things on deck and below and generally making ready for the bad weather which seemed likely with a falling barometer and the wind veering westerly. Among other precautions they made sure that storm sails were easily accessible, that all movable gear on deck was lashed down, and that Thermos flasks were filled with hot soup and coffee. That they had done so was just as well for by midnight it was blowing hard from the north-west, the seas growing large and angry.

This posed problems for Jan. Anxious to get away from the Cape as quickly as possible, he was confronted with windward sailing in worsening weather. He decided against sailing close to the wind because it would mean unacceptably slow progress. So he put the ketch four points off the wind and began a long beat to the west with double reefed main and mizzen and a small headsail. With this rig *Sundance* was logging four to five knots.

But it was miserably uncomfortable, the ketch plunging and pounding into head seas, the bows flinging icy water over the deck, drenching the cockpit. Goddy and Pippa, suffering severely from seasickness, had long since given up and gone below. Jan and André were now the only effective members of the crew.

Although the Bretsmar brothers were working in three hour watches, Jan had spent most of the night in the cockpit. André had protested that this was not necessary, but Jan had insisted. In fact, though he did not admit it, he was in his element. Heavy weather sailing with its taste of danger was for him one of the more exciting challenges of ocean cruising. And he was aware, too, that he had considerably more experience than his brother and was a lot stronger.

Throughout the night *Sundance* was held on long beats to windward, steering a westerly course on the starboard tack and a northerly one on the port. Twice in the early hours of morning increasingly bad weather made sail changing necessary and in that wind and sea it was hard and hazardous work. When daylight came with leaden skies and foam-streaked seas, the ketch was making slow progress under storm jib and close reefed mizzen. In Jan's judgement it was all the sail she could safely carry in that weather. They were not in a race and he was anxious not to strain *Sundance* or make life too difficult for those on board.

The gale had blown itself out by dawn on the third day, ending as suddenly as it had begun. The barometer rose, the wind backed round to the south then fell away several hours before blowing steadily from the south-east.

'The south-east Trades,' declared André exultantly.

'About bloody time,' said Jan.

With the wind astern, main and mizzen set and a big blue and white genoa pulling hard, *Sundance* was bowling along at between seven and eight knots. Jan and André shed their foul-weather gear and looked out on the new day with grateful but weary eyes.

The pounding and crashing had ceased and the ketch's motion now was largely a comfortable surfing on the crests of small but helpful following seas. A pale and wan Pippa came on deck to announce that she felt better.

'Water seems to have got in everywhere,' she said. 'Everything's soaking below.'

'It always does in a gale.' Jan was unsympathetic. 'As soon as we've had some breakfast we'll get stuck in and clear up below. Get everything we can up here and let the sun do its stuff.' He didn't add that he and André had at intervals throughout the gale gone below and pumped the bilge while Goddy and Pippa were fast asleep in their bunks, held there by lee cloths the brothers had rigged. Despite the pumping, water had continued to find its way in through small leaks and a faulty gland where the mainmast passed through the coachroof. That was something Jan planned to tackle during the coming day. In order to get away from the Cape earlier than intended, the ketch's refit had been postponed, and she wasn't as tight as she could be.

'Where's Goddy?' he demanded.

'Still in his bunk. He's been taking Valium for the last few days.' She brushed tresses of hair from her eyes. 'I think he's drugged himself into deep sleep.'

Jan frowned. 'Get him back on deck, André. This is not a bloody passenger ship. He'll get over it up here. He won't in his bunk.'

André went down the companion hatch and before long came up with a bedraggled, somewhat dazed Goddy who slumped into a corner of the cockpit and gazed helplessly at the sea.

André said. 'I'll go below and do a cook-up.'

'More likely a cock-up.' Jan grinned cheerfully at his brother. 'What's it going to be?'

'Sausages, onions, bacon and bread and jam – the last of the bread incidentally – and coffee. Any complaints?'

'Sounds great.'

A groan came from Goddy and he turned his head at that moment to vomit over the cockpit coaming.

'Not on the deck for God's sake,' implored Jan. 'Get him a bucket, someone. Clean up the mess.'

Red-eyed, white-faced and miserable, Goddy sank back into his corner. Pippa brought the bucket and André, looking anything but pleased, sluiced down the Pole's offering with seawater. When he'd finished he put the bucket between Goddy's feet. 'Use that next time,' he said.

The men had stubble beards and everyone including Pippa had a crushed, unwashed look. Jan had had little sleep during the gale and signs of fatigue showed clearly in his drawn face and bloodshot eyes.

Wisps of cirrus cloud looking like pulled-out cotton wool stretched across a blue sky and the morning sun shone down warmly on *Sundance* causing white patches of salt to form on her decks and coachroof.

After breakfast Jan was on deck, checking running gear and carrying out urgent repairs. Goddy, having declined food with a hoarse moan, had sunk back into his cockpit corner, crumpled and lifeless. André and Pippa had begun cleaning out and clearing up down below. For a start André pumped the bilge while Pippa mopped as best she could with bucket and rags. During the gale sea water from the bilge had washed about below as the ketch plunged and rolled, and a lot of it had got into lockers and splashed up and saturated bedding. Later Pippa went up top, wedged herself in the companion hatch, and took from André the bedding, clothing and other gear he passed up for drying. These included their canvas carrier bags. He failed, however, to warn her that the zipped top of Goddy's bag was open and when she threw it forward on to the coachroof it up-ended, some of its contents spilling out. Among them were Goddy's automatic pistol and his brown leather shoes, both of which slid off the coachroof on to the narrow strip of deck alongside it. Until then the Pole had been inanimate, apparently unaware of what was going on around him. This incident, however, brought him to life. For a moment he frowned incredulously at what had happened, tried to get up, slipped and shouted. 'My shoes, my shoes! For God's sake, Pippa.' His shout, his demeanour, everything about him, seemed strangely irrational as he clutched the cockpit coaming and gazed desperately to where his possessions lay on deck. Pippa retrieved the shoes and pistol, and passed them back to him. He grabbed the shoes, put the automatic in a pocket and fell back into the cockpit. 'My God,' he said. 'My shoes nearly

95

went. They're sopping wet. What on earth's happened to them?'

Jan said, 'Like everything else below they got wet. W.E.T.,' he spelt it out. 'That's what water does. They'll dry out. No need to go beserk.' Goddy's strange outburst had done nothing to improve his image with Jan. But whatever else the incident might have done, it proved to be the turning point for the Pole's seasickness. Hugging the shoes to his chest, he staggered towards the hatchway, turned and made his way slowly down the ladder.

André looked at Pippa with inquiring eyes. 'What was all that about?'

Pippa said, 'The poor guy's been dreadfully sick. He's full of Valium. Not himself. Those are new shoes. The only ones he's got apart from his joggers. So he was upset. Thought they'd gone over the side. Try to understand.'

'I thought you said he was full of guts.' Jan looked at André reproachfully. 'He behaved like a bloody kid.'

The incident became known to all but Goddy as *The Great Shoe Drama*.

For the rest of the day the coachroofs fore and aft, most of the deck and much of the cockpit, were festooned with bedding, clothing and sails laid out to dry.

FOURTEEN

The General unlocked the office safe and took from it Badenhorst's briefing sheet for the meeting with Muller, Engelbrecht and Henning held on June 27, a week after the raid on Godeska's flat. Though familiar with its contents he began to read it again, slowly and with intense concentration. It was, of course, in Afrikaans.

Ernst Stanislaw Godeska

The following information concerning the above has been obtained from Security Branch Investigations, West German Intelligence (BND), Bonn, and the Secret Intelligence Service (SIS), Whitehall.

1. Godeska entered the Republic of South Africa in February 1979 on a passport issued by the West German Government. He was born in Britain in June 1944, the son of a Polish father, Ernst Jozef Godeska, born in Cracow, Poland, and a German mother, Paula Hoffman, born in Frankfurt, West Germany, in 1923, but educated in England. Godeska's father, serving in the Polish wing of the RAF, was killed in action in November 1943. Godeska received primary and secondary education in Britain.

His mother appears to have left Britain with her son in 1958, having informed friends that she was returning to Germany where her sole surviving relative, a sister, was living in Frankfurt. It has been ascertained that this sister died in 1963.

2. There is no record of Paula and Stanislaw Godeska's re-entry into Germany in 1958 but it is known that she died in Munich in 1962. Her son, Ernst Stanislaw Godeska, was a student at the Munich Polytechnic during the period 1961–1963, where he studied electronics. In 1972, at the age of twenty-eight, he joined Adgarf of Dusseldorf, a firm of scientific instrument makers. In his application for employment with Adgarf he stated that he had worked in the electronics business in the USA and the Argentine during the period 1964–1971, and produced suitable references. This period of his life is still under investigation. He made good progress at Adgarf and in 1979 was appointed as their sales representative in the Republic with headquarters in Cape Town. The creden-

tials supplied by his employers at the time of his entry into the Republic were satisfactory.

3. (*Note: To protect our informant in what follows she is identified hereunder as Mrs X and her employers as the Blank Company Ltd*)

On June 20 last Mrs X called at Security Police Headquarters, Cape Town, and said she wished to see a senior officer about a security matter. She was interviewed by Major Muller. She told him she wished to make a voluntary statement about something which was troubling her conscience, but she would only do so on condition that her name would at no stage be revealed and that she was fully protected in every way. These assurances were given.

4. In brief her statement was as follows:

In November of the previous year she had met Stanislaw Godeska on holiday in Plettenberg Bay. They were staying at the same hotel. She had been married for several years but her husband, called abroad unexpectedly on business, was not able to accompany her as intended. During the three weeks in Plettenberg Bay she had established a relationship with Godeska which was in her words 'one of those silly, lightning, holiday affairs', and they had discussed with each other the work they did. After that holiday Godeska appeared to have dropped out of her life but on June 16 he phoned to say he wished to discuss something important with her. Since she liked him and was not averse to a private meeting she agreed. He picked her up after work that evening and they drove up to Signal Hill where they parked. He then said he had not only wanted to see her again for old times sake but because he wished to ask a favour. He was apparently charming and considerate and she was pleased to be in his company again.

5. The favour, he explained, concerned a business matter. He wanted a microfilm copy of an important document which he had to send to his principals in Dusseldorf. It was highly confidential, a tender for a Government defence

contract, and because of its nature Adgarf had requested that it be sent on microfilm. He said the firm operated a microfiling system in Dusseldorf but the Cape Town office was still too small to justify one. He knew from their conversations in Plettenberg Bay that she was in charge of microfiling at the Blank Company, so it was no surprise to her when he said, 'If I can come to the office after hours and use your equipment I can do the job myself.'

Since she liked Godeska and the request seemed a reasonable one she had agreed that he should come to her office on the following day.

After that they exchanged news of developments since their last meeting and discussed in light vein the Plettenberg Bay holiday. At about six-thirty that evening he drove her back into town and dropped her at the railway station.

6. Next day, as arranged, he arrived after hours at the offices of the Blank Company. Having met him downstairs she took him to the microfilm service room where she worked. There she showed him the equipment, a 3M 1050 Processor Camera with its reader, and demonstrated their use. He remarked that the equipment was much the same as Dusseldorf's and added that he'd have no problems, so she told him to get on with it.

He had produced an envelope from his briefcase and taken from it a document. 'Only three pages,' he'd said, unfolding it in such a way that she could see the top page. Glancing at it briefly she'd seen the printed heading *Adgarf (South Africa) Ltd*, and the words TENDER DOCUMENT printed beneath it. She was not able to read the text and headings which filled the page but they had the usual characteristics of a tender document. She'd moved to her desk and left him at the processor camera desk.

7. A few minutes later she asked how he was getting on and he said he'd nearly finished. She saw him remove a microfiche from the camera and noticed that in doing so his elbow dislodged one of the sheets of paper immediately to

the right of the camera bed. There had been a stack of Blank Company documents there awaiting filming and she'd presumed it was one of these. While he was at the reader she picked up the dropped sheet, satisfied herself that it was one of his and put it back, typed face down, on the stack beside the camera bed. He had looked up then and remarked sharply, 'What are you doing?'

She replied, 'You knocked a page off the desk. I put it back.' She realized it would be unwise to let him know what she had seen, so she smiled and asked if the fiche was okay.

8. He had looked at her in a curious, worried way and said, 'Yes. I think everything's okay.' He then picked up the three sheets of the document he'd filmed, stapled them together and put them back in his briefcase. At that stage he turned and faced her. 'If ever you mention this incident' – his expression had been unusually severe – 'you'll compel me to do something unpleasant.'

Frightened by the way he looked and what he'd said she asked what he meant. He meant, he explained, that she must never mention that he'd been there, or that there'd been any microfilming of any document.

She replied, 'Of course I won't. Why should I? It could only do me harm. The company wouldn't like it, nor would my husband.'

At that he'd said, 'You're right. If you ever did talk about it all sorts of unpleasant things might come out.' He'd hesitated before adding. 'Like our fun with the Polaroid and tapes.'

Upset by this she'd said, 'You told me you'd destroyed those at the time.'

He laughed. 'Of course I destroyed them. I was only joking. But I am serious when I say you must *in your own interests* treat all this as absolutely confidential.'

She promised that she would and again pointed out that it was in her best interests to do so. He then thanked her for the help which she'd given him and they parted on good terms.

9. During the journey home she thought over what had happened and became increasingly worried. In her brief glimpse of the page she'd picked up she'd seen it was a high quality photocopy with the words MOST SECRET printed in bold type above the Republic's coat-of-arms, beneath which was the printed heading MINISTRY OF FOREIGN AFFAIRS. Below that, typed in capitals, there'd been a four line heading which, to the best of her recollection, referred to discussions between the US Secretary for Defence and South Africa's Minister of Foreign Affairs about United States action in the event of a Soviet military presence in the Namibia–Angola area.

When asked how much time she'd had to read what she'd seen she said it had fallen typed side up. She'd looked at it while stooping to pick it up, again while coming upright, and then for a few moments afterwards. She demonstrated this action to Major Muller who timed it and found that it took six to seven seconds. This was in his opinion a sufficient period in which to record visually what she said she had seen.

10. Unable to confide in her husband who was of a jealous disposition, she had kept the problem to herself for two days, after which it had become too much of a burden. So she had gone to the Security Branch on June 20.

11. Major Muller at once reported these facts to the Chief of Security Police, Pretoria, who then contacted the Ministry of Foreign Affairs giving details of the document alleged to have been seen by Mrs X. Mr Engelbrecht, who handled the matter at the Ministry, had reported back shortly afterwards to the effect that the document in question was still in the files in the confidential registry, but he conceded that what Mrs X had seen appeared to have been a copy of the document in question. He pointed out that there were also copies in the offices of the Prime Minister, the Chief of the Defence Force and the US Secretary for Defence in Washington.

12. The Chief of Security Police then contacted these

authorities and it was established that their copies were still in the files. After discussions with the Prime Minister, the Minister of Foreign Affairs and the Chief of the Defence Force, the Chief of Security Police had given orders that Godeska should be arrested that night and his flat and offices searched. The Security Police had gone to the flat at 10 p.m. to find that he was not there. While awaiting his return they searched the flat but found nothing incriminating other than the pencilled note referred to below, and a West German passport made out in the name of Willi Helmut Braun. The photo in it was of Godeska.

The pencilled note found on the floor under the bed had probably been blown there by a draught. It had been scribbled hastily on a page torn from a loose-leaf notebook. Dated the 15th of June it read: *Called last night but you were out. I'm away for the next few days but feel you should see this as soon as possible. It arrived through the post this morning, plain envelope, Pretoria postmark, otherwise anonymous. If released to overseas media at appropriate time could have big impact. What do you think?*
Yours H
The identity of H has not yet been established.

13. The passport in the name of Willi Helmut Braun, purported to have been issued in Mannheim three years previously, contained exit and entry stampings for various countries in Western Europe, an entry stamp made at Cape Town on the date upon which Godeska entered the Republic in 1979, and thereafter several exit and entry stamps for neighbouring African countries covering the period 1979 to 1981. Details of this passport were communicated to West German Intelligence who replied that though it bore the same number as a passport issued to Willi Helmut Braun in Mannheim in February 1968 it was clearly a forgery. The Willi Helmut Braun to whom it had been issued had been killed in a motor accident near Frankfurt in October 1968.

14. During the search of Godeska's offices in Cape Town, carried out while his flat was being searched, his safe was forced and in it was found an air ticket to Dusseldorf for July 15, and a West German passport in the name of Ernst Stanislaw Godeska issued in Dusseldorf in November 1978. West German Intelligence has confirmed that this is a valid document. The photograph of Godeska it contains is identical with that in the Willi Helmut Braun passport.

15. A summary of the information contained in this briefing has been sent to the CIA in Langley, Virginia, and to the SIS Whitehall, together with the photo of Godeska which appeared on the forged passport.

(Copy of photo annexed hereto)

These authorities have been asked to assist in identifying Godeska who is probably a secret intelligence operative of an Eastern European power. In the meantime every effort is being made to prevent his escape from the Republic. Investigations into his background and activities in Cape Town continue.

Signed J. J. Badenhorst

June 26 1981   Deputy-Director

The General put down the briefing sheet, massaged his eyelids with bony fingers and looked at the picture on the wall facing him.

'Cunning bastard,' he muttered. It wasn't the picture on the wall he was seeing but Godeska's bearded face staring at him from the passport photo. And there's another one like that about, thought the General; the traitor who sent the photocopy to H. In an envelope with a Pretoria postmark. The departments concerned had been instructed to supply confidentially the names of any members of their staff suspected of harbouring anti-apartheid sympathies. There would be a thorough sifting out there and God help the guilty party if he were found, for no-one else would.

Who was H? A scribbled note on a sheet of paper from a

ringbound notebook? Students used ringbound notebooks. Somebody at the University of Cape Town? Muller's men would have to look into that.

FIFTEEN

At noon on the fifth day at sea – it happened also to be the fifth day of July – *Sundance's* position was 31° 10′ S: 11° 00′ E, approximately 440 nautical miles north-west of Cape Town. Jan was moderately pleased. He'd expected the gale to slow the ketch even more. That it hadn't was due to the favourable current.

The weather continued fine, the south-east Trades blowing steadily as *Sundance* surfed and dipped through azure seas, the waves dappled with white horses. The temperature had risen and though there was a chill in the air the sun beat down from an almost cloudless sky to warm the deck and raise the spirits of the crew – and to dry Goddy's shoes.

Now over his bout of seasickness the Pole was a different man, cheerful and eager to help. Aware of his concern about the new shoes Pippa had said, 'Give them to me, Goddy. I'll put them in cellophane bags and tie the ends. You can stow them on the top shelf of my locker in the after cabin. André says it's always dry there.'

Goddy frowned, hesitated, then smiled. 'Yes, please. That's very good of you, Pippa.' Later, apologizing to the others for the fuss he'd made, he said. 'Sorry I got so neurotic. I wasn't myself, you know. They're new shoes. About the only decent things I've got left. I thought they were going over the side.'

'You didn't seem too worried about the Walther pistol.' Jan watched him quizzically.

'I wasn't. Couldn't have cared less about it.'

'Why did you bring it?'

'It was in my gear when I ditched the Volkswagen. Like most South Africans I carry a firearm when driving long distances.'

Jan smiled. 'Fair enough.'

Since the gale Jan and André had continued to share the watches. With the ketch on auto-steering there was no need for anyone at the wheel during the day when they tackled the endless round of tasks inseparable from ocean voyaging: checking and repairing running gear, pumping the bilge, charging batteries – for this they used the Villiers two-stroke – drying out and repairing sails, fixing the ketch's position with sun and star sights and writing up the deck log.

Pippa had taken on the job of ship's cook, subject to André's insistence that she learn the rudiments of sailing; these he promised to teach her as the voyage progressed. Sleeping arrangements had been settled: Pippa was now installed in the after cabin with its own shower and loo – referred to in the yacht builder's glossy brochure as 'the owner's suite' – Jan had the navigator's bunk at the after end of the saloon, Goddy the saloon's starboard bunk while André had settled for the forward cabin which was also a sail locker.

Early that afternoon they had an unexpected visit when a distant rumble from astern grew rapidly into the thundering of jet engines and an aircraft appeared in the southern sky. Heading for the ketch it grew steadily larger.

'Get below right away.' Jan shouted at Goddy and Pippa who were on the coachroof near the mainmast. 'Make it snappy. There's a plane coming up from astern.'

They clambered aft and dropped down through the companion hatchway. Shortly afterwards the aircraft passed overhead.

'SAAF Buccaneer,' said Jan to André. 'Maritime reconnaisance. All we need. If they're bored they'll want to chat.

Hoist the Union Jack on the mizzen cross-trees.' He went down to the saloon, switched on the VHF radio telephone. Almost immediately a deep voice came through the speaker. 'Calling yacht below. Calling yacht below. Do you read me? Over.'

Jan pressed the speak-switch on the R/T handset. 'Yes. Loud and clear. Over.'

'What is your name? Where are you from and where bound?'

'*Sundance* from Hong Kong, bound Plymouth.' A good mimic, Jan affected a stylized English accent. He also took the precaution of jiggling the speak-switch and turning down the volume as he spoke.

'Roger,' came the airborne voice. 'But please repeat. Your signals are dodgy. Over.'

'Sorry. We've been in a gale,' replied Jan. 'Probably got water in the transmitter.' He continued to fiddle with the speak-switch and volume control. 'Yacht *Sundance* from Hong Kong, bound Plymouth. Do you read me now?'

'Not very well. I get *Sundance* from Hong Kong. Is that right? Over.'

'Dead right,' said Jan.

'Okay. Best of luck. Roger and out,' was the Buccaneer's last signal.

'Thank God for that.' Jan switched off, turned to Pippa and Goddy who'd been watching anxiously. 'Okay. I think they're happy. But don't come up for a while. I'll tell you when.'

Back in the cockpit he told André what had happened. The Buccaneer, still several miles away, was making a long sweep from west to south when the engine note changed and it went into a shallow dive. Moments later it flattened out, came racing towards them from astern flying low over the water.

Jan said, 'They'll be checking the name on the transom. Probably photographing it.' The Buccaneer roared over them, went into a steep climbing turn, waggled its wings, and flew off to the east.

It had soon disappeared.

Before dark a genoa was hoisted in place of the spinnaker they'd rigged during the forenoon. Jan felt the latter was too big and unhandy a sail to risk with auto-steering at night.

After supper in the saloon that night Pippa, André and Goddy were chatting over mugs of coffee.

'That was a great meal,' said André.

Goddy agreed. 'Absolutely brilliant.'

'Good recipe.' Pippa bowed. 'Heat one tin of stew and onions, one tin of new potatoes, *and serve*. Open one tin of apricots and one of cream, do not heat *but serve*.'

'No end to what higher education can do.' André took his mug over to the sink.

'Hey,' it was Goddy. 'It's five to eight. We *must* listen to SABC news tonight, André.'

'Good idea. Haven't heard one since the night after we rounded the Cape.' André came back to the table. 'That was some days ago.'

Goddy looked away. 'I was laid out then.' His tone was casual. 'You too, Pippa. Was there anything relevant – to us I mean?'

André yawned. 'Not a word.'

'Might be something tonight.' Goddy examined his fingernails. 'Stefan should have sent the MAYDAY yesterday.'

'Yes. Of course. It was the fourth, wasn't it? I'd almost forgotten.'

So they called Jan, switched on the radio and tuned in to the Cape Town service. While they waited Goddy was thinking about what the news might contain. He had that day given André and Pippa a brief account of his time on the run. How, driving through the night, he'd got to a farm some distance from Beaufort West and spent the days there in hiding, going for walks in the evening with his friend – a recluse living on five hundred morgen, whose sole activity was the cultivation of vegetables for his own consumption. The journey back to Rooiels Bay after leaving the farm had, explained Goddy, given no real trouble. The engine had packed up once, round about midnight, and after a lengthy check-up in the dark he'd at last found the trouble – a loose battery terminal. The rest of the journey he'd described as uneventful but for two incidents: the one an accident, a big truck fallen across the road with police on the scene directing traffic – that, he admitted, had been scary. The other, a talkative stranger who'd lost his way and was difficult to shake off. And of course the drama of ditching the Volkswagen, a story which lost nothing in the telling. While giving this largely fictitious account of his adventures two pictures had persisted in his mind: one of the African night watchman sagging to his knees, the other of the traffic officer cartwheeling through the air ahead of the BMW.

His thoughts were interrupted by the 'pips' of the time signal from Cape Town. The item they were waiting for came at the end of the news:

The search continues for the crew of the yacht South-wind, *reported sinking in bad weather yesterday morning twenty-five miles south-east of Mossel Bay. The weather is deteriorating and hopes of finding survivors are beginning to fade.*

'Well done, Stefan.' Pippa's eyes shone as she touched back strands of hair from her eyes.

'Anything one gives Stefan to do he does well.' There was smugness in the Pole's voice.

André said, 'Does he know we're bound for Europe?'

'No, definitely not. Thinks we're making for Maputo. Really believes that. Useful if he's interrogated.' Goddy's teeth showed in a humourless smile.

'Interrogated?' Pippa shrilled. 'Why should he be?'

'The Security Police may catch up with him. He's at risk. Like all of us.'

Jan went to the companion ladder, looked back at them. 'Don't include me in that "all of us". I'm not one of your lot, thank God. Another thing – I might as well mention it now – I don't want politics talked while I'm around. You people believe in one man one vote, I don't. The blacks have got numbers, time, world opinion, history – the bloody lot – on their side. It's up to the whites to look after themselves.'

Pippa laughed derisively. 'Having said politics are not to be talked about, you've just delivered a political dissertation. I certainly don't want to talk politics with you, Jan. Our views are a million miles apart. It would be a waste of time.'

Goddy held up a restraining hand. 'Although Jan doesn't feel as we do, he's put himself at risk to help us. That's a pretty decent thing to do, isn't it? He's entitled to his views as we are to ours.' He hesitated, managed a patronizing smile. 'Even if they are a little naive.'

Jan came back to the saloon table, looked at Goddy with undisguised contempt. 'You'd better watch your step. I don't take cheek from people like you even if you are fifteen years my senior. I'm a South African. What are you? Pole, German – Christ knows what? Go back to your own country if you don't like the South African set-up. You won't be missed.'

Pippa banged the table with both fists. 'Oh, for God's sake stop this stupid childish haranguing. We're going to be together for weeks, maybe months. Let's try and behave like civilized human beings.'

The next week went by without any untoward incident, the pattern of the days much alike, *Sundance* continuing to make steady progress towards the Equator. The day's runs were in the 100–125 mile range, the south-east Trades blowing at force four for most of the time. The warmer weather and following seas under blue, cloud-scattered skies made life on board relaxed and comfortable. At times there were rain storms and when they came water from the sails was collected in buckets hung on the main and mizzen booms. Under André's tutelage Pippa and Goddy were learning something about sailing, and as each day passed they became increasingly useful members of the crew.

The diet of tinned food was supplemented at times by fish caught with trolling lines, but this was infrequent. Though

André and Pippa had brought a fairly selective batch of paperbacks not much reading was done, sleeping and sunbathing enjoying higher priorities. Other than water, the only drinks on board were beer and Coke and these Jan rationed carefully; as indeed he did the food stores and fresh water.

Since their row the relationship between Jan and Goddy had been one of uneasy neutrality. For the most part they avoided talking to each other and this reduced the chances of friction. Other relationships were more harmonious. Goddy, André and Pippa continued to get on well. They would discuss politics when Jan was not present, speculate endlessly about the future in general, and in particular about what would happen when they reached Europe. Jan was in many ways the odd man out, though the bond between him and his brother was strong.

SIXTEEN

A week after their first meeting those concerned met again in the office of the Chief of Security Police in Pretoria: sitting opposite the General were, as before, his deputy Badenhorst, Muller of the Cape Western Division, and Engelbrecht from the Ministry of Foreign Affairs. On this occasion Henning of Intelligence was not present. Muller was summarizing developments since they'd last met. 'Carralin,' he said, 'is still in a deep coma. It is impossible at present to question him.'

'Do you have a man in his room at Groote Schuur?'

'Outside his room, General. The hospital authorities don't like us in the intensive care unit.'

Engelbrecht shuffled his papers. 'May I ask why there was this delay of four days before Carralin became a suspect?'

The General frowned, looked to his right. 'Please explain that Muller.'

'Carralin's accident was dealt with by local police. The garage which salvaged his car did not hand over the jerry cans and Marconi radio telephone until yesterday – four days after the accident. The police became suspicious then and referred the matter to us. I flew up from Cape Town first thing this morning.'

'Why didn't the local police check the contents of the boot at the time?' The General seemed engrossed in the design he was fashioning with his gold ballpoint.

'The car rolled off the road after the collision, General. The boot was badly crushed. It couldn't be opened at the time. That was done later by the garage.' Muller looked down at his notes. 'Once the matter had been referred to us it took most of the day to complete preliminary investigations into Carralin's background. We learnt at the University that he was a post-graduate studying clinical psychology. He is the only son of a widow who lives in Salisbury. He was known to hold strong views on apartheid but there is no evidence that he was an activist. At least not in a big way. Spoke at campus meetings, that sort of thing. The usual pseudo-intellectual claptrap. Later he appears to have dropped out. We found nothing of importance in his bed-sitter other than a snapshot taken on the beach at St James. It was of Godeska with a girl we have since identified as Philippa Brown – known at UCT as Pippa. We tried to find her but she'd left her room in Rondebosch some days before. We searched the room of course. No evidence of any significance. Her father and step-mother live in Durban. They had not heard from her for a couple of weeks; said that was not unusual. Otherwise nothing beyond a statement by a UCT lecturer who said he'd seen Carralin, Godeska and André Bretsmar together on several occasions. Godeska used to visit the University in connection with the sale and maintenance of scientific equipment. Bretsmar was a student reading politics and philosophy.'

'That's where the trouble starts.' The General shook his head. 'Know anything more about him?'

'We searched his room. A few letters from Pippa, his girl-friend. Nothing incriminating. He was known to be anti-apartheid. But that's not unusual among undergraduates. It's a disease these days.'

'I was a bit of a rebel myself at that age. But anti-British, not anti-apartheid.' The General all but smiled. 'That was more natural.'

Muller said, 'Quite so, General.'

'What were your assumptions on the evidence you then had?'

Muller poked at the bridge of his steel-rimmed spectacles with a bony finger. 'We know Carralin was in his flat at eight-thirty the night before the accident. At what time he left it, or where he'd gone, the caretaker couldn't say – nor had he any other information on that point. There was no luggage in the boot, but the two empty jerry cans suggested the possibility of a long journey. More suspicious was the Marconi marine radio telephone. Using it, Carralin could have communicated with a vessel at sea. Godeska's car was last seen on Houwhoek Pass by the traffic officer pursuing it. Godeska and the car had disappeared. On those facts I assumed – or shall I rather say suspected – that Godeska was in the car with Carralin *before* the latter's accident; that the Marconi radio telephone was used to communicate with a vessel at sea, possibly a Soviet submarine.' Muller looked up to see what effect his words were having.

'So?' The General watched him with narrowed eyes.

'I assumed then that the vessel at sea had subsequently taken Godeska on board, after which Carralin must have begun his return journey to Cape Town.'

'And the girl, Philippa Brown?'

'She was possibly with them.'

The General left the desk, began pacing the room. The deep frown of concentration told Badenhorst that his chief's brain was working with the precision of a computer, rejecting or accepting a series of hypotheses fed in at high speed. 'What was the frequency setting on the Marconi R/T?' The General shot the question at the men sitting round the desk.

Muller blinked, looked embarrassed. 'I'm afraid I don't know, General. The set is in our office in Cape Town.'

The General stopped pacing, his mouth set in a hard line. 'Well find out – NOW!' He barked the words, pointed to the telephones on his desk. 'Use the red one. They'll put you through at once. To any person at any place at any time.'

The others watched the unfolding drama with mixed feelings: sympathy for Muller, interest in what his inquiry might reveal, speculation as to what lay behind the General's question. The answer was not long in coming. Muller put the question to his deputy in Cape Town, received the answer and turned to the General. The setting was 2182 kiloHertz,' he said.

'Ask the Navy if that frequency would be used to communicate with a Soviet submarine?'

Muller picked up the red phone again. After a brief conversation he put it down. 'They say most unlikely. It is the international distress frequency.'

The General sat down, rested his elbows on the desk, made pyramids with his fingers, his eyes apparently focused on some distant object. 'We know from Muller's report that Godeska, André Bretsmar and the girl Pippa were well known to each other. We know also that the yacht *Southwind* sent out a MAYDAY in the early hours of the fourth of July – stating that she was sinking thirty-five miles south-east of Mossel Bay – that the crew consisted of two young brothers, Jan and André Bretsmar – that despite a long sea and air search there was no trace of the yacht or her crew.' He paused, tapped his fingertips together. Quite suddenly, he leant forward, 'You know why, gentlemen? Because the yacht *Southwind* did not sink near Mossel Bay. She left Cape Town on the twenty-eighth of June with the Bretsmar brothers on board and probably the girl. Today is the ninth of July. MAYDAY is the international distress call. 2182 kiloHertz is the international distress frequency. Carralin sent that signal some hours before the accident on Sir Lowry's Pass. *Southwind* must have passed Mossel Bay several days before the MAYDAY. She has been on passage now for ten days.' He turned to Badenhorst. 'Ask the Navy how long it would take a ketch of the *Southwind* class to sail from Cape Town to Maputo in Mozambique — assuming that it left Cape Town on the twenty-eighth of June.'

Badenhorst picked up the red phone. The General got up, went to a window, looked down on the street. Muller touched Engelbrecht's arm. 'Fantastic brain,' he whispered, looking admiringly at the tall figure.

Badenhorst returned the phone to its cradle. 'They'll check the weather conditions and currents along that route over the days concerned, General. Then phone us back.'

They did — fifteen minutes later. After a short exchange Badenhorst replaced the phone. 'Under sails only, they reckon anything from twelve to fifteen days. If the auxiliary engine was used the journey could take from seven to nine days. They have allowed for the adverse effect of the Agulhas and Mozambique currents. Not possible, they say, to be more precise than that.'

'H'm. Not very helpful.' The General's cold grey eyes fixed on Badenhorst. 'If the yacht has not yet reached Maputo the Air Force and Navy have got to stop her.' He picked up the red telephone: 'Get me the Chief of the Defence Force — at once.' Still holding the handset, he addressed Badenhorst. 'Get on to our agents in Maputo immediately. Explain the latest development. If *Southwind* has already arrived they must try to find Godeska. If she hasn't they are to keep a sharp lookout for her arrival.'

'And if they find Godeska?'

The General smiled briefly. 'They'll know what to do.'

By dawn on July 15 *Sundance* had passed the latitude of St Helena, and that of Ascension five days later. Jan had kept the ketch well to the west of both islands. To have gone within sighting distance might have invited communication, something he was anxious to avoid. For the same reason he had kept the Marconi Falcon radio transmitter locked to ensure that it was not used.

Since the gale off Cape Town sailing conditions had been almost perfect. Day after day they ran before the south-east Trades, the wind blowing a steady force four to five, the ketch lifting to the following seas, then surging forward before settling gently as they passed, like an elegant woman lowering herself on to a settee. As *Sundance* drove north the sun shone with increasing vigour and the bodies of her crew, leaner and fitter now, had tanned to a deep brown. The men's beards and hair had grown, but Pippa cut her's short because she had found the long tresses hot and difficult to manage under those conditions. Little clothing was worn, the men settling for bathing trunks or shorts, and Pippa for a bikini, the top of which by general consent she'd shed after passing St Helena. Young, lithe and slim, she had an almost perfect figure; long thighs, and breasts which were round and firm.

Each day Jan and André took sights in the morning – stars or sun depending on cloud – a meridian altitude at noon, and another sight for longitude in the late afternoon or evening. One day was much like another but there was a minor incident after passing Ascension Island when André, on watch in the cockpit, shouted, 'Periscope on the port bow.'

Jan who was working on a winch forward called out, 'Close or distant?'

'Close. About a hundred metres.'

And there it was, a tiny steel stick with a feather of white foam stretched out behind it as it raced down the port side. A few seconds later it had disappeared.

Pippa and Goddy who'd heard the shouting came up from below as fast as they could.

'What was all that about?' asked Goddy.

'Periscope. It's gone now. Came down the port side. Quite close.' André pointed astern.

'A submarine?' said Pippa. 'So close. How thrilling. I wonder whose?'

Jan said, 'Who knows? US, British, French, Soviet, Italian? You tell me. Shouldn't be surprised if it were Soviet. Could be checking on Ascension. The island is the terminal of an important NASA rocket range. I expect the Soviets keep an eye on it.'

'Couldn't the submarine be South African, Jan?' Pippa looked worried.

'No. Too far north I reckon.' He watched her affectionately. 'You should have been on deck, Pippa. Given the randy sods a kick. They don't often see topless ladies on patrol.'

Pippa smiled, looked down at her breasts. 'Think they'd have approved?'

'Sure they would have. Perhaps it's just as well you didn't show up. They might have surfaced and boarded.'

'Coo! Think what I've missed.' She looked up at the sails. 'Isn't it magic? Those tall white sails against the brilliant blues of sea and sky.'

André broke the spell. 'What's for supper?'

'Wait and see.' Pippa held a finger to her lips. 'I've found some exciting new tins.'

'Oh, God,' groaned André. 'Like that is it?'

'She cooks like she looks,' said Goddy. 'Superbly.'

'You can't look *superbly*. Not in English anyway.'

'You can in Polish. To me she looks superbly.'

'That'll do.' Pippa made a face. 'I don't fall for flattery, not . . .'

'Must fix that bloody winch,' interrupted Jan. 'It's still in pieces.'

Otto Bretsmar got back to *Schoongesicht* that afternoon to find a white-faced Mrs Bretsmar waiting for him in the drawing room.

'Oh dear,' she said. 'I'm so glad you're home early, Otto.'

Mr Bretsmar knew from her voice and expression that she was upset. He held up a warning hand. 'I'm glad to see you, my dear.'

'Let's go into the garden, Otto. I want to show you where I plan to put the new rockery in the spring.'

Mr Bretsmar knew what that meant. Ever since the first visit of the Security Police they'd assumed the house might be bugged. Anything confidential was now discussed in the garden. They crossed a lawn, went past the swimming pool and stopped below the tennis court. It was a typical July afternoon, cold with the sun setting in the west under a cloudless sky.

'That young Security Branch man, Claasens, was here again today, Otto. He asked me if we'd by any chance had news of the boys.'

'I had a call, too.' Bretsmar spoke in a low voice. 'From Smit. The chap who came to my office last time. I expect we were asked the same questions. Tell me first about yours.'

'I said how could we have news? The boys were lost when *Southwind* sank off Mossel Bay. I reminded him that he'd seen the press cuttings last time he came. I even managed some tears. Real ones because I was afraid for the boys. I always am. Especially for my darling André.'

'What did he say then, Kate?'

'He said perhaps they'd drifted a long way south with the Agulhas current and been picked up by a steamer and landed in some other country. I said we'd certainly have heard if that was the case, and he said, "Yes, you would have heard. That's why I'm asking you." He was quite friendly really. I gave him a cup of tea and he told me of their problems with these well-educated young men and women – so eager to put the world right but with so little knowledge of the problems involved. He said they were often used by dangerous people. Those who wanted to make trouble in South Africa. The agents of unfriendly powers. I asked him what powers and he said he didn't want to be specific, just unfriendly foreign powers.'

'Anything else, Kate?'

'No. That was about all. He drank the tea, we discussed the weather. Afterwards he thanked me, then went back to his car and drove off.'

'Interesting,' said Mr Bretsmar thoughtfully. 'Smit asked me the same questions. Said more or less the same things. I gave much the same answers as you did. It's that man Godeska they're after, I'm sure.'

'Funny they don't mention his name.'

'They'll have good reasons for that. These people know what they're doing. You can be certain of that.'

Mrs Bretsmar pulled the shawl about her shoulders. 'It's so cold. Let's go in and have tea.'

'Yes. I'd like that.'

They went back to the house.

SEVENTEEN

Contrary to the Admiralty Sailing Directions and Jan's expectations the south-east Trades persisted until the ketch had all but reached the Equator.

On July 23 he made the noon position 1° 47′ S: 21° 15′ W, and it was not until that afternoon that the wind faltered. By evening it had fallen away altogether and for the next few days winds were light and variable with rain squalls and occasional thunder-storms. The calms, alternating with winds which came and went, meant a lot of sail changing for *Sundance's* crew, and tempers frayed.

To Goddy and Pippa whose experience of sailing was, but for one gale, limited to running before a trade wind, the uncertain weather of the Doldrums was anything but pleasant. Sleep was difficult for various reasons: the heat was intense, in calms there was constant noise on deck — sails flapping and blocks banging — the squalls and rain storms made life uncomfortable and, as if that were not enough, crew were frequently on deck for sail handling. Jan was a demanding skipper but since he worked more and slept less than anyone else on board no-one complained though their language grew stronger.

They crossed the Equator on a grey day, the sea oily smooth under a sky massed with dark clouds. They had all made the crossing before though Pippa and Goddy had done it only by air; nevertheless the ceremony of crossing — it was in fact a drifting more than a crossing — was duly honoured with the right mixture of boisterousness and beer.

During calms Jan had permitted swimming but subject always to stringent safety precautions: never more than two crew in the water at one time, a rescue line with lifebuoy streamed astern and swimmers to remain close to the ketch.

Immediately after the crossing-the-line ceremony *Sundance* was becalmed and a small foresail, the only sail hoisted, flapped idly as she rolled to the long swell. Goddy, the last of the swimmers still in the sea, was floating on the surface about thirty yards on the port quarter when a sudden gust of wind filled the sail and the ketch began to make way through the water.

Jan was down below when Goddy shouted but André and Pippa, sun bathing on the coachroof, heard him. They looked up to see the Pole swimming furiously for the lifebuoy which was moving away from him. André jumped into the cockpit, tended the sheets and began to bring the ketch round to port. Jan arrived in the cockpit as Goddy's arms went up in a despairing gesture of surrender. He disappeared momentarily, came up again and let out a shrill, 'For God's sake help me.'

André said, 'Oh, God. I wonder if it's a shark?'

Jan snapped, 'Could be,' and dived over the side. A strong swimmer, it was not long before he'd reached Goddy. Holding the Pole to his chest with one arm, he turned on his back and began an almost leisurely swim in the general direction of *Sundance*.

Having manoeuvred the ketch so that the rescue line led across the men in the water, André let fly the sheets. Jan grabbed the line with his free hand and André and Pippa hauled them alongside. When they'd got the two men aboard an exhausted but grateful Goddy explained that he'd suffered a severe stomach cramp as he tried to reach the buoy. 'Jan saved my life,' he wheezed.

Jan grunted something unintelligible, turned to André: 'Let's get some more sail up. This could be a wind.'

It was. With main, mizzen and a genoa set and sheeted hard-in, *Sundance* began beating into a head wind; later it veered through north to the east but by midnight it had once more fallen away leaving the ketch ghosting, scarcely making way through the smooth sea.

'So that's it,' said a disgusted André who was on watch in the cockpit with Pippa. 'Now we mess about again looking for a wind. What a life.'

Earlier they'd been discussing Goddy's rescue. André had explained that he hadn't used the auxiliary engine because the battery terminals were disconnected. It was quicker to turn and make for Goddy under sail. 'I thought he'd had it,' he confessed. 'Thought a shark had got him.'

'Lucky Jan didn't think so.'

'He did. Said so at the time. Told me afterwards he reckoned he could deal with a shark. Had a sheath knife in his belt.'

'Some guy, your brother.'

'He is. Sort of superman. Super at sports, super swimmer, surf rider, yachtsman, scuba diver, the lot. You name it, he's super at it.'

'Your genuine macho man,' said Pippa sardonically. 'Pity he's so thick. And arrogant,' she added.

André didn't much like that. 'Can't be everything,' he protested. 'I don't really think he's thick, just a bit *verkrampt* – Conservative with a capital C.'

'To be Conservative with a capital C these days *is* thick.' Pippa spoke with all the assurance of her twenty years.

The General looked unusually grim as Badenhorst began his summary. 'Our agents continue to report no trace of *Southwind* or Godeska in Maputo. Nor have the Navy or Air Force found any sign of the yacht at sea. In Maputo the yacht harbour, the yacht club and the harbour generally have been fine combed. The islands of Inhaca and Chefine off the port have been visited. Inquiries have been made and are being made at all these places . . .' Badenhorst paused, put down his papers, shook his head, 'with absolutely no result.'

Engelbrecht tapped nervously on the wooden arm of his chair. 'My Minister is taking a most serious view of your –' he hesitated, 'of *the* I should say – failure to apprehend Godeska. He agrees with the Prime Minister that more urgent steps should have been taken initially.'

The General narrowed his eyes. 'Such as?'

'They feel that roadblocks should have been established immediately after Godeska's failure to return to the flat. They also believe that the police themselves should have opened the boot of Carralin's car at the time of the accident. Failure to do so involved the loss of four valuable days.'

The General stared at the man from the Foreign Ministry for some thirty seconds before speaking. 'That failure, as you put it, was due to the local police, not the Security Branch. Roadblocks could not have been set up in the time available. In any case they are at best no more than ten per cent effective. You can assure your Minister that I share the Prime Minister's concern. So does my Minister. We do our best – and it's a pretty good best by any standards – but we cannot perform miracles.' The General put a hand to his forehead, sighed noisily. 'From the start, when someone must have given Godeska the tip-off, things have gone against us.'

Engelbrecht brushed the underside of his moustache with a well-groomed forefinger. 'Perhaps I should now mention that . . .,' he cleared his throat, 'that my Minister is of the opinion that an important possibility appears to have been overlooked . . .'

'What's the trouble now?' interrupted the General, his head coming up abruptly from the pattern he was drawing on his notepad.

'The possibility that *Southwind* never went up the *east* coast to Maputo. That she may have gone up the *west* coast to Lobito Bay or Luanda. Although the journey to these Angolan ports is considerably longer, Godeska would know that once there he'd be safe. That he'd be given every assistance.'

The General smiled with his lips but not with his eyes. 'Nothing was overlooked, Engelbrecht. At our first meeting I drew attention to the possibility that Godeska might make for Maputo or *Luanda*. I gave instructions for doubling up gangway control of ships in Cape Town docks bound for those ports. You were present at that meeting.'

Engelbrecht blushed, rearranged the papers in front of him. 'I had overlooked that, General. My apologies.' He took a deep breath. 'But surely that precaution was not enough. Why were steps not taken to look for *Southwind* on the west coast?'

'Steps were taken.' The General's tone hardened, his eyes focused on Engelbrecht like steel spikes. 'Immediately after the meeting I discussed with the Chief of the Defence Force the need to watch the west coast route in case an Angolan port was Godeska's destination. The CDF at once instructed the Navy and Air Force to keep the west coast route and port approaches under strict surveillance. The Navy reported back that *Southwind* had been sighted on the twenty-ninth of June by two frigates returning to Simons-town. She had already rounded Cape Point; was heading up the east coast. On receipt of that information the CDF gave instructions that surveillance was to be concentrated on the east coast route and the approaches to Maputo.'

'I see.' Engelbrecht frowned. 'I was not aware of that. I was not told.'

'You didn't ask.' The General returned to the design on his notepad.

The intercom buzzed discreetly; they heard the secretary's voice. 'Top priority for you, General. Shall I bring it in?'

'Yes. Immediately.'

There was a knock on the door, the General released the lock-switch under his desk top, the door opened and a tall man of indeterminate age came in. He handed a message to the General.

As he read it the General's facial muscles contracted. He looked up at the tall man. 'Thank you. That'll do.' When the secretary had gone he stared at the men opposite him. 'Stefan Carralin died half-an-hour ago. Never came out of a deep coma.' He turned almost savagely to Engelbrecht. 'That is what I mean by things going against us. Is your Minister now going to say that we should not have let Carralin die?'

Engelbrecht looked away. There was silence in the room for some time after that. The General was not a man to be trifled with.

At last he said, 'Carralin under interrogation would have told us a lot. Now the man is dead.' He shrugged his shoulders. 'Still no trace of the yacht or Godeska in Maputo. That doesn't mean he isn't there. They could have scuttled the yacht in the bay. Gone ashore in the rubber dinghy. It's an ideal locality for that. So Godeska and the others have not been seen in Maputo. That doesn't mean they're not there — or haven't been there. The authorities will have given them every assistance. Brought them in from wherever they landed. Taken them to the airport. Most probably flown them to Europe immediately after landing. It is now the twenty-third of July. Unless *Southwind* met with trouble on passage I assume that she arrived in or off Maputo some days ago. The Navy also takes that view. But . . .,' he held up a finger, 'there is to be no relaxation of vigilance in Maputo. The Navy and Air Force must continue their patrols. That is all gentlemen.'

Sundance spent five days in the Doldrums during which time she covered only sixty-three miles. It was a frustrating time for her crew and not surprisingly tensions increased. Shortly after noon on the fourth day Jan was in the cockpit dismantling the windspeed indicator which had developed a fault. André was down below working out the noon sight, plotting the ketch's position and writing up the log. Pippa and Goddy having emptied and re-stowed the forward sail-bin, a long and tiring task, were lying on the coachroof in what little shade they could find under windless sails. They lay on their backs, side by side, talking in low voices; Goddy in his bathing trunks, Pippa in her topless bikini. Jan, streaming with perspiration and irritated by the intricacies of the wind indicator, looked up from his work to see Goddy's hand stroking Pippa's naked thigh. He shouted, 'Cut that out, Godeska.' It was his custom now to use the Pole's surname when annoyed.

Frowning, Goddy said, 'What's eating you, Jan?'

'Stop fondling Pippa. I'm not having any sexy nonsense in this boat. Cut it out.'

Pippa said, 'What *are* you saying, Jan?'

Goddy sat up. 'You go too far, Jan. You've no right to talk like that.'

Jan straightened himself, put his hands on the coaming, glared at the Pole. 'That's where you're wrong, my friend. You do that again and see what happens.' Flashing eyes reinforced the threat.

'Are you threatening me?'

'Yes, I am. I'll chuck you over the bloody side if I see you doing that again.'

Pippa laughed. 'You're pathetic, Jan. You really are. For goodness sake, you don't think Goddy was doing something indecent. I rather like my thigh being stroked. It's soothing.'

'Cut it out,' said Jan brusquely. 'You're supposed to be André's girl. Stop mucking about with your Polish *friend*.'

'For your information I'm nobody's girl. I happen to belong to myself.'

'All right.' The Pole got up slowly. 'If you feel so strongly about it I'll do as you say. Not for you, but for her sake. Because you have created a ridiculous situation with your threats. But,' he shook a finger at Jan, 'let me warn you, young man. Be careful. There are limits to what I'll take.'

Jan's hand went up in a dismissive gesture. 'Piss off before I really lose my temper.'

'I can't really believe this is happening,' Pippa said, shaking her head. Goddy went below and Jan, trembling with inner rage, resumed work on the windspeed indicator.

That night when Goddy was on deck with André and Pippa escaping from the heat below, Jan went to the Pole's locker, found the Walther pistol in his carrier bag, took out the ammunition clip and removed the eight cartridges in it. He slid the clip back into the pistol and returned it to the carrier bag. Later he threw the cartridges over the side. The clip held ten. He wondered casually what had happened to the other two.

The row between Goddy and Jan had strained and complicated relationships on board *Sundance*. Jan's outburst was due to more than the frustrations of the weather. The two men had always disliked each other but as the voyage progressed and Europe came closer Jan's concern grew at the irrevocable step he'd taken. Sailing the ketch on the long ocean voyage, the other elements of the adventure which lay ahead, were still exciting but what had become clearer each day was the bald fact that he'd outlawed himself from his country. Neither he, André nor Pippa could in the foreseeable future return. For all this he held Goddy responsible: Goddy the foreigner; the man without roots in South Africa; the left-wing trouble-maker; the older, more experienced man. It was he, in Jan's opinion, who had led André and Pippa astray and was thus responsible for all that had happened.

There was another less evident reason why he disliked the Pole. Pippa made no secret of her admiration for Goddy, seemed to attach more importance to his views than to anyone else's. She and Goddy shared private jokes, held whispered conversations, touched each other sometimes. Jan saw all this as an attempt by Goddy to supplant André in the girl's affections. Intensely loyal to his younger brother, he resented it. There was, however, a yet more compelling reason why the incident on the coachroof had upset him; the fact of the matter was that he was finding Pippa increasingly attractive as the voyage went on. Though he wouldn't have admitted it, and was possibly unaware of it, he was suffering from jealousy.

For his part André was not upset when Pippa and Goddy told him about the row and the reasons for it. Fond though he was of Pippa he didn't regard himself as being in love, nor had he any proprietorial notions. He couldn't understand why Jan had made such a fuss about something so trivial. He, Pippa and Goddy had been a trio for some time before the journey; at first simply because they worked in the same cell, but later because they'd got to know each other better and a meaningful friendship had developed. He knew that Pippa and Goddy got on well; as far as he was concerned that was a good thing. He liked them both and had no fears because his relationship with her was a secure and satisfactory one. They'd been close to each other for two years, there were emotional and intellectual bonds, and he saw the escape in the ketch and the problems which lay ahead as strengthening them. He liked and admired Jan and Goddy – though for very different reasons – so the row between them, the unpleasant atmosphere it had created, upset him. Sadly, he admitted to himself that Jan was responsible.

Pippa, the unwitting source of all this – or perhaps she wasn't altogether unwitting – had mixed and understand-ably feminine feelings about what had happened. While Jan's behaviour had surprised her she had not been upset. She'd sensed for some time that his manner towards her was changing, that he was becoming more interested, and she was flattered though she found him arrogant and uncaring. With Goddy something more intimate was developing. She didn't have to sense how he felt about her because things he said privately made that clear.

There was no threat to André, she told herself; their's was a well-tried understanding. But here she was, stuck in *Sundance* with three men who seemed to find her attractive. They were so different; André, sensitive, caring and thoughtful; Goddy, the much older, more experienced man, with loads of charisma and a foreign accent which made the whispered intimacies more exciting. I have to be frank, she told herself, I wouldn't mind sleeping with him. Come to that, Jan too. And of course I *have* slept with André. God, wouldn't it be awful if they could read my thoughts? As it happens there's no opportunity to sleep with anybody. Thank goodness for that!

Another day passed before *Sundance* found a wind. It came from the south during the night, fitfully at first, then backed to the east and steadied there for the best part of twelve hours, the ketch making good progress on a broad reach to the north-west. In late afternoon the wind fell away once more. After a few hours of calm it switched back to the south. There were heavy rain squalls that night and while they lasted Jan kept the ketch under bare poles. The next two days saw frequent sail changing, short beats and reaches on mostly unsatisfactory headings, the ketch chasing winds which failed to materialize. There was little rest for the crew.

On July 31 the barometer rose and the wind came in freshly from the north-east. Jan was at the wheel in the cockpit. He pointed to the wind burgee fluttering on the mainmast. 'North-east Trades, Pippa. We've found them at last.' He smiled, put a hand on her shoulder. 'Take the wheel. Feel a real wind again.'

While she steered he sat watching her, thinking how good she looked, her body deeply tanned, the wind ruffling her hair.

'Where are we, Jan? Tell me in language I can understand.'

'About five hundred miles sou-sou-west of the Cape Verdes.'

She nodded but said nothing.

Under a blue sky scattered with puffs of white cloud *Sundance* reached across the wind, her bows slapping into small seas, throwing up whisps of spray, the sails taut and trembling. Pippa took a hand from the wheel, touched Jan's arm. 'Isn't it magic?' She laughed happily.

EIGHTEEN

The intercom buzzed on the General's desk, he leant forward, tipped the switch. 'Yes.'

'Badenhorst, sir. Can I see you at once? Most urgent.'

The General looked at the wall clock, then at the appointments' list on his desk. 'Yes. Right away. I have an appointment at ten.'

Soon afterwards Badenhorst came in with a roll of thick paper under his arm.

'Morning, Badenhorst. What have you there?' The General's tone was genial, he liked his deputy. A good màn, quick, intelligent, thorough and reliable.

'A chart of Table Bay and False Bay, General. From the folio the Navy gave us some time ago.' Badenhorst went to the African mahogany table on the far side of the room and unrolled the chart. The General joined him.

'Well. What is it that's so urgent?'

'Muller has just phoned from Cape Town, sir. The Volkswagen has been found.'

'Where?' snapped the General.

'In deep water below the cliffs – about two and a half kilometres north of the causeway at Rooiels.' Badenhorst pointed to the mark he'd made on the chart. 'It was found by a coloured scuba-diver. Says he was looking for an old wreck. Probably diving for crayfish. It's illegal there of course.'

'Has the Volkswagen been recovered and searched?'

'Yes, General. It was in seven fathoms of water. Lifted out an hour ago. They wanted to identify it as Godeska's before phoning us. They confirm it is. The OB number plates stolen in Uitenhage, the dented rear bumper, a forged licence disc with the TJ registration numbers he was using when chased in Port Elizabeth, and the buckled front wing on the off-side where it struck Marais's BMW.' Badenhorst stopped, pinched his chin. 'There's one more important detail.'

'What's that?'

'The Volkswagen's clock, General. It stopped at forty-one minutes past four. Traffic Officer Marais was killed on Houwhoek Pass at approximately fifty minutes past three. That was the time of his last report. From the place where the BMW crashed to the point at which the Volkswagen was found was fifty kilometres. Godeska must have ditched the car within an hour of running down Marais. The times and distance fit.'

The General narrowed his eyes, squinted at the chart. 'Quite so. But the information comes too late. It's the tenth of August. *Southwind* left Cape Town on the twenty-eighth of June at five p.m. But wait . . .' Peremptorily he held up a hand, went to his desk, sat down, rested his head on the back of the chair and closed his eyes. 'Let me think.'

Badenhorst waited, looking at the chart, doing his own thinking. Several minutes later the General came bolt upright as if a spring had been released under him. 'What's the distance by sea from Cape Town to Rooiels Bay?'

Badenhorst measured off the distance with dividers. 'About sixty-eight nautical miles, sir.'

The General concentrated on balancing a gold ballpoint on the knob of a brass paperweight. When he'd succeeded he said, 'The Volkswagen was ditched around five in the morning of the thirtieth. That's thirty-six hours after *Southwind* left Cape Town. She was sighted by the Navy's frigates on the twenty-ninth. She could have reached Rooiels Bay after dark that night, even if she'd only made good three knots.' The General walked to the window, turned and spoke with sudden conviction. 'Here's a probable scenario. She picks up Godeska in Rooiels before daybreak on the morning of the thirtieth, then sails for . . .' he shook his head. 'That's the crunch, Badenhorst. Sails for where?' He got up, paced the floor vigorously before stopping at a window. 'The first we hear of her is on the fourth of July when the MAYDAY is sent off Mossel Bay. But that was a phoney. Carralin sent it. So where is she? On the way to Maputo we thought. Yet weeks have gone by and there's no sign of her there. So maybe having picked up Godeska at Rooiels Bay she doubles back on her tracks, rounds the Cape well to the south, keeps out to sea and sails up the west coast making for an Angolan port – Lobito or Luanda.' He slapped his thigh. 'That's it, Badenhorst. An Angolan port. Now listen – instruct our agents in Lobito and Luanda to make urgent and intensive inquiries. It's almost certainly too late – *Southwind* must have arrived in Angola weeks ago – but we *must* know.' He stared at his deputy. 'The Prime Minister *must* know. The White House

Each morning and evening Jan now listened to Portishead for weather forecasts. On the evening of August 27 when *Sundance* was 480 miles west-sou-west of Lands End and the crew's spirits were running high – only four or five days now before the ketch would be in the English Channel – Portishead broadcast a gale warning: wind westerly, force eight to nine.

On board *Sundance* preparations began for what was to come. The life-raft canister, the inflatable dinghy, the spinnaker poles and other movable gear on deck were securely lashed down, and steps were taken to stow and make fast things below. Storm sails were bent on and warps made ready for streaming. Pippa filled Thermos flasks with hot Bovril and coffee and put snacks of oatmeal cakes, corned beef, cheese lumps and chocolate slabs in the ready-use basket. She swallowed more seasick pills and insisted that Goddy did the same. By nightfall Jan felt they were ready for the gale to which in a strange way he looked forward. It promised yet another struggle with the elements, another man-sized challenge. And so he waited, his mood a mixture of eagerness and apprehension.

The General looked at the men facing him from the far side of the desk – Muller, Badenhorst and Engelbrecht – and wondered how many more meetings would be necessary and how many more days would pass before this, the most difficult and important case of his career, could be brought to finality. Not only was his own future involved but that of his country: of this he was acutely aware. The men round his desk noticed how strained he looked, the muscles of his face flexing as he stared at the Pieter Wenning landscape on the wall behind them. Only Badenhorst knew that the picture had been hung there because his chief liked to use it as a focal point.

'I must apologize,' said the General, 'for having called you together at such short notice. There has been a most important development. First, however, let me tell you that reports from our agents in Luanda and Lobito have been negative. No trace of *Southwind* or Godeska, nor of those with him. So we have drawn a blank there.'

Engelbrecht cleared his throat, shuffled his papers as he always did before speaking. 'It is already the twenty-fifth of August. My Minister would like . . .'

'That can wait,' interrupted the General, his blank stare quickly subduing the man from Foreign Affairs. The General opened a file, took from it a sheet of typed paper, looked once more at the faces across the desk. 'This report came to me from the CDF yesterday evening. It is highly classified. I will read it to you: "South African Air Force Intelligence has received the following from SAAF Operational HQ in Namibia. Begins: Captain le Roux of the Buccaneer Squadron now operating here states that recently when looking through an old yachting magazine he came on a report of the loss of *Southwind* off Mossel Bay. The item included a black and white photo of the yacht under full sail. He noticed that its general appearance, its sail rig and particularly the unusual striped pattern of the spinnaker was identical with that of a ketch he had investigated 350 miles north-west of Cape Town on July 5. He had spoken to the skipper by radio telephone but communication was so bad that he'd gone down to sea level and flown over the ketch from astern. The navigator of the Buccaneer had then photographed the stern transom which bore the name and port of registration: *Sundance* of Hong Kong. The ketch had, reports Captain le Roux, a green hull with yellow upperworks. One crew member, apparently male, had been seen in the cockpit. From the little that could be heard of his voice the skipper had a marked English accent. Captain le Roux, himself a yachtsman, stressed that he was not saying the ketch was *Southwind* in disguise, but he thought it his duty to draw attention to the similarity so that the matter could be further investigated if thought necessary. He states that he noted the sighting of *Sundance* in his reconnaisance report which was accompanied by a film of sightings made on that patrol."'

The General looked up. 'Well, gentlemen, SAAF Head-quarters fortunately did think it necessary to make further investigations. Captain le Roux's reconnaisance report was extracted from the files, the photo of *Sundance* taken by the Buccaneer was compared with photos of *Southwind*, the position of sighting was found to be consistent with what the latter's position could have been if she'd left Rooiels Bay at dawn on June 30. Finally SAAF Intelligence spoke to British Intelligence in Hong Kong asking for particulars of the ketch *Sundance* registered in that port, and information if possible as to her whereabouts.

'Two days later, that was yesterday, the 26th August, Hong Kong reported that no such vessel was registered in Hong Kong, nor had it ever been heard of in maritime and yachting circles there.' The General put down the report sheet, drew a hand across his forehead. 'Gentlemen, the ketch *Sundance* sighted by Captain le Roux was un-doubtedly the *Southwind*. Her crew must have painted the hull and upperworks and changed her name and port of registration during the night of the twenty-ninth of June while at Rooiels Bay. The heading *Sundance* was on when sighted by Captain le Roux suggests that she could have been making for West Africa, the Canaries or Cape Verde islands, Europe, North Africa, any number of places. However, I believe Europe to be the most likely destination.'

In the discussion which followed a number of decisions were made. Before the meeting closed the General summarized them:

'Badenhorst, you will report developments to the CIA at Langley, Virginia, and to MI5 in Whitehall. Langley and Whitehall will brief their agents world-wide. The CDF is already reporting directly to the chiefs of staff in the Pentagon and Whitehall. They will presumably instruct their naval and air forces to keep a sharp lookout for *Sundance*.' He referred once again to his notes before turning to Engelbrecht. 'And you, Engelbrecht – you will please report to your Minister on these developments. I've no doubt he will speak to his opposite numbers in Washington and Whitehall.'

'And the Prime Minister? Do you wish me to report to him?' inquired Engelbrecht.

'Certainly not.' The General's eyes froze on the Foreign Affairs man. 'I intend to do that myself.'

Muller fiddled with his steel-rimmed glasses, caught the General's eye. 'Should we not at this juncture request Interpol for assistance on the grounds that Godeska is wanted on two charges of murder and that the Bretsmar brothers and the young woman are involved as accessories after the fact? If we bring Interpol into this we are spreading the net.'

'No,' said the General emphatically. 'As long as this matter is restricted to the intelligence services of the countries concerned the story will not reach the media. Two things are imperative. One, it must not be known why we want Godeska – the political implications of that are too dangerous. Two, Godeska must not know what we know. The yacht has a radio. We must assume they listen regularly to news bulletins. As long as Godeska believes that we have swallowed the story of the loss of *Southwind* off Mossel Bay, that we do not associate him with the murders, that we know nothing of *Sundance* – as long as he believes these things there remains a reasonable chance of getting him.' The General got up, began pacing the length of the office. 'I've discussed with the Prime Minister a brief statement we will prepare for the media. It will be to the effect that a KGB agent, Boris Krasnov, alias Willi Braun, alias Stanislaw Godeska, for whom the South African Security Police have been searching for some time, is now believed to have escaped from the Republic and crossed the border into Mozambique. The statement will infer that information to this effect has been given by a prisoner presently held in Cape Town pending charges under the Terrorism Act. Because of its political implications we are clearing the statement with Washington. Since it will contain no reference to the missing document they are not likely to object.'

Engelbrecht teased at his moustache with a forefinger. 'How will that help, General? What is the purpose of such a statement?'

The General stopped in his stride and looked at the Foreign Affairs man as if he were beyond help. 'It will do two things, Engelbrecht. One, it will mislead Godeska, make him feel safe. Two, those with him in *Sundance* will learn the real identity and purpose of the man they have been associating with in anti-apartheid activities – the man they are now helping to escape.' He turned to the others. 'Well gentlemen. If there is nothing further to discuss I suggest we adjourn for lunch.'

The statement prepared by the General was duly approved by Washington and released to the media in Pretoria and Washington at noon on August 28. It made no reference to the missing document known to be in Godeska's possession, nor did it reveal that his real identity had been established only five days before the statement was issued. That information had come to the General in a computer-scrambled telex from CIA Headquarters in Langley, Virginia.

It read: CIA Station in Buenos Aires reports Stanislaw Godeska disappeared overnight from that city in October 1971 while working for local electronics firm. He left behind his personal belongings and automobile but no personal documents. The passport photograph you provided of Godeska has been identified as that of Boris Krasnov, known to have been a KGB operative in Buenos Aires during the period 1969–1971 when he worked in the same firm as Stanislaw Godeska, using the cover name Willi Braun.

It is presumed that Stanislaw Godeska was abducted or otherwise disposed of in Buenos Aires in October 1971, and that his personal documents were thereafter used by

Krasnov as cover for clandestine operations in West Germany and South Africa. The two men are said to have been remarkably alike in build and appearance. It is known that Krasnov established a close friendship with Godeska, presumably with the object of studying the latter's history, mannerisms and other personal characteristics. Investigation continues: message ends.

NINETEEN

The gale forecast by Portishead was not long in coming; at ten-thirty on the night of August 27 the glass began to fall and the wind backed in stages to sou-sou-west. As the barometer fell, wind and sea increased, and by morning *Sundance* was running before a gale force wind under a storm jib. Daylight revealed a desolate scene, the sky a dark mass of cloud racing with the storm, beneath it foam-streaked seas rolling in endless succession, the wind shriek-ing through the rigging, tearing wave crests into flying spray.

Jan and André had been together in the cockpit without a break since the gale began, doing two hour spells at the wheel, the auto-steering having long since been disengaged. Pippa and Goddy were again suffering from seasickness; she had taken to her bunk but the Pole somehow kept going and gave a hand as best he could with bilge pumping and other essential tasks.

During the afternoon the glass continued to fall and by eight o'clock that night the windspeed indicator was touching the sixty knot stop. The storm jib had been taken in and *Sundance* was running under bare poles with warps streamed to keep her stern to wind and sea. The seas were mountainous but flying spray which blanketed the night shut out visibility so that for the crew it was all sensation;

the lift of great waves picking up the ketch and hurling her forward on their crests, then racing past in the darkness to leave her wallowing in the valleys. The violent motion, the power of wind and sea, called for concentration and quick reaction by the man at the wheel.

Some time after midnight a rogue wave, a secondary sea doubling across the crest of another, lifted the ketch's stern high and pitch-poled her down its face into the trough below. Jan was at the wheel when *Sundance* fell into the trough upside down and he was hurled forward. Fortunately the lifeline of his safety harness held despite the violent tug, but he was winded by the binnacle and badly bruised.

André had gone below shortly before to investigate a banging noise. When *Sundance* pitch-poled – that is to say cartwheeled stern over bow – batteries, gas cylinders and other heavy gear below broke loose. Afterwards, as the ketch slowly righted herself, he slid back on to the floor from the deckhead where he'd found himself. At that moment another wave threw *Sundance* on to her beam ends and a flying gas cylinder struck him on the head.

When dawn came the gale was moderating and at ten o'clock the wind veered to the north-west, its velocity down to twenty knots. The seas, no longer mountainous, had become confused and lumpy as they quarrelled with the westerly swell. It had been a terrifying experience for *Sundance's* crew but they'd got off surprisingly lightly. Except for André who was suffering from concussion, their only injuries were bruises.

With daylight it became possible to take stock of the damage. Down below was a shambles; gear which had broken loose had splintered the saloon table, locker doors and other woodwork and smashed both radio sets, the radio direction-finder, and a number of dials and instruments above the chart-table. These included the windspeed indicator, the automatic log and the echo sounder. Little had been spared. Fortunately the hatch over the companionway was shut when *Sundance* went over and the washboards had remained in place. But for that she would have shipped a great deal more water. Damage to the batteries and circuits had upset the electrics and for some time after the disaster they used torches. When things were more settled two oil lamps which hung in gimbals in the saloon were lighted. Luckily they had come through unscathed.

For most of the morning André lay in his bunk with his head bandaged while the others set about doing what had to be done. Goddy pumped the bilge and mopped, and Jan and Pippa cleaned up the worst of the mess, re-stowing countless tins of food, pots and pans, plastic plates and mugs, sodden books and much else. After that Jan worked on the radio sets but found them too damaged for on board repairs.

The damage on deck was even more serious than below; the mainmast had gone, broken at coachroof level, taking its boom, stays and shrouds with it. Guard-rails, coachroof ventilators and the spray screen across the fore-end of the cockpit had been smashed by the falling mast and the force of the sea. Lashed to the coachroof, the inflatable dinghy and the metal canister which housed the life-raft had escaped damage. Jan's only recollection of the mast breaking was the fearsome noise it had made buckling across the deck when the ketch pitch-poled. At the time, submerged in the inverted cockpit, trapped in an air pocket, he'd had little idea what was happening. Evidently the impact had been so severe that the stays and shrouds had collapsed, and when *Sundance* came back on an even keel, the mast and its boom must have fallen into the sea, taking most of its rigging with it.

Surprisingly the mizzenmast was still intact although leaning precariously to port, its boom trailing. A mizzen forestay had carried away, probably broken by the falling mainmast. It would not, Jan decided, be difficult to rig a jury stay and get the mizzenmast back into some sort of shape.

That done they'd have something on which to hoist a sail. But for the moment there were more urgent tasks. First priority was the steering gear which had jammed. The warps streamed during the gale were still holding *Sundance* stern to wind as she drifted, but one of them must have fouled the rudder, and probably the propeller, during the capsize for instead of leading astern it now hung over the port side at a peculiar angle. No amount of heaving on it with sail winches made any impression. It was evident that the rudder could not be used until the jammed warp had been cleared, but there was still too much wind and sea to go over the side and tackle the job under water. Putting the task aside Jan and Goddy plugged the holes on the coachroof where the ventilators had torn away. Next they tackled the jury forestay. Having rigged it they hauled the mizzenmast upright, tightened the shrouds and stays and got it in pretty good shape.

In the late afternoon Jan managed to start the Volvo diesel after switching batteries and drying out wet leads. When he engaged the clutch his fear that the warp had jammed in the propeller was confirmed; it would not move. At that stage exasperation turned to despair.

'Here we are,' he said to the others as they sat in the saloon drinking mugs of coffee from a Thermos. 'Mizzenmast okay, but no mainmast. Nothing to hoist a foresail on, though we can probably rig a mizzen staysail. Jammed propeller so we can't use the engine, and jammed rudder so we can't steer. On top of that – no radio.' He looked at them through bloodshot eyes. 'How's that for a complete bloody screw-up?'

'And no stove,' added a bedraggled Pippa. 'The gas-pipe junction has bust and we can't get any gas.'

André, head still bandaged, had left his bunk. 'I can fix that,' he said wearily. 'But it'll take time.'

'Where are we?' Grimy and bearded, his hair in tangles, Goddy looked as though he was near the end of his tether.

'About two hundred miles north-west of Cape Finisterre.

The gale has pushed us a long way south and east of our course. About a hundred and fifty miles, I reckon.' Jan ran a hand through his hair. 'With this nor-westerly wind we're still drifting south-east. That's towards the land. The current's with us. I reckon we may be making three to four knots. The further south-east we drift the nearer we get to the shipping lanes. We're bound to see something sooner or later.'

'Sooner for me,' said Pippa. 'I'm scared and I'm lousy. I want a lovely scented foam bath. Sure to be one in a big ship.'

'If we are drifting like this, where do you think we come?' The Pole's speech had become more foreign with disaster.

'Spain or Portugal. Difficult to say.' Jan looked at his watch. 'Just after six. It's dark about eight o'clock. I'll fix the oil navigation lights. The electrics have had it. After that we'll make a start on rigging a jury foremast with spinnaker poles. Step them in the hollow stub of the mainmast. It'll be something to hoist a foresail on. Goddy can help me.' He turned to André. 'See if you can trace that diesel leak. It's getting in here, stinking the place out. The bilge is full of the stuff. After that, have a shot at Pippa's stove. I don't fancy cold meals.'

During the gale there had been no opportunity for rest let alone sleep, and there seemed little prospect of either in the immediate future. Still in their foul-weather gear they were a sorry-looking lot, their drawn faces smudged with oil and grime.

With Goddy's help Jan made ready two white, all-round oil lamps, and rigged boat-hooks fore and aft to carry them. Next they repaired and re-rigged the damaged guard-rails as far as possible. It was dark when they'd finished. Jan went below, lit the oil lamps and lashed them to the boat-hooks. By then it was too dark to do any more work on deck. Leaving Goddy to keep a lookout in the cockpit he went down to the saloon where André had got the stove going.

He hadn't been able to do anything about the diesel leak. 'It's coming from the underside of the fuel tank,' he said. 'Probably a strained seam. There's no way we can get at it. Just have to pump the bilge and hope for the best.'

Jan sniffed the air. 'I reckon I smell gas as well as diesel,' he said.

'It's a hangover from when I repaired the stove junction. Getting less all the time. The fore and aft hatches are open. There's air through the boat. Not to worry.'

Throughout the night and on into morning the wind blew from the north-west at about twenty knots and *Sundance* with warps still streamed lay quarter on to the seas, riding them with reasonable comfort.

When daylight came Jan and Goddy began rigging the jury foremast. 'We can't use the rudder but if we can get a foresail up with the mizzen we should be able to steer some sort of a course by juggling with the trim.' Jan pulled at his beard. 'Anyway it's worth a bloody try.'

With the ketch pitching and rolling as the seas swept past, the task was a difficult one and progress was slow. Jan abandoned it to take sunsights at ten in the morning and again at noon. He entered the noon position in the log that day, August 29, as 46° 12′ North: 10° 05′ West and plotted the position on the chart. *Sundance* was 180 miles north-by-west of Cape Finisterre, which was much as he'd expected.

Several times that morning they saw ships in the distance and on each occasion fired flares but there was no response. 'We're too far away and the light's too bright,' complained André. 'Last night would have been great for flares – if we'd seen anything.'

With André's help Pippa had got things below into reasonably good shape and the wet pillows, sleeping bags and other gear had been laid out on the coachroofs to dry under a strong sun. They looked like being ready for use by evening.

In mid-afternoon Jan and Goddy finished rigging the jury foremast: two spinnaker poles lashed together were stepped in the stub of the broken mainmast and fitted with improvised stays, shrouds and halyards. At last they were able to hoist a storm jib. To their joy it filled and *Sundance's* bows came slowly downwind; once again she was moving through the water.

'Great.' Jan grinned with satisfaction. 'Now for the mizzen and we'll see if we can hold her on a course.'

The Pole looked at him with admiration. 'Jan, you're a fine seaman.'

'Couldn't have done it without your help,' Jan conceded, looking embarrassed. The gale and its aftermath seemed to have healed the breach between him and Goddy. With André suffering from concussion and unable to give much assistance, Goddy's performance had far exceeded Jan's expectations. The Pole had worked hard, intelligently and cheerfully, in spite of his limited experience and tendency to seasickness. Jan decided that his judgement of Goddy had probably been harsh. He wasn't a bad guy really.

They were about to go aft to hoist the mizzen when there was an explosion followed by Pippa's scream. A whorl of smoke rising from the companionway hatch was snatched away by the wind.

Jan shouted. 'Christ! What was that?' and scrambled aft to the cockpit.

André, who'd come on deck just before the explosion, was first to reach the companion hatch. He started down the ladder but flames and smoke drove him back.

Jan shouted, 'Try the forehatch. I'll go for the after one.'

TWENTY

Jan reached the after-hatch to find Pippa looking up at him, her face smudged, her eyes wild with fright. She was trembling, shaking her head. 'Quick, Jan. Get me out. It's burning madly.' She was close to hysterics. 'I *must* get out.'

He leant down, took her hands and heaved her clear of the hatch. 'You all right, Pippa?' He watched her closely.

'I think so. I tried to stop it with the extinguisher but it was no good.' Her eyes were red and streaming. He bundled her into the cockpit, then went to the hatch from which whisps of smoke were rising. Lowering himself into the stern cabin he made first for the extinguisher on the WC bulkhead. It had gone. He grabbed a hand towel, wet it in the WC bowl and tied it round his head to cover his mouth and nose. When he got to the saloon he was confronted with clouds of smoke through which flames darted and hissed. The companion-ladder and the bulkhead aft of it, the saloon table and other woodwork were burning fiercely, fizzing and popping as the fire took hold. There was an extinguisher in the rack over the stove but the flames there put it beyond his reach.

The pictures! He had to save them. He forced himself through the heat, smoke and flames to the chart-table but it was too late. It was on fire. The heat was intense and movement was hampered by the rolling of the ketch. His next thought was for the radio spares and passports. They were in the stern cabin in the owner's safe above the double bunk. The smoke had begun to penetrate the wet towel, acrid fumes from burning wood, varnish, plastic and upholstery made breathing painful. He knew he couldn't last there much longer as he made for the stern cabin. As he went he heard André calling from the forward end of the saloon; he couldn't see him or hear what he was saying.

In the stern cabin a figure was kneeling on the bunk, hands reaching upwards. It was Goddy and Jan thought for a moment that the Pole was trying to open the safe. He got close and saw him take a brightly coloured shopping bag from the overhead locker. Jan tapped him on the shoulder, pointed to the hatch, indicated that he must go. Goddy went up through it, clutching the bag. Jan took a bunch of keys from his pocket, unlocked the safe and lifted out the radio spares package and passports. He took a lifejacket from the rack under the bunk and hauled himself up through the hatch, coughing and wheezing. When his head and shoulders were clear he took the towel from his face and breathed in lungfuls of fresh air. The hair on his arms was singed, his face streamed with sweat, his T-shirt and denims were wet with it and dark with smoke grime. He slumped into the cockpit. Goddy was already there. They were joined by André and Pippa, their blackened faces striped with runnels of perspiration. Pippa had a lifejacket in her hand, and André a canvas bag in which he'd put his binoculars, shaving gear, and a spare T-shirt before leaving the forward cabin. He looked at Jan. 'Couldn't do a thing. Absolutely hopeless.' His breath came in gulps. 'The fire extinguisher was useless against that blaze.

'I heard you shouting but didn't know what you were saying,' said Jan.

'I said I was going to get the Mercury up from the forward cabin. We got it up, Pippa and me.' The Mercury 20 was the inflatable dinghy's outboard motor.

The noise from the fire was increasing; a roaring, snapping sound, punctuated by small explosions, columns of smoke billowing up through the hatches as it spread.

Jan again wiped his streaming eyes. 'We'll have to abandon her,' he said breathlessly, 'before the fire gets at those drums of diesel. Let's get the dinghy inflated. Come on, time's short.'

They inflated the dinghy, lowered it into the sea and secured it alongside. The emergency rations, water containers, flares, medical pack and paddle oars were taken from the life-raft and placed in the dinghy. Then the Mercury was lowered into it; it was heavy, the ketch was rolling and they had to be careful. Once the engine was safely aboard Pippa and Goddy got in, wearing the two lifejackets salvaged from the fire. Jan passed down a coil of rope, the end of which he made fast to the foot of the mizzenmast. 'Our tow rope,' he explained as he joined them in the dinghy. They cast off and *Sundance* moved away, drifting faster than the dinghy. As she went Jan paid out the rope until the dinghy was forty or so feet astern of the ketch when he made it fast. *Sundance* drifted steadily downwind towing the dinghy.

Jan said, 'We stay like this as long as we can. We've got fuel for eighty miles. Land's at least a hundred and fifty to the south-east.'

Clouds of dark smoke were drifting downwind from *Sundance*. 'That's as good an emergency signal as any.' Jan's bearded chin pointed to it. 'Should attract attention. Safer to stay with it.'

'Three men in a boat,' quipped André in an attempt to be cheerful.

'And a woman,' said Pippa.

'Yah. Sorry, Pips.' He looked at the Pole. 'What have you got in that shopping bag, Goddy? Knickers?'

The Pole grinned. 'My new shoes, man. Everything else has gone, *kaput*.'

'There wasn't much else to go,' said André. 'But let's check what we *have* got. It'll be good for morale. My carrier-bag with binoculars, toilet things and a spare T-shirt; Jan's carrier-bag with the radio spares; Goddy's new shoes, the emergency rations, first-aid kit, two lifejackets and of course the gear we're wearing. Great, isn't it?'

Pippa let out a wail. 'I've left my little shoulder-bag.'

'So what?'

'All my face things.'

'That's bad.' Jan shook his head. 'Really bad.'

André looked at him. 'Why the hell did you bring the radio spares? A chart would have been more to the point.'

Jan wiped the sweat from his eyes with a lump of cotton waste. 'I tried bloody hard to get one. The chart-table was a blazing fire. Hadn't a hope.'

'Okay. But why bother with the radio spares?'

'Because, my boy, there's folding money in that parcel. Dad put it there. For us when we get to Europe.'

'If, not when,' suggested Goddy.

Jan said, 'Important thing is we've got emergency rations and water. We're okay for a few days.' He touched Pippa's shoulder. 'Tell us about the fire, Pips. How did it start?'

'Don't honestly know, Jan. I was refilling the oil lamps at the sink. Then I had to go to the loo.' She gave an embarrassed smile. 'One of those can't wait calls. I was there when I heard the explosion. I think I screamed. Then I . . .'

'Pulled up your pants?' suggested André.

'Don't be vulgar. Then with a fire extinguisher I went back to the saloon, pulled the extinguisher toggle but nothing happened. I tried two or three times, but no good. There were flames all over the place. I rushed back to the stern cabin. Dead scared, thought I'd be trapped below. When I got to the hatch you were there, Jan.'

He looked at her quizzically. 'Where did you put the paraffin can when you'd finished doing the lamps?'

'I'd only done one when I had to go to the loo. I put the can in the crockery rack so that it couldn't move around while I was away.'

'Was the stove on? Any burners on, I mean?'

'Yes, one. I was boiling water for coffee.'

André let loose a low whistle. 'Was the screwtop back on the paraffin can when you put it in the rack?'

Pippa looked bewildered. 'I honestly can't remember.'

'Ah,' said André thoughtfully. 'Perhaps a gas pocket had formed somewhere near the stove. Left over from when I fixed that junction. Or maybe diesel fumes from the bilge made a gas pocket. A lot of diesel got in there you know. I was working on the electrics this morning, trying to fix the light circuit. I did some work on the wiring where it passes along the bulkhead behind the stove. A short could have ignited the gas pocket. That might have been it.'

Pippa said, 'But the fire seemed to be everywhere at once. It spread in no time at all.'

Jan agreed with André. 'I accept the gas pocket theory. The blast of the explosion probably shot the paraffin can across the saloon, spilling out the contents. The explosion itself, and the lighted burner, would have been enough to set that lot off.'

'Oh, God! How awful.' Pippa was tearful. 'What can I say? It must have been my fault.'

'Can't be helped, Pips. We all make mistakes. Anyway we're only guessing what happened.'

Tears moved slowly down the sides of Pippa's nose. Jan put a hand on her arm. 'It could have started in quite another way, Pips. Probably nothing to do with you. Cheer up, love.'

They spent the rest of that day and the night which followed waiting for help which didn't come. For warmth during the night they huddled together. Pippa and Goddy at first suffered from seasickness but recovered as the weather improved towards morning. By then the wind had fallen away and long oily swells from the west were all that remained of the gale. When daylight came the ketch was still there, a black and smouldering hulk, down by the stern and listing to starboard as she rode the swells.

Jan said, 'She'll be gone soon. Another hour or so I guess. When she does we cut the tow rope.'

'Poor old *Sundance*,' said André. 'What a lousy end.'

'How d'you think I feel?' Jan was bitter. 'She meant a lot to me. Done thousands of miles in her, South Atlantic race and all.'

Goddy was saying something when Jan interrupted with an excited shout. 'Look! There's a ship.' He pointed a long arm to the north.

It was early morning, visibility was poor, but when the dinghy lifted on the next swell there she was some miles away; a small ship making for the ketch.

Jan watched the approaching ship through binoculars. 'Can't make out her name yet but . . .'

Goddy interrupted. 'You realize,' he said with urgency, 'that we can't use our real names. The Captain is bound to report by radio that he has picked us up. He'll have to say who we are, give the name of the yacht, where we've come from, where we're bound for. I haven't got a passport – I'll give my name as Pieter Berg. But you people have still got your passports, haven't you? Shouldn't you ditch them?'

Jan, eyes still pressed to the binoculars, said, 'We'll say we lost them in the fire. But we must keep them. They may be essential later. Pity this ship is south-bound. If it were going the other way there'd be no problem. Maybe she's making for a Spanish or Portuguese port. Corunna, Vigo, Oporto. That'd help. They're not far away, those places. Within twenty-four hours I'd say. But I agree about our names. If they're published in South Africa we've had it. The Security Police are after Goddy and we're supposed to have drowned off Mossel Bay. You can't make it more difficult than that. Tell you what,' his eyebrows drew together in a frown. 'We'll say our surname is Bennet. Pippa is our sister and Goddy – Pieter Berg – is a friend.'

'For God's sake remember I am Pieter, *not* Goddy,' urged the Pole hoarsely.

The ship was little more than a mile away now. Small, about four thousand tons, she looked like a mini-tanker with her bridge, funnel and superstructure aft. As she approached Jan put down the binoculars, turned to them. 'I've bad news. She's the *Island Enterprise*. Seen her before in Cape Town docks. That's where she's bound for. Via

Ascension and St Helena. She belongs to the Inter Island Navigation Company. They operate three small cargo/passenger ships to serve the islands. They began after the Union Castle service packed up.'

'Cape Town!' Pippa sounded appalled. 'We can't possibly go back there.'

André said, 'But what's the option? We can't refuse to be rescued. If we do . . .' He stopped, his mind contemplating the impossible.

'Why can't they land us in Ascension or St Helena?' asked Pippa.

'Maybe they could,' said Goddy. 'But that'd only complicate the problem and give the Security Police time to catch up with us. Where do we go from there, and how? Safest places for us are England, France and Holland. Three countries that can be counted on to give political asylum.'

Jan said, 'What about Portugal?'

'Not too good.' André shook his head. 'They're still sore at losing Angola and Mozambique to the Africans, and they have close ties with the South African government. Not likely to be keen on helping anti-apartheid activists. We'd be crazy if we counted on political asylum there.'

There was silence after that, each of them agonizing over the problem as they watched *Island Enterprise* approaching.

An urgent and rather wild discussion followed – how could they avoid being carried back to South Africa once the ship had picked them up? André suggested taking over *Island Enterprise* by force – 'take the Captain hostage, Goddy, using your pistol' – and compelling him to close the land and let them go ashore in their dinghy. But even André conceded defeat when they pointed out that that would be piracy on the high seas; it could only make things worse.

Goddy interrupted the discussion. 'Listen. I have a plan. It's basically this: *Sundance* has almost gone, the stern's already under water.' He looked across to where the ketch was sinking. 'We tell the Captain that she was the ketch *Chicuala* of Beira.'

'Beira,' echoed André and Pippa more or less simultaneously. 'That's Mozambique.'

'Yes. That's the whole point. It's our safest cover now. We've somehow got to persuade *Island Enterprise's* Captain to delay reporting that he's picked us up. A delay of at least twenty-four hours is vital, forty-eight hours would be better. I'll explain why.'

With *Island Enterprise* less than a mile away and already slowing down, Goddy unfolded the main points of his plan. He had to talk fast, there was little time for questions, but by the end of it he'd convinced them that the plan was their only hope.

'We'll discuss it in more detail once we're on board,' he added. 'But in the meantime you know enough to stick to the main story line. I think Jan should do the talking to the Captain. He's our skipper. Is that agreed?' It was.

Pippa thought it was interesting that in this sudden crisis it was Goddy who'd taken charge and not Jan who, until this moment, had always been regarded as their leader.

The approaching ship was close now and had all but stopped. André cast off the tow line in the dinghy's bows and Jan started the Mercury. The engine spluttered into life and the dinghy skimmed across the water towards *Island Enterprise*.

TWENTY-ONE

Passengers chatting excitedly, their cameras much in evidence, lined the deck as the dinghy approached *Island Enterprise* where a rope ladder had been dropped over the side.

'Don't forget,' Jan warned his companions during the final approach. 'We're exhausted, we haven't slept for days, we're suffering from shock and all we need is rest. Most of that's true. Keep clear of the passengers and stay in whatever accommodation we're given until I join you.'

The next moment they were alongside, a sailor threw down a line, André made it fast and they went up the ladder. The chief officer met them on the foredeck, there was an exchange of greetings, he introduced himself as Eric Smithers. Jan shook hands. 'I'm Tony Bennet.' He nodded towards Goddy, André and Pippa. 'Pieter Berg,' he said, 'and Mike and Mary, my brother and sister.'

The chief officer smiled sympathetically. 'You people look as though you've had a tough time.'

'We have,' said Jan. 'Thank God you turned up. We had three days of gale. Got pitch-poled and dismasted. Fire broke out yesterday. She's burnt out, sinking.'

'I can see that. Been at sea long?'

'Yes, a long time.' Jan changed the subject. 'I'd be grateful if you'd hoist our dinghy on board. It's all we've got left.'

'Certainly.' The chief officer looked over the side. 'Worth flogging with that Mercury 20.' He spoke to the bridge by walkie-talkie, got permission to hoist the dinghy and told the bosun to get on with it. A number of passengers who'd come down from the promenade deck had gathered round, listening attentively, their cameras clicking at the motley group of survivors: three bearded men and a girl with corn coloured hair, all deeply suntanned, their clothing fouled by smoke and grime, their faces streaked with sweat.

'Shame,' whispered a young woman in scarlet slacks and a vest. 'They look exhausted. It must have been terrible.'

The chief officer looked at Jan. 'You're the skipper, I take it.'

'Yes.'

'Come along with me to the Captain. The chief steward will look after the others. I expect you'd all like a hot shower for a start and something to change into.'

'I'll say we would.' Pippa was emphatic. 'And some sleep.'

They followed the chief officer up a steel ladder to the promenade deck.

The dinghy was hoisted on board, engine room bells clanged, *Island Enterprise* trembled as her propellers began to turn and she moved slowly ahead.

Rehearsing mentally what he was going to say, Jan followed the chief officer to the Captain's stateroom under the bridge. There he was introduced to Captain Daniel Briggs, a bearded, thickset man with a friendly, open countenance.

'We're very grateful,' said Jan as they shook hands.

'Glad we were around, Bennet. You seem to have had a pretty rough time. Incidentally, we heard no MAYDAY.'

'Our radio was written off in the gale. We were pitch-poled by a big sea, lost the mainmast, rudder and propeller jammed by a warp, and a lot of other damage on top and below.'

The Captain pointed to a chair, took one himself and pressed a bell. 'What would you like? Coffee, a stiff drink or both?' A steward arrived.

Jan opted for coffee. The chief officer left them and soon afterwards the steward came back with the coffee. When he'd gone the Captain said, 'Now, let's have your story.'

Jan explained briefly what had happened since they'd sailed from Beira in mid-June, the uneventful voyage up to the gale, the capsize, the loss of their radio, the other damage suffered and finally the fire. They were all from Beira, he said. His father owned a wine import business there, the control of which had been taken over by Frelimo when Samora Machel came to power. Though his father continued to run it under political supervision with Pieter Berg as manager, the business had steadily declined. The Bennet family, feeling that there was ño future for them in Mozambique, had decided to leave the country; their sons and daughter to get out first taking with them some of the family's more important possessions, notably the ketch *Chicuala*. They'd had on board, Jan said, a few good pictures, some family silver and other valuables, all of which were lost in the fire. They'd been able to save nothing but what they stood up in plus a few personal odds and ends. Their passports and *Chicuala's* registration papers had been in the lower drawer of the chart-table but because of the rapidity with which the fire spread it had not been possible to get at them.

Clearly impressed, Captain Briggs said, 'It's amazing you people got away with it. Bad luck having that fire so soon after weathering the gale. But that's the way of the sea, I'm afraid. Where were you bound for?'

'Falmouth.'

'I see. Would you like to talk to anyone there by radio-telephone?'

'Not for the moment, Captain.' Jan looked him squarely in the face. 'I must explain that our situation is dodgy. My parents are still in Beira. They're leaving for good on September the first. Before we sailed from there we had to inform the port authorities of our destination and the time we'd be away. We said we were going to Inhambane. That's a few days down the coast but it's still Mozambique. We said we'd be gone for about two weeks. They'd never have given permission for the ketch to go to Europe, that's for sure. If the Frelimo authorities now learn we were picked up from the *Chicuala* off the Portuguese coast there'll be hell to pay. They'll assume at once – and correctly I'm afraid – that we were without permission removing assets from Mozambique. That's strictly forbidden. They'd certainly arrest my father. God knows what would happen to my mother. As it is, they'll long ago have accepted that *Chicuala* was lost at sea on the way to Inhambane.'

The Captain was puzzled, 'But surely the Mozambique authorities would learn of the ketch's arrival in Falmouth?'

Jan agreed. 'I know, but my parents will have left Mozambique by the first of September. That's in two days' time. We had arranged that *Chicuala* would not make Falmouth before the third of September. That was to give them time to get down to South Africa. My family comes from the Cape. We went to school there.'

For some time the Captain considered the problem in silence. 'This is a bit awkward,' he said, frowning. 'You see I must report to my owners that I've picked you up. Say who you are. Where from and where bound, name of vessel, etcetera. Another problem. Where do I put you ashore? We call at Ascension, St Helena and Cape Town. But you've no passports. That means trouble with the immigration authorities, possibly refusal to permit you to land. We can suffer voyage delay, extra port charges. That sort of thing.'

Jan sighed. 'Yes I can see that. It's very awkward.'

They watched each other without speaking until Jan, quite suddenly and with some exuberance said, 'Tell you what, Captain. If you can delay that report for twenty-four hours — and leave out the name of our boat — simply say we were rescued from a burning ketch — or get its name wrong — that would do the trick. I mean I could have given you the wrong name, couldn't I? Said she was *Frisco Boy* from Port Louis, Mauritius. Something like that. A delay of a day or two will give my parents time to get away.'

The Captain studied the young man with cautious, inquiring eyes. 'I don't quite follow. If I do that, where do we land you?'

'Preferably twenty or thirty miles off the Portuguese coast. That's more or less on your course, isn't it? Say off Oporto. We can go ashore in our dinghy. We've got fuel for eighty miles. The Mercury 20 gives us eighteen knots and the weather's fine at the moment. You'll be off Oporto sometime tonight or in the early morning, I imagine.'

'Why Oporto? What do you do when you get there? No passports.'

'Dad has good business connections in Oporto. For years he's bought a lot of his wine there. Using the dinghy, we don't have to go into the harbour. We can land on the beach

156

well to the south. It'll be dark. Antonio Ferreira, an old friend and business associate of Dad's – he's a wine merchant – lives on the coast south of Oporto. We'd land there. He'll give us all the help we need to get to Falmouth. Ferreira's an influential guy – well in with the government. If any questions are asked by the authorities we'll say the ketch was the *Frisco Boy* from Port Louis. By the time they've sorted that one out with Mauritius my parents will be safely down in South Africa.'

'I see.' The Captain sounded dubious. 'A bit complicated, isn't it? What happens if the Mercury packs up? You'll have to give me time to think about this. Not sure that I really like it, although the sooner we can land you the better. In the meantime go down, have a shower, change and rest, and we'll discuss it later in the day. Say 1600. Suit you?'

'Yes. Of course. But you won't send that radio message until we've settled things, will you?'

'No, I won't.' The Captain lit a cigarette. 'You can count on that. I'll tell our radio officer that I'll be giving him a radio message to transmit in due course. Nothing to go out until then. You must tell your crew not to discuss this with passengers or ship's staff. It's better they say nothing. Keep the name of the ketch to yourselves, and don't let on where you're from or your destination. Preferably stay in the cabin.'

With the hint of a smile Jan said, 'I've already told them that, Captain.'

The survivors had been given a four-berth cabin on the lower of the two accommodation decks. 'The only unoccupied cabin left,' apologized Bill Snell, the chief steward. 'You'll have to share it.'

Pippa brushed the hair from her eyes. 'We'll manage somehow. We've spent a long time together in more or less zero space. Used to it now.' She looked round the cabin. 'Our own shower and loo. How marvellous. I'm going straight into the shower.'

'Better hurry.' André poked a finger into her side. 'There are three men in the queue.'

The chief steward said, 'Your gear looks a bit of a disaster. I'll send you down some jeans and T-shirts.' With a critical eye he appraised them for size. 'One average-lady – one average gent – two large gents. You okay for shoes and socks?'

There was a chorus of assent. 'Especially Pieter,' said André. 'He carries spares.'

'What about breakfast?' The chief steward looked at his watch. 'Getting on a bit. Could send you a tray with coffee, toast, rolls, jam, cheese, fruit. Any good?'

'Dead right,' said Jan. 'I don't know about the others, but my top priority is sleep. That's something we haven't had for quite a while.'

There was a parental beam in Bill Snell's eyes. 'Bet you haven't. Get your heads down as soon as you can. You look a pretty clapped-out lot.'

When the chief steward had gone Jan told the others of his talk with the Captain. 'He seems a reasonable guy. Bit worried about letting us go it alone in the dinghy, but I reckon he'll agree. It solves various problems for him if he can get rid of us quickly. At four o'clock this afternoon he and I will have another chat. He'll let me know his decision then. He's promised not to make any radio report until we've settled things. I reckon he'll play ball about giving us a head start.'

'D'you think he swallowed the *Chicuala* story?' André had lowered his voice. 'Beira, Dad, the wine business and all?'

'Yes. I think so. He didn't query anything.'

'That's good.' Goddy nodded approvingly. 'So if he agrees we get into the dinghy between one and two in the morning?'

'That's right. I'll ask him to let me see the chart. Look for a suitable spot. The weather's just right.'

'If it stays like this,' said Pippa anxiously.

'When we do get ashore I reckon we make for Lisbon,' said Goddy. 'It's only a few hundred kilometres south of Oporto. Less than a day's train journey.'

André shook his head. 'No. I'm dead against that. As I said before, the Portuguese government is well in with ours. They're not going to offend Pretoria.'

'There are embassies in Lisbon.' Goddy frowned his disagreement. 'We can go to them and ask for political asylum.'

'We certainly can't go to the South African Embassy,' said Jan. 'What embassy do *you* propose going to? Polish?'

'No, German.' The pale eyes flickered. 'My mother was German. I worked there for a long time. Represent a German firm, travel on a German passport. Told you that some time ago. You people can go to the British Embassy.'

'There'll be Portuguese police guarding embassies,' said André. 'They might think we're terrorists and ask to see our passports. Ours are South African.' He shook his head. 'No. You can forget Lisbon, Goddy. I'm not holing up in any embassy in Lisbon, British or otherwise. Even if they'd have me, which I doubt. Let's make for the north. England's the place. We *know* they'll give us political asylum. So probably will France. Not sure about Spain, but I reckon it's a lot safer than Portugal.'

'You'd better stay with us, Goddy.' Pippa smiled at him affectionately. 'We've got passports, *you* haven't. Jan's got the money, *you* haven't. You'll be safer with us. We'll be able to vouch for you.'

'*We'll* be safer, too.' Jan looked at the Pole as if trying to read his thoughts. 'If you go off on your own and get nicked they'll soon learn about us. I'm not risking that. You stay with us, my boy.'

Goddy shrugged, sighed, looked unhappy but said nothing.

A St Helena stewardess brought clean jeans, T-shirts and a

tray of food and took away their soiled clothes. They'd have them back by evening, she said. Having showered, changed and eaten, they climbed into their bunks and slept soundly until four o'clock that afternoon when there was a knock on the cabin door.

'The Captain would like to see Mr Tony Bennet now,' said the St Helena steward.

The Captain was sitting in his day-room when Jan arrived. 'Sit down, Bennet. I've thought things over, discussed them with the chief officer. We've considered the pros and cons and I've come to a decision.' His blue eyes fixed on his visitor with disconcerting directness.

Apprehensive about what that decision might be, Jan said nothing. Silence, he felt, was likely to be more effective than speech.

The Captain went on. 'Provided you people sign this indemnity,' he took a sheet of typed paper from the desk, 'and provided the weather stays as it is, I'll slow down, keep steerage way, and put your dinghy into the water at two o'clock tomorrow morning. We'll be just south of Oporto then, about fifteen miles offshore. Suit you?'

'Sounds great, Captain. There are just a couple of points I'd like to settle. One, what's the indemnity about? Two, what are you going to do about the radio message?'

The steward came in with a tray of tea, put it on the table by the settee. When he'd gone the Captain poured the tea, passed a cup to Jan. 'It means you people are indemnifying me and my company against any loss or damage you may suffer and from any penalties you may incur in Portugal or elsewhere once ashore.' He smiled as he handed it over. 'In fact it indemnifies us against just about everything. You'd better read it.'

'I'll do that later, Captain. We'll definitely sign it.'

'Now about the radio message.' The Captain looked at a note he'd made. 'I've decided to send that in an hour's time – that's at 1700.'

Jan looked startled. 'One hour!' he echoed.

'Yes. Let me explain. All it will say is that we've picked up four people in their powered dinghy, survivors from a yacht which had burnt out and sunk. Details to follow. That will be the end of the first message. At the same time tomorrow – that'll be at 1700 again – I'll send a second message. Say that I closed the coast off Oporto in fine weather during the morning to enable the survivors to proceed ashore in the powered dinghy, thus saving the company harbour charges and voyage delay. I'll add that you people signed a comprehensive indemnity safeguarding the company's position.'

'When d'you give our names – name of the ketch, etcetera? I'm thinking of my parents.'

'So am I,' said the Captain. 'But for that I'd have given all the gen by now – as I should have done. In fact I don't propose to give your names, or that of the ketch, until somebody asks for them.'

'And when they do?'

'Well, it won't be until after 1700 tomorrow anyway, and in that event they won't get our reply – I'll see to that,' the Captain smiled, 'until the following morning. That'll be September the third. Then I *will* have to give your names and the ketch's, and report you were making for Falmouth. Entries to that effect will have to be made in my deck log and voyage report.'

'I understand that,' said Jan. 'Can't tell you how grateful we are, sir. It's really super of you. I'll tell my lot that we will be leaving the ship at two in the morning.' He hesitated. 'I wonder if you could let me see a chart of the coast round Oporto?'

The Captain opened a desk drawer, took out a sheet of paper. 'Had this photocopy made for you. It's a section of the Admiralty chart showing Oporto and the coastline south as far as Praia de Barra. That's about fifty nautical miles down the coast.'

Jan took it. 'That's great. Just what we need.'

'I suggest you and your crew remain in the cabin until you leave in the morning. The chief officer will prepare the dinghy for launching. The chief engineer is providing an additional can of fuel, and Bill Snell is fixing some sandwiches and coffee. How's your crew getting on by the way?'

'Sleeping their heads off.'

'Good. Keep them at it.'

Jan said, 'One more thing, Captain. The chief steward sent us a change of clothing, new jeans, T-shirts and socks. We want to pay for those and for anything else we're liable for. We've only got two smallish bags for our gear. We'd like to buy two more from the ship's shop. I saw some in the showcase as I came up.'

'Better you don't go into the shop yourself. I'll tell Bill Snell to let you have them. Don't worry about paying.' The Captain's eyes twinkled. 'You're distressed mariners.'

TWENTY-TWO

Awakened by his wristwatch alarm Goddy switched on the cabin lights and called the others. 'Half past one,' he whispered conspiratorily. 'Time to get ready.'

There was restrained excitement as they washed, put on jeans and T-shirts and generally prepared themselves for the journey. They packed their few possessions, mostly spare clothing; Pippa and André in the carrier bags from the yacht, Jan and Goddy in those brought down by Bill Snell the night before; blue canvas bags with ADIDAS on them in big white letters. Bill Snell had performed other useful services: he'd changed their remaining South African rands into US dollars and bought for them the toiletries they needed, including cosmetics and a hairbrush for Pippa.

As arranged with the Captain they gathered on the foredeck shortly before two o'clock. Jan checked that the paddles, boat-hook, spare fuel, hand-compass and other gear were in the dinghy which the bosun and a sailor were making ready for lowering. *Island Enterprise's* engines had stopped and all was silent but for the lap of water along the side. It was a dark night, the sea calm, a light breeze ruffling the surface of the long swells from the west. The bags were put into the dinghy and it was lowered into the water. The chief officer wished them good luck, they all shook hands, and Jan and his crew went down the rope ladder. He started the Mercury 20, the bow line was cast off and with the engine throttled back they drew away from *Island Enterprise*.

Once clear of the ship Jan opened the throttles, the dinghy's bows lifted and the little craft leapt, skimmed and bounced over the hills and valleys of the swells, leaving a phosphorescent trail in its wake as it sped to the south-east. Before long they had picked up the light at Oporto broad on the port bow. Using a torch Jan kept a watchful eye on the chart the Captain had given him and on the time. The dinghy was showing no lights but they saw those of ships in the distance and twice passed fishing vessels, one of which hailed them but they made no reply. As time passed the scattered lights along the coast drew nearer and when he judged the dinghy to be about a mile offshore, Jan altered course and ran parallel to the coast. They roared on through the darkness of early morning until he estimated their position to be a mile south of Praia de Torrera. There he turned the dinghy in-shore and throttled back. With André sounding ahead with a boat-hook, they moved slowly through the shoaling water until they reached the shallows. Jan tilted the Mercury's propeller clear of the water and they paddled in until the bows of the little rubber craft nudged the beach. With shoes round their necks and carrier bags over their shoulders, Goddy and Pippa clambered ashore. Jan stripped, put his clothing in his bag and passed it to André. 'Wait for me on the beach,' he said as he fastened a leather belt with his sheath-knife round his waist. 'I won't be long.'

'Take care,' said André apprehensively. He pushed the

dinghy clear of the sand and Jan paddled it out to deeper water where he lowered the propeller, started the engine and motored seawards. When he was some distance from the beach he stopped the engine, took his knife from its sheath and slashed the dinghy's rubber compartments. Deflated, weighed down by the outboard engine, the dinghy quickly sank. Once it had gone Jan swam back to the beach where André and the others were waiting.

'Bloody cold,' he complained. 'Give me that towel, Pips.' He rubbed himself down vigorously, pulled on his clothes and they set off again along the beach. After a short distance they turned inland and made their way through brushwood broken up by clumps of firs and sand dunes. They came to a tarred road which ran parallel to the beach and followed it in a northerly direction, the sensation of walking on firm ground strangely unreal after two months on a constantly moving deck. Ahead of them a causeway showed up in the light of early morning. Beneath it a small stream gurgled and trickled on its way to the sea.

'Marvellous,' said André. 'Fresh water. Just what we need.' They left the road and followed the stream back towards the beach. They'd not gone far when they found it had led them into a sandy depression surrounded by undergrowth. It was near to five o'clock and the light in the eastern sky was growing stronger.

'Right,' said Jan. 'Let's stop here and get on with it.'

They dropped their bags and for nearly an hour were busy with soap, water, scissors and razors. Pippa cut the men's hair, André cut hers; the men removed their beards and moustaches, and Goddy and Pippa completed the transformation by putting on their sunglasses. Bearing little resemblance to the survivors picked up by *Island Enterprise* they retraced their steps upstream, reached the causeway and followed the road to the north.

'We've landed on a narrow strip of coast,' explained Jan, 'little more than a kilometre wide. According to the chart the sea's on one side and a sort of lake or inland sea – the Ria d'Aveiro – on the other. It's what we wanted, a pretty deserted stretch, but when the day starts up properly there's bound to be road traffic. If we can get a lift we must reach a town or village before long. Then we can buy a map. That's top priority. After that we should . . .'

'Eat,' suggested Pippa. 'I'm rattling inside.'

Jan ignored her. 'We should work out a route.'

André said, 'I reckon we head inland first. Get as far as possible from where we landed. Then go north. The Spanish border can't be more than a few hundred kilometres to the north. With hitching and bussing we ought to reach it by tonight.'

'Don't forget I have no passport,' said Goddy gravely. 'Frontiers will be a problem.'

'Same for all of us.' Jan was abrupt. 'Our passports are useless except for establishing identity when we get to the UK. We've no visas or entry and exit stamps. To use them now simply draws attention to the fact that there's something phoney about us. We'll have to sleep rough and cross borders at night in remote places. Keep well away from frontier posts and human habitation. Shouldn't be difficult once we've got a good map. The important thing is to get one, and then clear out of Portugal as quickly as we can.'

With daylight now established André noticed something unusual. ''ullo, 'ullo, 'ullo,' he mumbled at Goddy. 'I see we're wearing our new shoes.'

The Pole looked at his feet, smiled sheepishly. 'Better for walking. The joggers have had it. Wet and sticky and torn. But I've still got them.' He patted his bag and trudged on, as always limping slightly.

The road came clear of the trees to reveal a vast sweep of water on their right.

'The Ria d'Aveiro I told you about,' said Jan.

They went on, walking in single file and came in time to an attractive building set in well-kept grounds near the water's edge. Cars were parked in the drive beyond gateposts on which bronze plaques bore the name *Pousada*

Ria. It was evidently an hotel; from its looks an expensive one.

Further on the road inclined to the right and ran alongside the lake, where gaily painted fishing boats with high prows and sterns lay close in-shore. Along the beach mounds of seaweed had been heaped for loading. The road led on to become a street with shops and apartments on one side and the lake shore on the other. At that hour it was deserted, the only signs of life wisps of smoke from chimneys, a woman sweeping steps, and a roaming dog which barked at them. A café on a small quay jutting into the lake looked inviting but had not yet opened. 'Seeing it makes me even hungrier,' declared Pippa. Later in the day when they'd bought a map they realized that the lakeshore village was Praia de Torrera.

They trudged on until some time later there appeared ahead the long arch of a bridge spanning the northern narrows of the lake. They'd not gone far when a truck loaded with seaweed came up from behind, but the men in the cab ignored their urgent signals and drove on. Two more trucks passed after that, neither showing the slightest interest.

'No good,' said André. 'Four of us together is too many.' So they split into two groups, Jan and Goddy going ahead, Pippa and André following some distance behind. The sign at the junction before the bridge indicated that the road branching over it to the right led to Murtosa, whereas that to Oporto lay straight ahead. They turned right and followed the road up on to the bridge. From its highest point they had a splendid view of the Ria d'Aveiro, the lake blue and shimmering in the sunlight of early morning. What Murtosa was, town, village or district they had no idea. But it was inland and that was the direction in which they wanted to go, and there they planned to meet again.

When splitting into two groups it had been decided that Jan and Goddy should go ahead. This was on the assumption that André and Pippa following behind would be more likely to secure a lift and, having done so, might be able to persuade drivers to pick up their plodding friends.

'Nothing like a dishy bird to get the drivers going,' Jan said.

Pippa gave him a dirty look. 'Chauvinist pig.'

He put an arm round her, rubbed his cheek against hers, said 'You lovely sex symbol, you!' and kissed her. That was just before he and Goddy had gone ahead.

Their plan succeeded in part. Soon after they'd left the bridge a truck came up from behind with farm produce. Pippa turned and signalled to the driver, the brakes groaned and the truck stopped beside them. The driver put his head out of the window. Pippa put on her best smile. 'Going to Murtosa?'

The driver, sunburnt and unshaven, stuck a rugged forearm through the window, shook a gnarled hand. '*Não falo inglês.*'

'Oh dear,' said Pippa. 'Murtosa?' She repeated slowly.

The driver looked puzzled. '*Como?*'

André took a hand. 'Murtosa.' He pointed down the road, said 'Murtosa' again, this time rolling the R and broadening his vowels. That worked.

'Ah – Murtosa.' The driver's eyes lit up. He nodded, thumbed towards the far door. '*Sim*. Okay.'

They clambered in, joined him in the cab. The truck moved forward, the clatter of its diesel rose as it gathered speed and quite soon they had reached Jan and Goddy who signalled frantically; the driver stared ahead, ignoring them but for a muttered unpleasantry. André put a hand out of the cab window and gave the hikers a rude two finger sign as the truck lumbered past.

The road turned and twisted through fields of maize and vegetables, outlying patches of water, spinneys of trees and distant farmhouses. They passed a farm cart drawn by oxen, the cart and cattle yokes patterned in bright colours. A woman in traditional dress led the oxen, and the children sitting on the hayload waved to them as they went by. Far ahead the outline of a small town showed against the skyline.

'Murtosa,' said the driver.

They reached the outskirts, gestured to him to stop, thanked him as best they could and got down. The truck moved on and they sat by the roadside to wait. It became a long wait for it was almost an hour before Jan and Goddy finally turned up. A new plan was discussed.

'Hitching's no good,' said Jan. 'It took us several lifts and a long time to get here. We haven't done more than twenty-five kilometres in the last two hours. That's useless. We're going to bus from now on.' He said it firmly as if expecting opposition. 'In twos – André and Pippa, and me and Goddy. We'll wait at the same bus stops, get on to the same buses, but we mustn't recognize each other. At the stops and in the buses keep as far apart as possible. We're two different lots, strangers. At least while travelling. That's the way it must look. Got it?'

Pippa said, 'I agree about using buses but why the two different lots idea if we're not hitching? What's so great about that?'

Goddy chimed in then. 'I told you on board, Pips. We've got to be careful. We've been out of touch with South Africa for two months. How do we know what's happened during that time? They're bound to have got something from Stefan and other UCTs if they've taken them in. How do we know Captain Briggs will keep his word about the radio message? We're on the run. That's something we can't afford to forget. We've done our best to cover and confuse our tracks with *Sundance* of Hong Kong and *Chicuala* of Beira, phoney names and all . . .'

'And all that jazz,' suggested André, his forehead puckered.

The Pole gave him a pale-eyed stare before going on. 'But the *Southwind* lost off Mossel Bay story may have blown by now – probably has. Let's assume the SP have guessed we sailed for somewhere abroad, that they've alerted police everywhere, Interpol the lot. We can't afford to take chances. When *Island Enterprises's* radio message gets through and is sorted out things are going to hot up.'

'Goddy the escape artist,' quipped Pippa looking unhappy; but the bussing plan was agreed and they got on to the subject of money. Jan said, 'I'll fix that. Give you enough to carry on with.'

'Good.' André pulled at his ear. 'Let's start now.'

Jan took a brown paper parcel from his carrier bag and tore off the paper wrapping. Inside was the radio spares box with its *Marconi Falcon* markings. A foolscap envelope was fastened with cellophane to the bottom of the box. From it he took a wad of £20 notes and gave one to André together with two $5 notes. 'You may be able to change the sterling here. If not wait for a larger town. If there's no bank try a post office, shop or café, whatever. Buy something. You and Pips will need food. They'll probably change the dollars for that – and fiddle the change.'

'I'll say we need food.' Pippa brushed the hair from her eyes and patted her stomach. 'I'm famished.'

With these plans made they walked into Murtosa, André and Pippa leading, the others some distance behind. They'd agreed to keep each other in sight as far as possible.

Jan found a small general store-cum-stationer where with the help of Goddy's French and smattering of Spanish they were able to buy a map, pocket notebook and a ballpoint pen. For these he used dollars. The shopkeeper told them there was a *cambio* down the street where they could change money. There they changed their remaining dollars and a £20 note into escudos and hunted round for a Portuguese/English dictionary. But Murtosa was little more than a large sprawling village and they had no luck. In a dingy café near the *cambio* they bought ham rolls and glasses of milk, took them to a table outside and studied the Michelin map.

'Main road will be best for buses,' Goddy suggested. 'Faster and more frequent services than minor roads.'

Jan agreed and with that in mind they settled on a route. The main Lisbon–Oporto road, the N12, lay about ten kilometres east of Murtosa. Once on the N12 a short journey south would bring them to the junction with the N16 which in turn would take them due east to Viseu. From there they could bus north by way of Lamego, Vila Real and Chaves to the Spanish frontier. On the final leg they'd leave the bus short of the border at Vila Verde and walk on into the mountains with the object of crossing into Spain at a remote point that night.

Jan did some mental arithmetic. 'That's going to be about three hundred kilometres,' he said. 'If buses average around fifty, that's six hours. Allowing for bus changes, waits at bus stops, getting something to eat, etcetera, let's say ten hours.'

Goddy looked at his watch. 'Nine-thirty now. In ten hours it'll be seven-thirty. Sun sets about six-thirty. Should be just about right. We rest for a few hours somewhere in the bush after leaving the bus near Vila Verde. That gives us most of the night to make the crossing.'

There was nothing wrong with the plan. It was simple, logical and sensible, but they were to find that, like so many well-considered plans, this one wasn't going to work out quite the way they hoped it would.

TWENTY-THREE

By ten o'clock they had boarded their first bus of the day. It took them from Murtosa to Albergaria-Velha where they changed to one bound for Viseu, a provincial town eighty kilometres to the east. The road – the N16 – dropped and climbed, snaking its way along the picturesque valley through which the Rio Vouga flowed westwards to the sea.

In Viseu they spent half an hour waiting for a bus to the north, and used the time for minor but essential shopping.

Before one o'clock they were back on the road, this time bound for Vila Real where they lunched at a pavement café before changing to a bus bound for Chaves. That, as it happened, was to be the first of their troubles on the way to the Spanish frontier.

In Viseu, when Jan took sterling notes from the envelope attached to the Marconi Falcon box, a watching Goddy had observed, 'Why d'you hang on to those radio spares, Jan? It's only more weight to carry around.'

Unable to duck the question Jan had said, 'They're ore samples belonging to my father – or rather to his syndicate. They didn't want them assayed in South Africa. Afraid the big mining groups might get to hear the results and check on the areas the syndicate has under option for mineral rights. I have to hand them to Dad's contact in London. They'll be assayed there.'

'Couldn't you have posted them?'

'Yes. But he'd have had to declare the contents. Always the risk of a leak, you know. Better to use a courier if you can.'

The Pole smiled understandingly. 'I see. I wondered why you went flat out to rescue those radio spares from the fire.'

'I was worried about the money, not the samples. But they were in the same parcel, and in fairness to Dad I felt I had to bring them along. It was the least I could do after all he'd done for us.'

'Of course.' Goddy looked thoughtful. 'Why were they in a radio spares box?'

'Customs men expect yachts to have radio spares.' Jan looked from the Pole to his watch. 'Let's go. It's getting late.'

While at sea in *Sundance* he had told André about the ore samples but he was sorry he'd had to confide this to someone outside the family. He reassured himself, however, with the knowledge that he'd substituted London for Antwerp – at least Goddy didn't know all the story. Not that he really mistrusted the man; it was simply gut reaction to keep family secrets. The long.voyage in *Sundance* had changed his opinion of Goddy. He felt now that the Pole was someone who could be relied on in spite of his anti-apartheid activities. But Jan was glad he'd told no-one about the pictures; the Renoir and the two Cézannes which had been lost in the fire. He'd not even told André. His brother was, he feared, too much of an idealist, too critical of materialism, to approve of that sort of thing.

It was a cold night in late winter, the wind off the Magakiesberg Mountains whistling bleakly through the wiremesh surround of the tennis court where Otto Bretsmar and his wife were discussing the letter he'd received that day from Simon Lutgarten in Antwerp.

'I hope he's been discreet in what he's written,' said Mrs Bretsmar apprehensively.

'Naturally. I wouldn't have left it in the office if he hadn't. A quite ordinary letter with a mix of business and family news. He says they're not taking a holiday for some months because Gerhard is expected home from Indonesia shortly and they don't want to miss him.'

'Gerhard?' Mrs Bretsmar's thoughts were elsewhere. 'Who's he?'

'You don't know Gerhard?'

'I don't think I do, Otto.'

'Well, you ought to.' It was said with a mirthless laugh.

'Why?'

Somewhat unnecessarily he lowered his voice. 'Because he's your son Jan. Code name "Gerhard". Don't you remember?'

'Oh, of course. I'd forgotten. Those poor boys. It's more than two months now since I've seen them or even heard of them. Being without news is terrible, Otto. You don't know what it does to me. It really is terrible. Anything may have happened.'

Mr Bretsmar put an arm round his wife's frail shoulders. 'Don't worry too much, Kate. You always think the worst. You must think positively. That's the secret of success. Look what it's done for me.' He dropped the butt of a cigar on the lawn, stubbed it out with his heel. 'It's the first of September. They should be approaching the English Channel any day now. Maybe they're already there. Harry Morris and Simon Lutgarten will let us know as soon as they have news.'

'Oh dear. I hope they're discreet about it.' Mrs Bretsmar, too, had lowered her voice.

'Yes. Very discreet.' A note of irritation crept into her husband's voice. 'What's worrying me at the moment is something quite different. The insurance brokers.'

'Why? They're not suspicious are they, Otto?'

'No. Not at all. But they're pressing me to accept settlement for the loss of *Southwind*. Lloyds want the matter concluded. I've explained that the yacht's no longer mine. Told them I made it over to Jan by deed of gift shortly before he sailed. They've seen the deed, but they say I'm still the insurer. Anyway, I told them we'd not given up hope – stressed that the yacht might have been dismasted – lost the use of her radio – drifted down into the Southern Ocean. I said we believed they may still be found; that to claim now would be to admit we'd given up hope, something we're not prepared to do.' He hesitated and in a brief moment of silence all that could be heard was the moaning of the wind. 'You see, Kate,' he went on. 'It's a matter of principle. I can't accept insurance settlement for a yacht I know is still afloat – *and* still an asset within the family. I mean, *you* know I wouldn't do anything dishonest.'

'I'm sure you wouldn't, Otto.' Mrs Bretsmar spoke with such lack of emphasis that her husband wondered what she really thought.

They left Vila Real for Chaves soon after half past four. It was a hot torpid afternoon and the motion of the bus, the monotonous drone of its engine, and the uninspiring nature of the countryside soon induced sleep. It was Goddy who first woke to find that they were in the wrong bus. The stubby distance posts along the road were marked N15, not N2 as they should have been. He woke Jan and broke the news. They saw from the Michelin map that the N15 led off to the east to a town called Murca. From there it would presumably be possible to get a bus to Chaves, but it would add something like sixty kilometres to the journey and a good deal more in time. 'Bloody nuisance,' complained Jan. 'Probably means at least another few hours.'

'Doesn't really matter.' Goddy was apathetic. 'We're not exactly pressed for time. Wonder where we went wrong?'

'Can't think. We asked that guy at the terminus. He directed us to this bus. I saw Chaves on its destination board when we got in. Perhaps it was switched after that. We were the first people into the bus. Wonder if André and Pippa have spotted the mistake?'

Goddy turned, took a quick look, grinned. 'They're fast asleep.'

In Murca, a grubby little market town, they learnt that after a turnround and change of crew the bus would leave for Pedras Salgadas later in the evening, arriving there at nine o'clock that night. It would leave Pedras Salgadas for Chaves on the following morning. Their informant, who introduced himself as Federico, was a wizened little man with a triangular face, small glittering eyes and a smile which exposed fragments of yellow teeth. He spoke broken English, learnt, he explained, during his years in London working as a waiter. He told them there was a good *pensao* in the amusement park at Pedras Salgadas where they could spend the night. 'Better you sleep there, *senhor*. Nice place. Very clean. Murca no good.' A disapproving arm encompassed the street. 'Too much bandito thees place.'

TWENTY-FOUR

It was dark when the bus reached the terminus at Pedras Salgadas. The passengers got off, Goddy asked the driver the way to the park, he pointed to a nearby road and they made their way down it, Jan and Goddy leading. They'd agreed to sleep rough that night; a hotel or *pensao* would want to see their passports.

'Goddy hasn't got one and we can't use ours,' Jan spoke with authority. 'So we've no option.'

'The night doesn't look too bad,' said André. 'Could be worse.'

The park turned out to be a rambling, somewhat neglected affair of lawns and gardens at the foot of a tree-covered hillside. There was a swimming pool, a children's playground, tennis courts, souvenir shops, mineral baths, a disco and a restaurant. A white building of medium size where people were eating and drinking in the forecourt appeared to be the *pensao* of Federico's recommendation.

At the far end of the park a weatherworn casino was decked with strings of coloured lights. Near it a drive led up through pine-covered slopes to an old hotel. Empty, deserted, with peeling sun-baked paint and broken windows, it stood among the pines with an air of lost grandeur, the relic of more elegant days when the mineral baths and casino were the haunts of the well-to-do.

Before they reached the *pensao* Jan and Goddy stopped in the shadows of a hedge. As André and Pippa passed Jan muttered, 'Find a table. Get something to eat. We'll look for a place to sleep tonight. Won't be long.'

It took them a little time to find and decide on a secluded place among the pines above the *pensao*. It was behind a

175

dilapidated aviary not far from the deserted hotel in which they planned to shelter if it rained. Back at the *pensao* they took a table near André and Pippa. The forecourt was well patronized and Jan felt more at ease and pleasantly anonymous than at any time since landing in Portugal that morning. He confided this to Goddy. '*This morning,*' said the Pole, 'seems like years ago.'

The waiter came, took their order and went. While they waited they made do with butter and rolls. Cheered by the knowledge that food, drink and sleep were on their way, they discussed the journey, laughed about the mistake over the bus and Federico's English, and were generally more relaxed than they had been for a long time. André and Pippa, a few tables away, seemed in much the same mood, and Pippa's cheerful laughter made Jan wish dearly that he could swop places with André. He was thinking what a super girl she was when he noticed a couple two tables away watching him. He and the Pole were evidently the subject of their conversation, for several times the woman had looked at her companion and nodded gravely before turning back to look again.

'There's a couple at a table missing one on your right who seem interested in us,' said Jan in a low voice. 'Know who they are?'

Goddy turned his head briefly. 'Yes. Seen him before. Car salesman from Cape Town. I think he's recognized me.' It was said casually but after that the Pole kept his back to the stranger. Shortly afterwards he said, 'This could be embarrassing, Jan. I think I'd better go into the *pensao* with my bag. He'll think I've gone to my room. I'll pick up a beer and snack in the bar. Tell the waiter I've gone for a pee. I'll wait for you up at the aviary. Okay?'

'Sure,' said Jan.

Goddy forced a laugh. 'Could be awkward if he came over for a chat.'

'I suppose so.' A flicker of doubt appeared on Jan's face. 'You'd better go,' he said. 'See you later. Coming soon. I'm dead tired.'

'Same here.' The Pole got up, took a carrier bag from the chair. 'If he comes over when I've gone, say you met me in the bar. We had a drink together, then decided to sit out here. Carry on as if nothing has happened. Don't hurry. It'll look suspicious if you do.'

Jan said, 'Right. You'd better get cracking.'

Goddy slung the strap of the bag over his shoulder, nodded to Jan. 'Bye now,' he said in a loud voice.

Jan was watching the Pole limp away when the stranger at the nearby table came over with a folded newspaper. He introduced himself. 'Tim McLean from Cape Town. Excuse me asking, but that man who's just gone? Friend of yours?'

Jan looked up in surprise. 'No. Met him in the bar half an hour ago. What's the trouble?'

'Know who he is?'

'No. He told me to call him Joe.'

McLean unfolded the newspaper, pointed to a paragraph. 'I'm not absolutely certain,' he said, 'but that's who I think he is. Beard and longish hair have gone, and he's wearing dark glasses. But if that's not him with that hoarse foreign voice and the limp I'll eat my hat.'

Jan looked up at McLean, took the paper. It was the *Herald Tribune*, international edition, dated 1st September. He read the paragraph McLean had indicated. The report from Washington was headed SOVIET SPY, STATE DEPARTMENT'S NO COMMENT ON SECRET DOCUMENT.

It read: *A State Department spokesman yesterday confirmed reports from Pretoria that KGB agent Boris Krasnov, alias Willi Helmut Braun, alias Stanislaw Godeska, for whom South African Security Police have been searching for some time, is now believed to have escaped from the Republic and crossed the border into Mozambique.*

Jan stopped reading, watched McLean with puzzled, disbelieving eyes. 'You mean to say that guy's a Soviet spy? You're sure that's him?'

'If it's the man I think he is then his name certainly was Stanislaw Godeska when I last saw him in Cape Town,' said McLean. 'But read on, there's more there.'

Jan read on: *The spokesman declined to comment on rumours current in Pentagon circles that Krasnov had in his possession a highly secret document relating to joint action to be taken by the United States and South African governments in the event of a Soviet military presence developing on the Angola-Namibian border.*

Jan said, 'Christ! That's really something. If he *is* the guy. What's he to you? How d'you know him?'

'He bought a used VW Golf from me in Cape Town last year. Low mileage, clean condition, good buy. Said he represented some German firm. Kept bringing the car back. Belly-aching about this and that. I don't forget that sort easily.'

Jan frowned his bewilderment. 'What are you going to do?'

'Don't know.' McLean shrugged his shoulders. 'The wife and I are here on holiday. Off to Spain first thing in the morning. Should report him, I suppose, but I don't know.' He looked doubtful. 'Don't want to get involved with the Portuguese police. Could be held up for days here. And I'm not *dead* certain he's the guy, though I'm pretty sure.'

Jan nodded. 'That's right. Never know what happens if you get involved with the police.'

McLean looked worried, worked his lips. 'You're a South African, aren't you?'

'Yah. But I'm in the UK now. Got a job in London. In the City. Over here on holiday. Sort of hitch-hike tour, you know.'

'I thought so. Your accent.' McLean laughed, '*Our* accent I should say.' The cheerfulness went, he looked unhappy. 'Think he's coming back to the table?'

'I've no idea. Shouldn't think so.'

'You reckon I should do something about this?'

Jan hesitated. It was impossible for him to say what he knew. The situation called for quick thinking. Eventually he said, 'Why not write to the police in Lisbon enclosing the cutting? Say you think you saw this guy here a couple of days ago. It'll take at least twenty-four hours to reach Lisbon. Don't see you can do more than that if you want to avoid getting tied up. You could do it anonymously, couldn't you?'

McLean looked relieved. 'You're right,' he said. 'Dead right. That's a really good idea.' He smiled. 'By the way what's your name?'

'Johan Smit,' lied Jan with easy familiarity.

McLean held out a hand. 'Well. Hope I haven't started a false hare, but seeing that he was with you I felt I had to come across and check up.' They shook hands. 'What'll you do if he comes back?'

'I don't think he will,' said Jan. 'But I'm going shortly. Don't want to get mixed up with a KGB agent.'

'I reckon you'd be wise to do that. To go, I mean. Well, so long. And good luck.'

'Same to you. Enjoy Spain.'

McLean went back to his table, spoke to his wife, she got up, looked at Jan and smiled and they left.

TWENTY-FIVE

Jan scribbled on a sheet in his pocket notebook: *Urgent — You two follow me discreetly*. He folded it, got up, slipped the strap of the carrier bag over his shoulder and walked past André's table dropping the note on it as he passed.

A few minutes later they met in the darkness behind the *pensao*. Jan told them about McLean and the *Herald Tribune* report.

'That's absolutely crazy. I just can't believe it.' André's sudden hoarseness conveyed incredulity and fear.

There was an agonized discussion, a hurried shaken exchange of views, the brothers dismayed, somehow at odds with each other. Pippa frightened, uncertain. 'So what do we *do*?' she implored. 'We can't just stand here talking.'

'We're not going to.' Jan was brusque. 'Go back to the table and wait there. We'll go up to the aviary. Confront Godeska – or whatever his name is,' he added bitterly. 'See how he reacts. If he's got that document we're going to get it. It's the least we can do. Helping a Soviet spy to escape – Christ! That's what sticks in my gullet. And once we've got it I'm handing him over to the police.'

'You can't do that. You don't *know* that he's a KGB agent.' There was pleading in Pippa's tone. 'May not be the same man. It's all guess work. I'm sure Goddy's not a spy. He's too decent for that. Can't be the same man.'

'What? Two Stanislaw Godeskas in Cape Town?' challenged Jan. 'Grow up! Of course it's the same man. If you want to keep out of it you can. But I'm going to get him. He's been using you kids, manipulating your precious anti-apartheid movement for his bosses in the Kremlin. The man's a bloody spy, *agent provocateur*, whatever.'

Pippa's only response was to sigh loudly before going off into the darkness with the money André had given her to pay the waiter. She was a frightened, disturbed and very confused young woman.

'We'll check the bar first,' Jan told André. 'Godeska said he'd pick up food and drink there on his way to the aviary.'

But he wasn't in the bar, nor was he in the WC which adjoined it. 'Might have gone back to the table,' André suggested.

'Not unless he knew McLean had gone.'

But it was worth checking so back they went to the forecourt. The Pole was not there but the waiter was, with a loaded tray. He glowered at them, grumbled irritably in Portuguese. Jan mumbled an apology and paid the bill.

'Now for the aviary,' he said when the waiter had gone.

They made their way round the *pensao*, stopped in the semi-darkness behind it. Jan opened his carrier bag.

André said, 'What are you looking for?'

'Torch and sheath-knife. It's dark by the aviary, Godeska's in a tight corner. He might get stupid.'

'Being a bit dramatic, aren't you?' suggested André.

'We'll see.' Jan fumbled away in the bag, stopped suddenly. 'For God's sake,' he roared, almost shouted. 'This isn't my bag. That bastard's gone off with it. Most of the cash is in it. Over a thousand quid. Dad's ore samples. My clothes. The sheath-knife. The Michelin map. The dictionary – every goddam thing. This is Godeska's bag. I'll tell you something else. The Walther pistol's not here.'

'He often keeps it in his denim jacket. And he could have taken the wrong bag by mistake,' André was doing his best to be cheerful. 'After all they're identical.'

'Mistake my foot. Point is where is Mister bloody Stanislaw Godeska alias Boris Krasnov now? That bloke knows what he's up to. He's been using us to get away. *Southwind* and the lot. He's a cunning sod – a quick thinker. No doubt about that. But McLean comes along and upsets his plans. So he takes *my* bag – knowing the cash is there – and clears out.' With sudden decision he said, 'Come on. Let's go after him. He can't have got far.' Zipping up the carrier bag he slung it over his shoulder and headed down towards the *pensao*.

They found Pippa at the table, told her what had happened.

'You stay here.' Jan gave her a bundle of escudo notes. 'If we're not back soon, get a room. If they ask for your passport, say your husband's got it. His bag was stolen and he's gone off looking for the guy. Pay for the room in advance, that'll satisfy them. You've got close on fifty quid there.' He put down the bag. 'You'd better deal with this, Pips. It's Godeska's. No use to me.'

André pointed to the carrier bag on the chair beside her. 'Mine too, Pippa.'

'Me with three bags. That'll look funny, won't it?'

'Not really. Don't forget you've got a husband,' Jan chuckled. 'Leave Godeska's under the table here. Couldn't care less what happens to it.'

'Can't I come with you?' Pippa looked at them with searching uncertain eyes. 'Don't want to stay here on my own.'

'No. You stay,' said Jan decisively. 'We'll be back. Pretty late maybe, but we'll be back. Don't hang about out here too long. Get a room. The wind's coming up. May be cold tonight. And you're dead tired.' He thought of something, half laughed. 'Don't forget you're a Bennet. *Mrs* Bennet now. Wish you were Mrs *Jan* Bennet,' he added, squeezing her arm.

André said, 'Bye Pips. Look after yourself.' The two men disappeared into the darkness.

They'd not gone far when Jan realized they'd overlooked a more than likely hideout. The deserted hotel. So back they went up the hill. An eerie search followed, hunting in the dark through deserted rooms, hurrying down dusty corridors, climbing creaking stairs, the wind whistling dismally through broken windows, their only light the small torch Bill Snell had given Pippa as a present before they left *Island Enterprise*. It had to be used sparingly.

At times they would stop and listen, believing that if Godeska heard them getting too close he might move. And they were right. They'd searched through the desolate building right back to the service quarters, the kitchen and pantries. Jan had gone down a ladder into a débris-filled cellar when he heard the distant slamming of a door, followed by André's shouted, 'Jan, quick!'

He raced up the ladder but André had gone. From the far end of the corridor to his left there came the sound of running feet so he hurried down it, turned a corner in the dark and collided with André.

'Shuush! Listen!' André put a restraining hand on his brother's shoulder. 'He was just ahead of me when I lost him.'

They waited, tense, straining to hear, but the only sounds were their own uneven breathing and the mournful whistle of the wind. Then, suddenly, like a distant gun shot, a door banged at the far end of the building. As they made off in that direction it banged again several times but without rhythm.

Jan stopped. 'Sounds as if the wind's got hold of an open door, André. Was it banging before?'

'No. It's just begun.'

'Come on then. Must have been him.' Jan ran on down the corridor with André close on his heels.

Lamp standards stood at intervals along the drive which led down from the deserted hotel through wooded slopes to the casino. It was in the light of one of these that they saw, briefly and several hundred yards ahead of them, the hurrying figure of the Pole, carrier bag over his shoulder.

'Come on,' Jan pointed. 'Run like hell.'

Godeska must have seen or heard them because he left the drive and took to the trees where it was dark. They followed, led by the sound of pine twigs snapping under the weight of running feet. They lost him then, only to see him again minutes later crossing the drive ahead of them and making for the casino's car park. It was a busy place at that hour, groups of visitors and cars coming and going against a noisy background of voices and the blare of taped music. They saw him break into a walk as he reached the fringe of this activity and disappear among the cars and people. They reached the car park and began a systematic search but it was fruitless. Breathing heavily from his exertions, Jan said, 'He must have faded away into the crowd. All these people moving about make it dead easy.'

'What about in there?' André looked towards the casino. 'Good cover inside.'

'Could be. Let's try.' Jan lead the way through parked

cars to the main entrance. 'I'll go in,' he said. 'You stay here in case he comes out before I see him.'

André nodded. 'Will do.'

Jan was stopped at the entrance by a commissionaire who pointed to the ticket bureau. That was an unexpected delay. He joined the queue but it was several minutes before he could buy a ticket.

The dimly lit casino was thronged with people, gamblers and lookers-on crowding round tables where roulette, baccarat and chemin-de-fer were being played. The steady hum of voices was punctuated by the calls of croupiers and the click and rustle of the counters they raked and tossed about the tables. Aided by his six-foot-four of height Jan could see over the heads of most of those around him but it was a large area with recesses, screens and passageways, and though he once caught a glimpse of the Pole on the far side of the hall – and made for him as fast as he could, dodging and darting through groups of people – he soon lost touch again. For some time after that he searched through the main hall, the recesses off it and even the lavatories but there was no sign of Godeska. In desperation he accosted a mild affable looking man. Were there any exit doors other than the main entrance? *Não falo inglési, senhor*, was the puzzled reply.

Eventually he managed to find two exit doors, one at each side of the building. They were guarded by uniformed staff who couldn't speak English. Instinctively he tried Afrikaans but that produced no more than head shakes. He had no doubt that Godeska must have left by one of the side exits, so he went back to André at the front entrance. 'No good,' he shook his head despondently. 'Saw him once but lost him again in the crowd. He's not in there now. Must have left by a side door. There are two of them.'

After a hurried consultation they decided to make for the bus station. 'Remember his keenness to get to Lisbon, to go to an embassy,' André recalled. 'There's bound to be a Soviet Embassy there. Once he got to it he'd be home and dry.'

'You could be right.' Jan nodded with slow deliberation. 'But his top priority now must be to get away from us. As far and as fast as he can. I reckon he'll take any bus that offers. Come on. Let's go.'

It was close to ten o'clock and a good deal cooler now, the wind blowing leaves and scraps of paper about the roadway beneath the steps down which they hurried.

To have run would have attracted attention, so they walked as fast as they reasonably could, back across the park to the main gates beyond which the road led into the town. Making their way down it they headed for the bus station. Once there they found a number of buses without crews and a few waiting passengers but little other activity. A bus at the head of the line with an idling engine had the name Vidago on its destination board. Jan and André watched while several people boarded and took their seats but Godeska was not among them. They were walking back down the line of buses when where was the sound of an engine revving up and they turned in time to see the Vidago bus pull away. As it moved forward a dark shape ran from behind a parked truck, grabbed a handrail and swung aboard.

It was Godeska.

Jan and André raced after the bus, shouting and gesticulating, hoping the driver would stop but it gathered speed and disappeared down the road, the pungent fumes of its exhaust blowing in their faces. Back in the bus station, using signs, gestures and André's smattering of schoolboy French they made urgent inquiries. Vidago was thirteen kilometres to the north, the bus that had just left would end its journey there. Their informant, a bus driver predictably without English, took them to the notice board, pointed with a stubby finger at the timetable. They saw that there'd be no other bus to Vidago that night. They saw, too, that there was nothing to Lisbon until the following morning.

Jan stared gloomily into the darkness. 'We've got to get after him right away. Let's get a taxi.'

'Taxi?' they inquired of the bus driver. He frowned, tapped his wristwatch, raised his eyebrows, shook his head doubtfully, went through the motions of telephoning. '*Dez, vinte minuto*.' He indicated ten and twenty with his fingers.

Jan turned to André. 'What's all that about?'

'He's trying to tell us we'll have to phone for a taxi and it may take ten or twenty minutes to get one because it's late.'

'That's no bloody use.' Jan looked across the road to a side street from which came the distant thump and blare of rock music. At its far end the lights of a disco flashed in the darkness. He said, 'Come on. I've an idea.' Walking fast they crossed the main street and went down the side street to the disco. It occupied one side of a small tree-lined square in which stood a few parked cars and many motorcycles. But for a mongrel urinating against a car wheel the dimly-lit square was deserted. Waves of amplified music beat and boomed from the disco shutting out all other sounds. Crossing over to the darker end of the square they walked among the parked motorcycles, small machines with names like Macal, Casal Sport, Voia, Puch and others.

'Looks like Portugal's two-stroke country,' complained Jan. 'Haven't seen a big bike all day. Most of this lot are between fifty and a hundred cc.'

The mechanics of motorbikes presented no problem to Jan and André who'd grown up with them, but the wheel locks and security chains did. Within a few minutes, however, they'd found two unlocked machines, one of 75 cc, the other 100 cc. There wasn't time to be choosy so they took what offered, started the engines and tested the controls.

'Ready?' called Jan, looking large on a little Zundapp.

The engine of André's Casal Sport was popping and hiccupping. He nodded.

They switched on headlights, the engine notes rose to a higher pitch and they pulled out of the square into the street at its far end. Some way down it they turned left, travelled a block, then right on to the N2, the main road to Vidago.

The bus had a fifteen minute start but the timetable had shown several stops before Vidago; it would be a close run thing but they believed they might just overtake it before it reached its destination.

With the little engines screaming in crescendo they roared into the night.

TWENTY-SIX

He was congratulating himself on having got clear when he saw them at the bus station. Fortunately he'd already moved into the shadows at its northern end where he stood against a wall behind a parked truck. When the bus for Vidago pulled out they were walking away, their backs towards him, so he ran from the shadows, grabbed the handrail at the passenger door and swung himself aboard. He'd seen them turn and chase the bus, waving their arms.

There were few passengers and he sat at the back where there were empty rows. At the station bureau he'd learnt that the bus was the last for Vidago that night. He realized that his pursuers might try for a taxi but it would mean delay. That too he'd learnt at the bureau.

Tired as he was he knew he couldn't relax. Once in Vidago he'd have to move on. The sooner he got away from there, the better his chances of escape. The encounter with McLean had been a disaster. From inside the *pensao* he'd looked back through a window and seen him talking to Jan. Two months had elapsed since *Southwind* left Rooiels Bay. A good deal about Stanislaw Godeska could have appeared in Cape Town papers since then.

He took the Michelin map from the carrier bag, studied it closely. Chaves was only 19 kilometres from Vidago. He'd make for Chaves as soon as the bus arrived there. Start walking if necessary; hitch, take whatever offered. Sleep rough outside Chaves – my God, he thought, how I need that sleep – and take the train from Chaves to Lisbon in the morning. He could do that now for at long last he had money, something he'd lacked since they'd landed in Portugal.

Once in the Soviet Embassy he'd be safe. What he had to deliver would be taken on to Moscow by courier. He'd follow later, report to the Chief personally. Borodin would be pleased, suggest a vacation on the Black Sea coast. Krasnov had no doubt he'd earned it.

The bus pulled into Vidago, the passengers climbed down and disappeared in the darkness. It was late and there were few people about as he made his way across the main street of the small country town, cursing the three-quarters moon which had just come clear of the clouds. Moonlight was the last thing he wanted. Entering a side street he heard the sound of motorcycles behind him. Drawing back into the shadows he turned to see two helmetless riders pull up beside the bus he'd just left; large and easily recognizable, they were calling to the driver, miming, gesticulating. Two of the gestures were unmistakable; one rider was indicating something carried over his shoulder, the other made circles with thumbs and forefingers and held them to his eyes. He'd seen enough. Hurrying down the darkened street he took the first turn left which offered, then the next right, moving away from the centre of the town towards its residential area.

He turned a corner, stopped suddenly. Some ten yards ahead of him a woman was getting out of the driver's seat of a small car. She went round to the boot, unlocked it, began to take something from it. He moved forward quietly, stepped into the roadway behind her, spoke in a low voice, '*Senhora. Un momento, faz favor.*'

She turned to face him, frail, middle-aged, her expression guarded, uncertain. He struck her left temple with the

Walther pistol. She sank to her knees, holding her head with both hands, puzzled eyes staring at him in the moonlight. He struck again, this time at the centre of the forehead, between the hands, and she rolled on to her side. He locked the boot, took out the keys, threw the carrier bag into the car, slipped on the seat belt, started the engine and drove away without lights.

He made several left and right turns only to find that he'd ended up in a cul-de-sac. The Bretsmar brothers would be searching Vidago for him now, he'd no doubt about that, but they wouldn't be looking for a motor-car. He wondered if he should change his plans, use the Opel for the journey to Lisbon? But he decided against that. The police would soon be hunting for the car, and he was too exhausted to undertake a long drive. Just keeping awake was going to be enough of a problem.

He took the Michelin map, the sheath-knife and the Marconi box from the bag, ripped the cellophane-attached envelope from the bottom of the box and put it in an inside pocket of his jacket. When he abandoned the car he'd leave the box and the bag behind; everything in the bag identified Jan Bretsmar. He slung it on to the back seat, put the Marconi box on the floor at his feet and the knife in his waistband. In the light of a small torch he consulted the map. To reach the main road to Chaves, the N2, would mean going back into the cente of Vidago. That would be dangerous. There was another road to Chaves, the N311–3, via Loivos. A little longer that way, but it was a minor road running through remote country. It would be less busy and therefore safer than the N2. The map showed it branching off east from the southern end of the town. He turned the car and using side lights only drove south through the residential area. There were a few lighted windows in the houses but he'd seen no-one in the streets other than two people close together against a wall in the shadows of a high tree. Lovers, he supposed. Switching on the headlights he turned into the main road and drove on for a short distance until he saw the sign *Chaves-Loivos*. He turned left, accelerated, changed up through the gears and soon the little Opel was bouncing along the country road at a useful speed.

It was a winding, tree-lined road, its tarred surface bumpy and broken at the verges. Fearful of falling asleep he kept the windows open. He was grateful for the moonlight now. It made it easier to see the road and watch the verges. He planned to stop well outside Chaves, hide the car somewhere and walk into the hills to find a place to sleep.

It was a pity he'd had to strike the woman but it was as unavoidable as it had been unpleasant. His safety against hers. There was no way he could have risked her screams, any more than he could have risked the noise of shooting her. Another operational necessity. He dismissed the incident from his mind and concentrated on what lay ahead.

With their engines at full throttle two helmetless motorcyclists raced into Vidago and slowed down before pulling up alongside the stationary bus, their engines popping and spluttering.

André said, 'We're too late. It's empty.'

'The driver's still there.' Jan jutted his chin towards the driver's window. 'Don't suppose he'll speak English.'

The driver couldn't. However, with gestures and miming they succeeded in getting their message across. The driver's visible emotions ranged from irritated frowns to understanding smiles, after which he pointed to the side street immediately to the left of the garage on the far side of the road.

'Thanks,' Jan shouted, accelerating away. André raced after him. Though bright moonlight helped the search they reached the end of the street without seeing anyone. Jan throttled to a stop, André drew up alongside him.

'Like looking for a needle in a bloody haystack,' said Jan.

André nodded. 'No future in dashing round like this. If the driver's right Goddy's on this side of the main street.

Let's split up, search with some sort of system. I'll do the northern half, you the southern. Say we meet again on this corner in five minutes? If no luck we do the other side in the same way. He may have doubled back there.'

'Might as well.' Jan was despondent. 'Got to do something.'

They met again on the corner five minutes later, dismounted, switched off lights and engines and parked the bikes. 'Nothing doing, haven't seen a soul. Vidago's gone to bed.' Jan yawned. 'Christ I'm tired. Nearly fell off a minute ago.'

André yawned in sympathy. 'Not much point in searching the way we are. If he sees our headlights or hears the engines he's only got to slip behind a hedge or get into a lane between houses.'

'Talking of hedges,' said Jan. 'I'm bursting to pee.'

'Same here.'

They went round the corner, relieved themselves against a wall under the shadows of a large tree. A car with sidelights came down the street, travelling slowly south. As it passed André yelped. 'Hey, look. That's him.'

By the time Jan turned to look the car had gone. 'You sure?' he asked doubtfully.

'Just about. Saw his face in the moonlight, dark glasses and all. Almost certain it's him. He must have nicked the car. Come on.'

Jan buttoned his flies as he ran. 'Once more to the breach . . .' He laughed exultantly. 'He'll be heading for the main road. Making for Lisbon probably.'

They leapt on to their machines, kicked the engines into life, switched on headlights and accelerated down the street in the direction the car had taken. They reached the main road just in time to see twin red lights ahead swing sharp left. With their two-stroke engines at full stretch they rode down to where the car had turned, saw the signpost *Chaves-Loivos*, and swept round the corner.

Distant lights showed up in the rearview mirror; two lights. At first he thought they were the headlights of a car but soon realized from their relative movements that they were two single headlights; two motorcycles.

He accelerated, drew ahead, but not for long. The lights began to gain on him.

The little Opel crested the hill and he changed into top gear, speeding down the winding slope, the tyres shrilling on the turns. At the bottom of the hill the road straightened out and he drove along it at high speed, clumps of trees, patches of cultivated land and isolated farmhouses rushing by in the moonlight.

The lights of his pursuers had faded from the rearview mirror as he drove over the top of the hill but now they showed up again and it was evident they were still gaining on him. He rounded a bend and saw a beam of light coming down the slope of the hill to his right. Moments later he realized that the lights were those of a farm truck which had stopped before gates which a man was opening as the Opel passed.

He raced on, distributing his attention between keeping the car on the road and watching the moonlit scene in the rearview mirror. The farm truck with its trailer had passed through the gates and stopped, straddling the road. He imagined the driver had got down to shut the gates.

The road ahead swung left and climbed again. Shifting to a lower gear he began the climb. The rearview mirror showed no signs of his pursuers and he assumed the truck had held them up.

At the summit of the hill he changed into top and drove fast down the slope into the valley below. It was the moment to take advantage of his lead. He reached back with his right hand, felt for the carrier bag and lifted it over on to the seat beside him. Pulling the Opel towards the left-hand verge he threw the bag out of the window. Next he took the Marconi box from the floor and hurled it well clear. Still no lights coming up behind. The road went left, climbed briefly over a low ridge before continuing its descent into the valley. He pressed the accelerator pedal into the floorboards and watched the speedometer needle climb through 100 to 110, 115 . . . the car swayed, he'd lost concentration, a front near-side wheel slipped off the verge, the back wheels slewed left; he spun the steering wheel left to correct the dry skid, half succeeded, but it was too late. The Opel left the road, slithered down the embankment, crashed through a thicket of gorse, rolled twice and ended up on its side, wheels spinning, some distance beyond the thicket.

Dazed, semi-conscious, he staggered into a grove of pines and sat down against the trunk of a large tree. Soon afterwards he heard the raucous buzz of two-stroke engines and through chinks in the trees saw lights flash by a hundred or so yards from where he sat. The sound of the engines grew fainter and was finally overtaken by the noisy clatter of the farm truck and its trailer as it went lumbering by. He felt a sudden warmth towards the driver of the truck. But he couldn't stay where he was, still close to the overturned car. He got up, moved his limbs one by one, tested them gingerly, realized he'd not suffered any serious damage, and made off through the trees.

It had been impossible to get round the truck and trailer. It was a narrow road and though the truck had turned full lock its radiator stood against the left hand embankment, the long trailer blocking the right hand side of the road. So they waited, hooting and revving the noisy little engines in sheer frustration. The farmer called out something uncomplimentary in Portuguese and showed his disapproval by taking time as he went back to the gates and shut them before returning to the truck.

Jan leant across to André. 'Unco-operative bastard,' he growled. 'He's cost us a couple of minutes.'

The truck pulled away, the empty trailer rattling along behind. They opened their throttles and raced past. A long straight stretch lay before them but there was no sign of tail lights and they realized he must have already topped the hill which loomed ahead. They reached its summit and swept down the long reverse slope, bouncing and swaying, their engines screeching, the little machines reaching towards the 120 kph mark.

At the bottom of the hill the road inclined left again before entering another straight. They tore along it, reached its end and climbed yet another hill from the top of which they could see the road stretching far ahead. But there was no sign of tail lights. They stopped then to consider the situation.

'We've missed him somewhere along the line,' said André. 'He couldn't have got that far ahead.'

'Yah. That bloody farm truck. Krasnov's probably switched off his lights and pulled in somewhere.' Since the meeting with McLean Jan had refused to use the name 'Goddy'. 'We'll have to go back. You take one side of the road, I'll take the other. Not too fast. Look out for places where he could have pulled off and concealed the car.'

Beyond the pine trees a gentle slope led up the hill; in the moonlight he saw an arid hillside with fields long fallow and crumbling stone terraces studded with the dried stumps of dead vines. He set off up the slope and when he reached the top moved cautiously along the summit towards the building he'd seen on the skyline when first leaving the trees. It was a ramshackle affair, isolated, with no sign of a farmhouse on either slope of the hill. Drawing closer he saw that it was an old barn, its wooden sides and corrugated iron roof broken and holed in places. He was about to inspect it when he heard the sound of two-stroke engines in the distance. Looking down into the valley he saw two single lights chasing each other along the road below. Heading south, they'd either given up the chase or were checking back along the route. He watched apprehensively, nerves stretched, as the two lights ascended the hill where the Opel had left the road. But they didn't stop there and before long they'd passed over the hilltop and disappeared from sight. Sighing with relief he went into the barn and with the aid of moonlight and the torch checked through it. A wooden ladder with broken rungs led up to a loft. He climbed the ladder, found the loft floor was covered in hay and set about heaping it into a corner where the roof was intact. He took off his jacket, folded it into a makeshift pillow, put the Walther pistol and the sheath-knife under it and lay down on the straw. Exhausted, he had soon fallen into deep sleep.

Riding back along the road at moderate speed they stopped at places where a car might have turned off and looked for tyre tracks. They continued this until they reached the gates where the farm truck had held them up.

Jan said, 'It's no good. We've covered the road all the way now. His car *must* be hidden somewhere between here and where we turned to come back. There's been no side road he could have taken. I reckon . . .'

'Hey,' interrupted André. 'I've an idea. Remember that wreck we saw way back? The one lying well clear of the road, near the foot of the hill?'

'You mean that job on its side with the bottom of the chassis facing the road?' Jan shook his head. 'That was an old rusted up wreck.'

'The underside of a car always looks rusty and old. When it's rolled down an embankment it's liable to look wrecked.'

'It's been there a helluva long time.'

'I'm probably wrong,' admitted André. 'But I'm going back to check.'

Jan yawned loudly, shrugged his shoulders. 'Okay. Will do. Let's go.'

Towards the bottom of the slope beyond which the wrecked car lay they found the faint track of skid marks and having parked their bikes they followed the trail of disturbed soil down the side of the embankment below the road. It led eventually to a crushed path through a gorse thicket.

Jan examined the broken gorse. 'I guess you're right. This is recent.'

The car had finished up on its side in scrub and brush some fifty yards from the road and they soon reached it. A yellow Opel, engine still warm, smelling strongly of petrol.

'He's probably in it,' André said with some misgiving. He hadn't properly adjusted to the fact that Goddy the old friend was now Krasnov the new enemy. 'I don't think he could have got away with this.'

But Krasnov wasn't in the wreck, nor was Jan's bag or anything else that indicated that the Opel had been used by the man they were chasing. The silk scarf, gloves, lipstick, powder compact and tissues in the glove box suggested a woman's car.

'He's lucky to have got away with it,' said André.

'Bloody lucky.' Jan kicked the broken door. 'He can't be far away. This must have happened within the last twenty minutes. He's probably injured. Let's go look for him.'

They found fresh footprints near the car, recognized the distinctive tread of the new shoes and followed them into the wood. There, on a carpet of pine needles, they disappeared.

'No sign of blood.' André sighed with private relief.

'He'll have got as far from the car as he can. We'd better hide the bikes out of sight of the road, then search.'

When they'd dealt with the bikes they hunted through the trees but there was no trace of Krasnov. Beyond the trees they found themselves confronted by the slopes of a hill. They were wondering what to do next when less than half a mile away, silhouetted against the moonlit sky, they saw a dark shape moving along the ridge.

'See the limp,' cried André. 'It's Goddy.'

'Yah. It's him all right.' There was excitement in Jan's voice. 'Come on. Let's get him.'

It was after midnight when they set off up the hill.

TWENTY-SEVEN

Krasnov shivered in the grip of a nightmare. He was running down a road in the dark, from behind him came the sound of pounding feet and the hoarse voice of the African night watchman; ahead a single bright light came down the road and he stopped, knowing it was the traffic officer on the BMW. He tried to leave the road and run down the embankment but his limbs refused to move. He was trapped. The bright light drew closer, dazzling him, and the voices grew louder as the spectral quality of the dream dissolved into reality and he realized that the voices were those of Jan and André. The light, too, was coming from them. He raised his left hand to shut out the blinding beam and with his right felt for the Walther pistol under the denim jacket.

'Come on,' Jan was saying. 'Get up.'

Playing for time he rubbed his eyes with his free hand saying, 'Oh. Hullo, Jan.' Then with both hands on the straw he pushed himself into a kneeling position, came slowly to his feet. As he did so he whipped an arm round from behind his back, aimed at the shape beyond the torch and pressed the Walther's trigger. Nothing happened. Desperately he slid back the chamber lever and again pressed the trigger; still nothing happened.

'Too bad,' he heard Jan say. 'No ammo. Clip empty, I presume.'

Krasnov's eyes dilated, his lips moved, but no sound came from them. Throwing out his right hand in a gesture of resignation he dropped the pistol. 'You win.' He managed a mirthless laugh. 'But I gave you a good run for your money, didn't I?'

Jan nodded, kept the torch on the Russian's face. 'For a

start, Mister Boris Krasnov,' he said, 'you can hand over that money.'

A shock of surprise showed on the Russian's face. 'I suppose McLean's been talking. It's a lie, of course. An absolute lie.'

'Is it? Willi Helmut Braun alias Ernst Stanislaw Godeska?'

Krasnov shook his head, stared into the torchlight before dropping his eyes. 'I suppose I'll have to hand over the money.' He bent down, put a hand beneath the folded denim jacket, fumbled there, came suddenly upright. André yelled, 'Knife. Look out, Jan. Knife!'

The flash of steel across the beam of light was followed by a scream as Jan's explosive kick landed in the Russian's crutch. Krasnov dropped the knife as he fell, clutching his genitals, his face contorted with pain.

Jan picked up the knife. 'Nothing like a kick in the balls to restore law and order,' he said. 'Now let's proceed in a friendly way.' He frisked the crumpled figure, found the money envelope and a wallet and checked through both in a silence broken only by the Russian's groans. Next he checked through the denim jacket.

'It's not here,' he said, dropping the jacket and pocketing Krasnov's wallet and the money envelope. 'Now we'll have to do a little interrogating, gentle but . . .'

'He's in terrible pain,' André broke in.

'I hope so. That was the object of the exercise.' Jan waited for the groans to subside. When they'd quietened down he said, 'Now, Krasnov. Secret document please.'

The Russian looked up from where he lay on his side, knees drawn up to his chin. 'I don't know what you're talking about.' he said hoarsely.

'Better jack-up your memory, Krasnov, if you don't want another kick in the balls.'

The Russian winced, turned away from his persecutor. 'No, no, not that. Remember all we've been through together. I've honestly not got any document. You can search me.'

Jan did so again, very thoroughly and anything but gently, but found nothing. 'Come on, Krasnov.' His voice was harsh, relentless, as he focused the torch on the Russian's face. 'Where is it?'

'In your bag,' muttered Krasnov.

'Where is the bag?'

'I threw it out of the car window. When I saw your lights coming up from behind.'

'Why?'

'It was instinctive, I suppose. I wanted to get rid of it in case you caught me. I took the bag only to get the money.'

Jan reached down, pulled Krasnov to his feet, held him at arm's length with one hand, directed the torch beam in his eyes with the other. 'You're a liar, Krasnov. You wouldn't throw away that document.'

The Russian was close to hysteria, mumbling, pleading in a mixture of English and a language Jan couldn't understand but presumed was Russian.

'Your choice, Krasnov,' he went on. 'You give me the document or I give you another kick in the balls. It's as simple as that.'

Krasnov was shaking, his eyes in the torchlight wide with fear, his hands crossed protectively across his crutch. 'In my left shoe,' he said in a low voice.

Still holding him at arm's length Jan said, 'A document? In your left shoe?' His eyes narrowed in disbelief. 'Too bad if you're joking. Take off that left shoe, André.'

André took it off, pulled out the cork insole. 'Nothing here,' he said.

'Now, Krasnov.' There was a fresh rasp of anger in Jan's voice. 'Quit fooling unless you want to be hurt. Where is it?'

'In the heel,' muttered Krasnov. 'Microfiche.'

'A microfiche,' echoed Jan. 'Bright boy, Boris, aren't you? How do we open the heel?'

Krasnov sighed. 'With a knife. I'll show you,' he quickly added.

'I'm sure you would *if* you had a knife. Go ahead, André. Take that heel off.'

With some effort André prized the heel free of the shoe and ran his fingers over it. 'I can feel a square hold in the upper part of the heel where it joins the shoe. Very small. Can't see what's in it without light.'

Jan increased his one-handed grip on the Russian, passed the torch to his brother.

It took André a little time to extract a minute water-proofed package the size of a rectangular throat lozenge. With the tip of the knife he removed the waterproofing and produced a photographic negative a good deal smaller than a postage stamp. He held it against the torch beam. 'It's a microfiche all right – two pages of it.' He laughed with sudden exuberance. 'Final episode of The Great Shoe Drama.'

'Great,' said Jan. 'Take good care of it.' With his free hand he took the torch from André, shone it in Krasnov's face. 'The radio spares. The Marconi box. Where's that?'

'It also I threw from the car window. It was extra weight. Ore samples were no good to me.'

Jan frowned, shook his head. 'You really are an awkward bastard, aren't you, Boris? Exactly where did you throw away that box?'

'I don't know,' pleaded the Russian with some truth. 'Somewhere beyond where that farm truck came on to the road. Two or three kilometres after that I'd say.'

A few more minutes of intimidating interrogation satisfied Jan that the Russian was telling the truth. The loss of the ore samples had to be accepted. It was nothing like as serious as the destruction of the Renoirs and the Cézanne in the fire on board. The ore samples could be replaced, the pictures couldn't. Nevertheless, he felt he'd let his father down by losing the samples. It would involve a lot of work, worry and delay for the syndicate. But to go back and search along the road for the box would be time-consuming and dangerous. The overriding priority was to cross the border into Spain during the coming night – and before that to get some sleep; it was already after one o'clock in the morning.

But Jan had a final question. 'Where did you get that car, Krasnov?'

'In Vidago. It was parked. Key left in the ignition lock.'

Using bits of old baling wire which lay about the loft they bound Krasnov's hands behind his back and lashed his legs together. The Russian protested. The bindings were too tight. They would interfere with his circulation. The protests left Jan unmoved.

'It really wouldn't be too tragic if you died, Krasnov. Think, they'd make you a Hero of the Soviet Union. Wouldn't that be quite something?'

André, concerned as always about the welfare of others, examined the bindings by torchlight, ran his fingers over them. 'You'll be all right, Goddy,' he said. 'As long as you don't try to force them.'

Jan's sense of what was proper was outraged. 'For Christ's sake stop calling him Goddy. The sod's a Soviet agent. He's used you and your anti-apartheid friends for his lousy spying. Got you into the most bloody awful mess. *And* me. Don't start feeling sorry for the guy.'

'He's a human being.' André spoke with quiet conviction. 'No doubt doing what he feels to be his duty.'

'So am I,' said Jan. 'Doing what I believe to be mine. And while we're on the subject of duty you'd better let me have that microfiche for safe keeping.'

André handed it over. Jan picked up the Walther pistol and slipped it into a pocket. Not long afterwards they lay down to sleep, one on either side of the Russian whom they'd placed face downwards on the hay, his lashed hands behind his back.

Despite shafts of sunshine and the cheerful song of birds it was close to nine o'clock that morning before they'd slept off their exhaustion.

André, first to wake, went to a corner of the loft to relieve himself and it was the sound of creaking floorboards which woke the others. Krasnov at once complained of aches and pains caused by the wire bindings which had bitten into his wrists, legs and ankles.

'We'll take them off for the time being. But don't try any funny tricks.' Jan threw him a menacing look.

So the bindings were taken off and the Russian was able to move about the loft until his circulation returned. Later, Jan made him take off the T-shirt he wore beneath his jersey and cut it into strips which they used as padding when they put back the bindings. That done, Jan said, 'We're going to gag you. Can't take any chances.'

The Russian protested. It was inhuman, he said, he could choke to death, he'd had no food or water since lunch-time the day before. Surely the months they'd spent together at sea, the hardships they'd endured, meant something? If they left him bound and gagged he'd never be found. In a few days he'd be dead. Had Jan no sense of moral responsibility?

'Not much,' said Jan. 'But possibly a little more than you have. Moral responsibility didn't seem to cramp your style when you put on your shooting and stabbing act last night. But I've good news for you, Boris boy. We'll ensure that help comes within the next twenty-four hours. It's more than you deserve but that's us – always generous. Sorry about the food and water. We haven't had any ourselves, you know. You'll just have to lump it until help comes. You'll find the experience character-building.'

'Who will come to me?' The Russian's pale eyes flickered a message of doubt.

'Don't really know except that they'll be Portuguese – and that they *will* come.'

At that Krasnov had given a deep sigh of resignation. Jan got on with the gagging, pushed a balled up handkerchief into the Russian's mouth and secured it with a crude muzzle made from baling wire tied tightly behind his head. They did what they could to make him comfortable on a bed of straw, but with a man trussed, bound and gagged it couldn't amount to much. André turned away from Krasnov's accusing stare; looking miserable, he said, 'Sorry about this but we've no option. Help *will* come. I promise you that.'

'For Christ's sake,' said Jan impatiently. 'Cut out the sentiment. Let's get going.'

He led the way down the ladder, through the barn and into the sunshine outside.

Seeing each other in daylight reminded them that they hadn't washed or shaved for some time. There was no way of doing either at that moment so they combed their hair, dusted hay from their jerseys and jeans and felt marginally better.

Before long they'd reached the spinney of pines at the bottom of the hill, gone through it and come out on to the road. They set off on foot towards Chaves, twelve kilometres distant according to a whitewashed stone by the roadside. They walked on, came to a bus stop and decided to wait. A bus arrived about twenty minutes later and they joined its handful of passengers, mostly farming folk.

The bus went on, passed through a village, Izei, and soon afterwards began the winding descent towards the plain where Chaves showed up in the distance. Before long the Tamega River was reached; the bus rattled across the old Roman bridge and entered the town, stopping in the square outside the Banco Pinto.

It was after ten o'clock when they got out and made their way up the Rua de Santa Antonio in search of a telephone, a barber and somewhere to eat.

The morning in Chaves was a busy one. First they went to a public call-box and after some difficulty André managed to get through to Pippa at the *pensao* in Pedras Salgadas. In a brief conversation he told her to take the next bus to Chaves; to meet them in the café opposite the square from which he was phoning. He told her its name, Café 5, and how to get there.

'Everything all right?' she asked anxiously.

'Yah. Fine. Tell you later. You okay?'

'Yes. See you soon. Can't be too soon for me. Bye, André.'

'Bye, Pips. Don't forget my carrier bag.' He rang off.

Next they found a barber, had themselves shaved and their hair washed, brushed and combed. They moved on to Café 5. It was a cheerful place, filled with students, the babel of young voices competing with taped pop music. They bought themselves the ubiquitous cheese and ham rolls and coffee, sat down at a table and ate ravenously. When they'd finished Jan looked at his watch. 'Now for some shopping,' he said. 'We'd better move around separately. Meet here again at noon. Pippa can't make it before then.'

'I'm all for shopping,' agreed André. 'But what about cash?'

'Haven't you any left?'

'Not much.'

Jan produced the money envelope from the inside pocket of his denim jacket, discreetly checked its contents. 'Okay,' he said in a low voice. 'There's still over a thousand quid here.' He gave André two £20 notes. 'Hunt around for the September first edition of the *Herald Tribune* and get Michelin maps for Spain and France.'

'Will do,' said André

They left the café and set off in different directions.

At noon they were back at Café 5. Jan had bought a pocket compass and a haversack in place of the lost carrier bag. In it were items of clothing, shaving and toiletries he'd purchased to replace gear in the bag thrown away by Krasnov. André had found the international edition of the *Herald Tribune* of September 1 and bought two copies. From these they cut the Washington report, each putting a copy in their wallets. He'd also bought sardines, cheese, biscuits and coke for the meal that night.

They were studying the maps over cups of coffee and discussing the onward journey when a cheerful 'hi' announced Pippa's arrival. She dumped the carrier bags, complained that they felt like lead and sat down. Quite joyously, her eyes shining, she said, 'Lovely to be with you. Thought I might never see you crazy kids again.'

'Same to you,' they said. 'What'll you have?'

She told them she'd had breakfast – 'and a bath,' she added with a suggestive wrinkle of her nose – but would join them in a cup of coffee.

Using the formidable noise level of Café 5 as cover, they told her what had happened.

'So he's still in the barn?' She looked worried.

'I sincerely hope so,' said Jan.

'What next?'

'Round about five o'clock this afternoon I'll phone the police in Lisbon. Ask for a senior security officer. I'll refer him to the *Herald Tribune* report, tell him where to find Boris Krasnov gagged and bound in a barn between Loivos and Chaves. I'll give pretty explicit directions. Tell him where to find the Opel and the two motorbikes. Ask him to see that they're returned to their owners in Vidago. I'll let him know that the missing document is on its way to London in safe hands. Finally I'll say I'm looking forward to seeing him in Lisbon shortly. After that I'll ring off.'

'Why Lisbon?' Pippa frowned.

'Red herring. May make things easier for us.'

'Will you tell him who you are?'

'No bloody fear. Now listen, Pips. André and I have got maps and made fairly detailed plans. We've checked bus times to Vila Verde de Raia. That's where we get off. Close to the Portuguese frontier post. The Spanish post is about five kilometres further on. From Vila Verde we walk, take a minor road to Santa Antonio and Maros. That's east of the Tamega so we're not faced with a river crossing. It'll be dark before Maros. We'll go into the foothills. Sleep rough until the early hours of morning, then cross the frontier in high country. Once across it, we'll make for Viladerbos. That's about five kilometres on the Spanish side.'

'Sounds all right.' Pippa nodded approval. 'Hope it works. What then?'

Jan regarded her with an affectionate smile. 'We'll deal with that in due course. Travel now, pay later.'

'Super.' She leant over towards André, whispered in his ear. 'I'm sorry for poor old Goddy, aren't you?'

'In a way.' André smiled sadly for lost innocence.

Jan said, 'When you two have finished we'd better make plans for the afternoon. We've got at least four hours to get rid of.'

Pippa insisted that she would have to have her hair done before she considered anything else. It was agreed that she'd meet them in the café at three o'clock. After that they'd do some relaxed sightseeing, preferably of the sort that included a good deal of sitting down. André and Pippa were to keep together, Jan to operate on his own. They would rendezvous finally at the bus station on the square in front of the Banco Pinto at five forty-five. By then Jan hoped to have made his Lisbon call.

TWENTY-EIGHT

Hands clasped behind his back, head bent forward, the General paced the room, oblivious it seemed to the men who watched him in curious silence. He stopped abruptly, turned to face them. 'Greyling was on the phone from Washington this morning.' His eyebrows contracted in a dark frown. 'He says the Pentagon gave the Embassy the standard reply. Their spokesman declined to comment on the *Herald Tribune* report which he described as journalistic kite-flying.' The gaunt figure resumed its measured pacing. 'So where does that leave us?'

Engelbrecht took a cheroot from his mouth, held it elegantly between thumb and forefinger. 'I don't understand,' he said. 'In Washington they impressed on us the importance of treating the arrangement as absolutely confidential. Stressed the dangerous consequences of breaches of that confidentiality. And yet . . .' He put the cheroot to his lips, drew on it and exhaled as if seeking time in which to order his thoughts. 'And yet,' he repeated, 'despite that the leak comes from them. They seem unable nowadays to control sensitive information. Yet they blame us.' His tone was defensive.

Through pebble-lens spectacles Henning of Intelligence stared myopically at Engelbrecht. 'Leaks of highly sensitive information are often deliberate. It is quite possible that the US Secretary for Defence ordered the Pentagon leak.' He nodded as if in confirmation of this conclusion before adding, 'In order to discourage Kremlin adventurism on the Angola-Namibian border.'

Engelbrecht shrugged, lifted his eyebrows in a deprecatory gesture. 'I can see that. But why the hard line towards us? We were not responsible.'

The General stopped pacing, glanced intimidatingly at the man from Foreign Affairs. 'Because, Engelbrecht, we are guilty of something more serious than a leak. It was Pretoria, not Washington, that permitted a top security document to fall into Krasnov's hands.' He moved round the desk to the high-backed chair, leant on it. 'Henning's right, of course. The Pentagon leak is probably deliberate. Gives Washington the opportunity of repudiating the existence of any agreement. I can tell you that the Prime Minister also takes that view. Washington will, I imagine, now suggest that the Pretoria document is a fake – a Soviet propaganda ploy.'

Engelbrecht said, 'It is not quite as simple as that, General. If the Kremlin has the document you may be sure it will be used effectively against Washington's Africa policy — to demonstrate to Black Africa that behind the USA's front of antipathy to apartheid there is commitment to the defence of Southern Africa.'

Henning smiled courteously but at no-one in particular. 'I agree with the General that the United States will deny the authenticity of the Pretoria document, having used the leak as a means of warning the Kremlin. I believe that view is taken in the US Embassy here.'

The General glanced keenly at the younger man. 'What makes you believe that?'

'I play golf with one of their men.' Henning shrugged as if in disapproval of his role. 'He didn't say as much. Very discreet. But that was the impression I got.'

'Who is the man?'

'Bob Ingram,' said Henning quietly. 'He's an attaché.'

The General nodded several times, very slowly, apparently digesting Henning's admission.

Engelbrecht put in an oar. 'But the central problem remains. You have failed . . .' He quickly corrected himself. '*We* have failed to apprehend Krasnov. By now the Kremlin must have that document. My Minister thinks . . .'

'I have my own ideas.' The General interrupted as if pre-empting the Minister's thoughts. 'Who in Pretoria sent that document to H? Who is H? Answer me those questions? Somehow, somewhere, we've got a rotten egg in the basket. That's where the failure lies.'

Engelbrecht turned away from the General's penetrating stare, concentrated on dealing with the ash of his cheroot. Badenhorst controlled an almost irresistible desire to laugh. The General certainly knew how to serve an ace into the court of anyone who displeased him.

The sun was low in the sky when they left the bus at Vila Verde de Raia and set off along the country road which led to Maros. The village in the foothills was reached as daylight faded; before that they had seen in the distance the mountain range, dark and forbidding. Once clear of the village they followed a track towards a col on the eastern side of the range and when darkness set in Jan used the compass and the stars to maintain direction. By midnight they had almost reached the summit of the col after a long climb. There, under the shelter of a rock overhang, they ate a frugal meal and made camp for the night, sleeping on layers of sage brush and heather. The twenty kilometres they had covered, much of it over rough terrain, combined with nervous tension, acted as powerful sedatives and they were soon asleep. It was after eight o'clock next morning when they were aroused by the bleating of a mountain goat grazing on a ledge above them.

They washed in a stream, packed up their gear and headed for Viladerbos, a small country town on the Spanish slopes of the mountain. There, a few hours later, they had a meal in a café before taking a bus to the nearest rail link at Orense which they reached at noon. Their spirits rose with the knowledge that they had safely accomplished their first frontier crossing without passports.

Two years earlier Jan had spent a summer holiday cruising in a yacht which belonged to the Morrises, London friends and business associates of the Bretsmar family; much of that cruise had been spent on the Brittany coast.

'There's a super spot, St Jacut-de-la-Mer, just west of Dinard,' Jan had told his companions in Chaves when making plans for their onward journey. 'We anchored there for three days. Quiet little place. What an estate agent would call "exclusive residential". It has a sheltered anchorage with a good few yachts belonging mostly to locals. We should be able to pick up something there. It's not a harbour – no port authorities, customs, immigration or anything like that. Ideal for us. Anyway, if no joy there we can always work our way north or south along the Brittany coast. It's stiff with marinas.'

And so St Jacut-de-la-Mer became their destination. To reach it they had to cross Spain and much of France. For this they allowed two days, and so planned the journey that they would spend most of the two nights involved in trains, thus avoiding the discomfort, risk and delay in sleeping rough.

At Orenso they caught the train to San Sebastian on the Franco/Spanish border, a journey which took them by way of Salamanca, Valladolid and Burgos. At intermediate stations where they had to change they used the time between trains for snatched meals. On the afternoon of September 4 they arrived at San Sebastian and took a bus to Irun, close to the French frontier; there they changed to another bound for Santesteban. At the end of a two-hour journey into the mountains they changed buses once again and finally disembarked at Errazu, near the French frontier. It was already dark and in the course of that night they made the crossing into France. It proved to be more difficult than anticipated, the going hard, the tracks rough and often precipitous, and the night much colder than expected. But for the compass bought in Chaves and a clear night sky they might have lost their way. Next morning they limped into the nearest French town, St Etienne-de-Baigorry, and found a café where they ate large quantities of rolls, croissants and cherry jam. Refreshed they took the train to Bayonne. While there Jan sent a telegram to Harry Morris in London. It read: *All well. Enjoying Europe en route London. See you shortly. Please inform Dad and send our love. Gerhard.*

Sunday morning breakfast at *Schoongesicht* was an occasion to which Otto Bretsmar always looked forward. On weekdays his breakfasts were slight, quickly eaten affairs since it was his custom to be in his office in the city by eight o'clock. On Sundays, however, breakfast at nine-fifteen was a relaxed occasion, its pleasures enhanced by the Sunday newspapers through which he would browse, his particular interest being the financial pages.

On this agreeable spring morning he was paging through the Johannesburg *Sunday Times* when a minor headline on a back page caught his eye. 'My goodness, Kate,' he exclaimed with some agitation. 'Just listen to this.'

Mrs Bretsmar, knowing from his tone that her husband was disturbed, replaced her coffee cup on its saucer with a nervous rattle. 'What is it, Otto dear?'

'It's headed, Steamer Rescues Yacht Survivors. I'll read it: *A small passenger steamer* RMS Island Enterprise, *bound for Cape Town, reports picking up the crew of a yacht which had caught fire and sunk after a gale off Cape Finisterre. The survivors, three men and a woman, were landed at Oporto. The yacht was on passage to the United Kingdom.* That's all it says, Kate.' His voice trailed away.

'Good heavens, Otto.' Mrs Bretsmar put her hand to her heart, leant back in the chair, her eyes half closed. 'Do you think . . .?'

'I don't know what to think,' Mr Bretsmar frowned. 'On passage from where? It doesn't say. Could be from anywhere. Anyway, there are only two men and a woman in *Southwind*.' He put down the paper, took off his spectacles, wiped them with a silk handkerchief.

'Well, I don't suppose it's them, but if it is thank God they're safe,' said Mrs Bretsmar devoutly.

'Yes, indeed. And *if* it is, you may be sure we'll soon hear. No point in getting worked up about it.' He spoke with such assurance that Mrs Bretsmar was momentarily silent. There were, however, questions which had to be put.

'Do you think, Otto . . .?'

Mr Bretsmar deeply preoccupied, was aware that his wife was saying something but engrossed with his own thoughts he was not listening. He was thinking that if by an incredible chance it was *Southwind*, the news could be disastrous. In a gale, caught fire and burnt out? In that case what would have happened to the pictures and diamonds? Even if Jan had been able to save them, how could he get them through the Portuguese customs at Oporto? The consequences of such a disaster, however improbable, all but overwhelmed Mr Bretsmar. And if it was *Southwind*, would the insurers pay out for the ketch's loss, observing that it had not happened as and where first reported? Complicated, potentially dangerous explanations would be involved. How could he possibly handle them without somehow embroiling himself?

Leaving unfinished his favourite breakfast of a kipper, he got up heavily from the table, went across to the French windows and looked out towards the Magaliesberg mountains his mind filled with gloomy forebodings not helped by his belief in the inaccuracies of press reports: *three men and a woman* might well have been *two men and a woman*; or *Southwind* might have called in somewhere on the voyage and picked up another crewman; at St Helena for example. It was worrying, to say the least.

TWENTY-NINE

The *Sundance* survivors arrived in St Jacut-de-la-Mer in mid-afternoon having made the journey from Bayonne by train via Bordeaux, La Rochelle, Nantes, Rennes, Lamballe and finally Plancoët. There they took a bus for the short stretch on to Trégon Giclais. The last seven kilometres to St Jacut were by choice done on foot for the exercise which they badly needed after so much time in trains. While waiting at Rennes for the train to Lamballe that morning they had used the station rest-rooms to wash, shave and change into their only spare T-shirts and jeans, set aside especially for the occasion.

The Bretsmar family were not alone in finding the Johannesburg *Sunday Times* report a disturbing one. Badenhorst had phoned the General's house in Waterkloof at seven-thirty that morning to draw attention to the report, and an hour later the two men were together in the town office.

'Three men and a woman.' The General frowned at the paragraph. 'In a yacht on passage to the United Kingdom. Where from and date of landing in Oporto not given.' He turned to Badenhorst. 'Contact the ship's agents in Cape Town. Ask for the names of the survivors, the name of the yacht and where she was from. I'll get through to Ferreira in Lisbon and ask him to check with Oporto.' José Ferreira was chief of security police in Lisbon, an old friend of the General's from the days when Ferreira had served in Mozambique, then a Portuguese colony.

Badenhorst went through to his office and the General picked up the red phone.

The fact that it was a Sunday complicated matters. The offices of the shipping agents in Cape Town were closed. Badenhorst at once phoned Muller at his home in Cape Town and explained the situation. 'Check where the managing director lives. Phone him there right away. Find out if he knows the name of the yacht, where she sailed from, the names of the survivors landed at Oporto and the date.'

Muller came back on the line a few minutes later. 'He knows nothing more than the *Sunday Times* report but suggests we phone *Island Enterprise* direct.' Badenhorst returned to the General's office, reported the result of the Cape Town call.

'Good,' said the General. 'We should have thought of that.' He picked up the red phone. 'Get me the Captain of RMS *Island Enterprise*, on passage from Falmouth to Cape Town. She's a day or so out of Oporto. Make the call immediate.' He replaced the phone.

'What's the news from José Ferreira?' asked Badenhorst.

'He's not pleased,' said the General. 'The time difference, you know. Portugal's a couple of hours behind us. Had to wake him up. He'll ask Oporto for the survivors' names and present whereabouts, name of the yacht, where from, and date of landing. Said he'll come back to me shortly.' The General frowned, shrugged his shoulders. 'Why must this happen on a Sunday?'

'Typical,' agreed Badenhorst. 'Crises seem to like Sundays.'

Before noon that day much had happened. Henning of Intelligence had joined them in the General's office. *Island Enterprise's* Captain, uncertain of his caller's credentials, had politely suggested that the inquiry should be made through British Intelligence in Whitehall. This entailed a delay of about an hour, a circumstance which irritated the General. However, the information so badly needed was at last forthcoming: Whitehall reported that the yacht was the *Chicuala* of Beira, the survivors were two brothers, Mike and Tony Bennet, their sister Mary Bennet – all in their twenties – and a friend aged about forty, Pieter Berg. All were from Beira where the Bennet family ran a wine business managed by Pieter Berg. The survivors had left *Island Enterprise* fifteen miles off Oporto in a powered dinghy. The weather was fine and they had expected to complete the journey into Oporto in an hour. The yacht was on passage from Beira to Falmouth.

The General's mouth tightened, he glanced at Henning. 'Check the Beira aspects of that report with your man up there. Let's hope he's not out fishing,' he added sourly.

Henning was phoning Beira when the red phone buzzed discreetly. It was Ferreira from Lisbon. Oporto had no record of yacht survivors being landed from *Island Enterprise* or any other vessel during the preceding week. The General then gave the information supplied by Whitehall. Ferreira said he would follow it up. He rang off, complaining that his Sunday had been ruined.

Later Henning came back from an adjoining office. 'There is no yacht named *Chicuala* registered in Beira, nor is there a wine business owned or run by persons named Bennet or Pieter Berg.'

The General massaged his eyelids with long fingers. 'I thought as much,' he said wearily. '*Southwind* of Cape Town is *Sundance* of Hong Kong is *Chicuala* of Beira. So where are Krasnov and his friends now?' He got up from the desk and paced the length of the room before answering the rhetorical question. 'On the run in Portugal, probably making for France, then the UK.' He turned to Badenhorst with sudden decision. 'Now we bring in Interpol. Krasnov alias Godeska alias Braun alias Berg is wanted by us on two charges of murder, one for car theft and . . . no . . .' he interrupted himself, 'we don't mention espionage or the Terrorism Act or the General Laws Amendment Act. For Interpol we keep this strictly on the criminal level.'

Badenhorst nodded agreement, left the office. The red phone rang. It was Ferreira from Lisbon again. 'We're holding a KGB suspect alleged to be Boris Krasnov.' He chuckled. 'You interested?'

'Interested,' echoed the General. 'You must be joking.'

Ferreira told the story of the anonymous phone call traced to a public call-box in Chaves. The caller, speaking English, had referred them to the *Herald Tribune* report of September 1. He had told them where to find Krasnov, said that the missing document was on the way to London in safe hands. He had ended by saying that he would shortly be in Lisbon and would call at police HQ.

The Lisbon police had thought it a hoax but ordered their people in Chaves to check the caller's information. Having found the overturned Opel and the two motorcycles where he'd said they were, Chaves' police began taking the matter seriously. In the barn on the skyline to which the caller had referred they found a man, gagged and bound. He'd no documents or other means of identification. Denying that he was Boris Krasnov, he refused to answer any questions except in the presence of an official from the Soviet Embassy in Lisbon. He was being held in custody in Chaves while further investigations were taking place. His request to see an official from the Soviet Embassy had been refused.

'Now that's a hell of a scenario.' The General chuckled

with unusual exuberance. 'Bloody marvellous. Who d'you think left him there gagged and bound?'

'Presumably the man who telephoned from Chaves.'

'His motive?'

'To get the missing document? I thought it might have been your men.'

'Wish it had been. Tell me, José, were there no clues in the barn? Nothing to suggest who'd left him there?'

'Nothing other than a balled-up handkerchief they'd used to gag him. It had the initials JSB. Krasnov refused to answer questions about that, or about those who'd put him there. Seems from the two motorcycles and wrecked Opel that several people must have been involved.'

Frowning at Badenhorst, the General whistled into the phone. 'JSB – John Sebastian Bretsmar. The older Bretsmar boy. So that's it. His brother André and the girl probably with him. But why would they do that to Krasnov?'

'Would they have known he was a Soviet agent, General?'

'Possibly. We released the news to the media on August 28. They could have heard radio bulletins while still at sea.'

'They could also have seen press reports after landing in Portugal,' said Ferreira. 'Are they communist sympathizers, fellow travellers?'

'No, José, I wouldn't say that. The older brother, Jan, is like his Dad, I'm told. A good Nationalist. The younger brother and the girl are mixed up in anti-apartheid activities. It was this that brought them into contact with Krasnov. He was using them for his own ends.'

'I see,' the Lisbon line faded, then came clear again, '. . . once they found out they wouldn't be pleased. So that could be their motive.'

'Yes. It could be. You're certain there were no papers on Krasnov? No trace of a microfilm?'

'No. None at all. There'd evidently been a struggle. He had a really bad bruise in his crutch. One of his shoes had lost a heel. Probably kicked off in the fight. But he wouldn't tell us anything.'

'So we've got Krasnov but not the microfilm. Listen, José. We've got to get the Bretsmars and the girl. That document mustn't get to Britain.'

'Not so easy, my friend.' Distance couldn't conceal Ferreira's scepticism. 'Europe's a big place. And if they are found, what then? Is it not probable that the document has already been posted to London? When a man tells you it's on its way in *safe hands* I don't think he means *his* hands. By *safe hands* he possibly means "safe" from your point of view. That you need not fear the microfilm will get into the wrong hands.'

'You may be right, José, but that's not going to stop me trying to get these young people. Anyway, you say Krasnov's being held in Chaves.'

'Quite so, General.'

'Well, that at least is something. He's wanted here on two charges of murder, one of car theft and others which concern internal security. But I won't bother you with those just now. What I will do, José, is send a couple of my men over right away to collect him.'

Ferreira's laugh suggested the idea was amusing. 'I think you've got a problem, General. He's wanted here for attempted murder, car theft and illegal entry. There could be more charges by the time we've finished with him.'

'Attempted murder? Who?'

'The woman whose car he stole.'

'I see.' The General's manner was guarded.

But nevertheless before the conversation ended Ferreira had agreed that Henning and Badenhorst should fly to Lisbon next morning. No final decision concerning the man alleged to be Boris Krasnov would be taken there until the matter had been discussed with the emissaries from Pretoria.

St Jacut-de-la-Mer lay on a finger of land which poked into the Atlantic to form one side of a narrow-mouthed bay. The peninsula was almost entirely residential, most of its attractive houses, some in large grounds, overlooking the sea; these, and the yachts anchored off them in the sheltered waters of the small bay, suggested a preserve of the well-to-do.

Towards evening the wind came from the south-west bringing with it heavy cloud, but well before then they had split up and reconnoitred the western side of the bay. The reconnaisance completed, they met as arranged outside the drive leading up to *Le Vieux Moulin*, an hotel they'd passed earlier in the afternoon. It was a pleasant stone building standing on high ground; in its original form probably a farmhouse. Set back from the road it could scarcely be seen but the windmill from which its name derived was a prominent landmark. After meeting there they walked down the road in the darkness discussing their plans for the night. Central to them was the target they'd selected, a sloop-rigged yacht, the *Aurore*, moored to a buoy off a private beach on which a rubber dinghy lay against a boat-shed. The anchorage where she was moored was sheltered by a stone breakwater. Late that evening the yachts at anchor off the beaches had been lying bows to seaward. That, taken together with the high water mark on the breakwater, told its tale for Jan.

'I reckon the tide's about half way through the flood,' he said. 'Should be ebbing in the early hours of morning.' He looked at his watch. 'We've got five hours to get rid of. Any suggestions?'

'For a start,' pleaded Pippa. 'Let's have something to eat. I'm famished. That café where we had the coffee and sticky cakes seemed nice.'

'You two can go there,' said Jan. 'I'll try that joint at Bior. After a meal, I'll walk and bus over to St Cast-le-Guildo. It's about fifteen kilometres from here.'

'That won't use up five hours. What else are you going to do?' asked André.

'Chat up French birds, I guess.'

'Well, don't get so engrossed that you forget the time,' said Pippa tartly.

Having agreed to meet again at the entrance to *Le Vieux Moulin* at midnight, they went their separate ways. André and Pippa decided to fill in time after the meal by walking to and from St Briac-sur-Mer on the eastern side of the bay.

It was well past midnight when Jan arrived at the rendez-vous more or less at the same time as the rain brought by the south-westerly wind.

'Thank goodness you're here,' Pippa said. 'We've been worried sick. Where on earth have you been, Jan?'

'Sorry. She wouldn't let me go.' He grinned in the darkness. 'Actually, it took longer than I expected.'

'The journey or what?' said Pippa.

André wasn't amused. 'Come on! For God's sake don't let's waste any more time. You're twenty minutes late, Jan. A police car came this way twice. We've had to spend fifteen minutes in the hotel grounds behind the hedge.'

'Lucky you,' said Jan. 'I'll go first, you two follow in five minutes. Okay?' The night swallowed him as he moved away down the road which swung left and right at the bottom of the hill. He went left and came soon to a small tree-lined lane which led to the private beach. He approached cautiously, stopping once for a barking dog, then deciding it was safer to go on. From ahead came the sound of water lapping the shore. When he reached the stone parapet above the beach he found the steps and went down. On his left loomed the dark bulk of the house to which the beach and yacht presumably belonged. There were lights in several windows. The sound of distant voices somewhere on the beach came nearer and he moved into the shadows beneath the wall. A couple passed close by, the man and woman talking in low voices. They went up the steps. He did not move until he heard the dog barking at them some way up the road. Not long afterwards it barked again. André and Pippa, he supposed. He made his way across the beach to the boat-shed, felt in the dinghy for oars or paddles. As he'd expected, there were none.

André and Pippa joined him and there was a whispered discussion. It was decided to wait until one o'clock before moving the dinghy. They went back to the shadows beneath the wall and waited there. By one o'clock the lights in the big house had gone out but for one in a room upstairs on the side facing the sea. 'We'll have to risk it,' said Jan. 'If we wait too long we'll be in trouble with the tide.' They took the dinghy from the boat-shed, put their bags, shoes and socks in it, rolled up their jeans and carried it down to the water's edge. There they launched it and climbed in. Using their hands as paddles they made for the *Aurore*. Once alongside they clambered on board, hoisting the dinghy after them. André forced the locked companion-hatch with the spike of his sail-knife and they went below, closing the hatch after them. Shutting the screens on the port lights they made a quick check by torchlight of *Aurore* below decks. The sloop was smaller than *Southwind* but well equipped. In the forward sail lockers they found and made ready the sails they'd need. The drawer under the chart-table yielded a chart of the North Brittany coast and another of the English Channel. 'All we need now,' said Jan happily, 'is a little bit of luck.'

An element of it came soon when Pippa, sent to keep a lookout on deck, whispered down a saloon ventilator, 'The last light in the house has just gone out.'

They waited another twenty minutes before hoisting the jib and casting off the mooring rope. With Jan at the wheel, *Aurore* moved out from behind the shelter of the break-water and headed up in the darkness towards the mouth of the bay. Helped by the south-westerly wind and ebbing tide, it was not long before they'd passed the flashing light on Pointe du Chevet, the seaward end of the peninsula, and cleared the bay. Only then was the mainsail hoisted. As it filled the sloop heeled over to starboard and was soon slicing through the water at a useful pace, rising and falling to the westerly swell coming in from the Atlantic. Steering a northerly course they passed between the little offshore islands of Ebihens and Agot, switched on navigation lights and headed out to sea. The jib was taken in and a genoa hoisted in its place. With the bigger foresail *Aurore's* log was soon registering six to seven knots. Some distance to starboard they could see the lights of fishing vessels outward bound from St Malo. When the flashing lights on the buoys marking the shoals at Plateau des Minquiers showed up ahead, Jan altered course to the nor-west and eased the sheets.

Pippa looked astern through shimmering rain at the ribbon of blurred lights which marked the coastline. 'Isn't it beautiful?' she said. 'Like a picture in a fairy tale.'

THIRTY

It was apparent to Kate Bretsmar that her husband was in high spirits that evening, for he came into the drawing room at *Schoongesicht* with shining eyes and a mysterious smile.

'Just listen to this, Kate.' He flourished the greetings cable at her. 'It's from London – from Harry. Reads: *Gerhard in France enjoying Europe en route London. Arriving here shortly. Reports all is well and sends love. Regards Harry.*'

'Oh, Otto. How wonderful.' Mrs Bretsmar leant forward on the settee, clapped her hands. 'We must thank the Almighty for his marvellous mercy.' Her eyes filled with tears.

Mr Bretsmar put a cautionary finger to his lips, pointed to the French windows. She nodded, they went out on to the veranda and walked across the lawn to the rockery below the tennis-court. It was a fresh spring evening with the sun low in the western sky.

Mrs Bretsmar touched his arm. 'Isn't it fabulous, Otto – the "all is well"? It must surely mean they're safe and in good health. We must thank God for that.'

'Yes. Indeed we must,' said Mr Bretsmar piously. He took his wife's hand. 'You realize, Kate, that "all is well" includes the diamonds and pictures?'

Mrs Bretsmar snatched her hand away. 'How can you be thinking of that, Otto, when you've just learnt that your sons are safe at last?'

'One *has* to think of these things, Kate. Those pictures and the diamonds must be worth close on three million rands. That's a lot of money. Now they're safely in Europe. It can be vital to us. And don't forget, it's not been roses all the way. I've lost the ketch.'

'Damn the blasted ketch,' said Mrs Bretsmar with unusual spirit. 'And your wretched money. I want to see my sons.'

Mr Bretsmar looked hurt, regarded his wife thoughtfully. 'You're going to, Kate.'

'Yes. But when?'

'Sooner than you think, dear.' His smile was secretive. We're flying over to London the day after tomorrow. I told Daniels to make the necessary arrangements before I left the office this evening. London, Kate – won't that be a nice way of celebrating?'

'Oh, Otto.' She looked at him affectionately. 'You are a kind man. When d'you think they'll arrive there?'

Mr Bretsmar, deeply involved in private thought, made no reply. So they *had* landed in Portugal. He wondered where they were now. The 'in France enjoying Europe' of Harry's cable must mean they'd left Portugal and passed through Spain. Belgium was next door to France. Jan would no doubt see Simon Lutgarten in Antwerp before making for London. How was he getting the pictures and diamonds through customs? Perhaps they'd gone from Oporto to France by sea. Crewed in a yacht. Youngsters were so resourceful nowadays. He'd every confidence in Jan. Such a practical, capable, young man. A chip of the old block. Must be in the genes, thought Mr Bretsmar with a satisfaction which would have been blunted had he known that Harry Morris had in all innocence transposed the 'all well' in Jan's Bayonne telegram to 'all is well'. The distinction was, as Mr Bretsmar was soon to learn, of some importance.

At four o'clock in the morning the Minquiers Shoal was abeam. No longer sheltered by the land the sea had built up and *Aurore* was behaving in lively fashion. With two months at sea recently behind her, Pippa was delighted to find she wasn't suffering from seasickness. 'I suppose I'm really half a seaman now,' she said.

'Just about.' Jan's tone was grudging.

André said, 'I like both halves.'

'That's sweet, André.' She gave him a warm smile.

At noon Guernsey was abeam to starboard. Though the rain had stopped, visibility was poor and they could not see the island but they celebrated progress by having their first meal on board. In St Jacut-de-la-Mer the day before they'd bought tins of beef, packets of dry biscuits, cartons of milk and some coffee; enough for four meals, which they hoped would see them through the passage across the Channel. Jan had estimated that the journey to Poole would occupy about thirty hours, depending on the weather and their ability to start *Aurore's* engine. He'd worked on it for an hour before noon but without success. In the afternoon he took over on deck and handed the task to André who quite soon identified the trouble. Several wires in the ignition circuit had been connected to the wrong terminals.

'The owner's way of putting the engine out of action,' he explained. The diesel tank was full so there was no fuel problem. *Aurore* was doing so well under sail that they decided not to use the engine until they entered the north-bound tanker lane. When they did, late in the afternoon, the diesel was started and *Aurore's* speed with sail and engine increased to ten knots. The estimated time of arrival off Poole Harbour was advanced to one o'clock in the morning.

It was not until early afternoon that Sophie Dubois, housekeeper to the Le Brun family in St Jacut-de-la-Mer, noticed that her employer's yacht *Aurore* was no longer moored inside the stone breakwater off the private beach.

Wondering if it had somehow broken adrift during the night, she called Maurice the gardener and together they went down to the breakwater to search the bay with M. Le Brun's powerful binoculars. There was no sign of *Aurore*.

'She has been stolen,' Sophie Dubois announced with indignation. 'I shall report this to the police at once. It would happen when the family are away in Greece.'

Nodding assent, Maurice juggled a Gauloise between his lips before croaking, 'France is not what it was.' His face was so gnarled and wrinkled that it concealed any show of emotion.

Sophie Dubois hurried back to the big house above the breakwater to phone the police at St Cast-le-Guildo, the nearest gendarmerie.

It was by no means the first time a yacht had been stolen from St Jacut-de-la-Mer and Inspector Chaillot at St Malo, who received the report of the theft from St Cast-le-Guildo, took the matter in his stride, putting out the necessary theft reports and informing the appropriate authorities. In no time harbours and marinas along the Brittany coast were alerted. On the following morning Radio Brittany's news bulletins referred briefly to the theft of *Aurore*.

It was a busy night for shipping in the Channel and on several occasions *Aurore* had to give way to tankers, bulk carriers and other vessels. But by seven o'clock that evening they had crossed the north and south-bound lanes and course was altered to the north-east. Soon afterwards the wind veered to the west and the sails were trimmed accordingly. With the wind now on her port quarter *Aurore* surged and plunged on her way to the Dorset coast.

At half past ten the light at Portland Bill was abeam and before one o'clock that morning they had rounded Anvil Point into Studland Bay to begin the run into Poole Harbour.

They'd not gone far when André called down to Jan who was in the saloon. 'There's a ship overtaking us.'

'Okay. I'm coming up.'

Jan joined him in the cockpit a moment later. Having examined the dark shape astern through binoculars he said, 'We'll hold our course. She has to keep clear. Looks like a naval job.'

The steaming lights of the overtaking vessel drew steadily closer. When no more than a cable away she directed a blinding beam of light on to *Aurore*.

'Bloody searchlight.' said Jan. 'Don't panic. They're checking on what their radar screens show them.'

The searchlight went off as suddenly as it had come on and soon the dark shape passed down the starboard side and drew ahead, the deep throb of its diesels clearly audible.

From below came Pippa's voice. 'What's going on up there?'

'Nothing to worry about, but don't come up,' replied Jan.

'What d'you make of it, Jan?' There was a tremor of anxiety in André's voice.

'Naval mine-sweeper about to enter harbour. Same as we are.'

'Thank God for that. I thought they were after us when that light came on.'

'Not to worry. Keen young CO doing his stuff. Probably a lieutenant with four years between his stripes. Now let's concentrate on getting this job safely into harbour.'

Two years had elapsed since Jan's visit to Poole with the Morrises. On that occasion they had for some days used it as a sailing base, and it was to him comparatively familiar ground. Not that it needed to be, for among the books in the rack above the chart-table was a copy of Adlard Coles' *Channel Harbours and Anchorages* which included a large-scale plan of Poole.

As the lights marking the entrance between Sandbanks and South Haven Point drew closer, the moon came clear of the clouds, sails were lowered and *Aurore* motored in at slow speed. Soon afterwards they left the buoyed channel and followed the line of stakes which marked South Deep, a narrow channel between Brownsea Island and the mainland. Several hundred yards down it they dropped anchor close to Furzey Island on the southern side of the bay, well away from Poole Quay and the harbour proper.

With *Aurore* riding safely to her anchor they went down to the saloon to discuss future plans. It was a subject they'd avoided, both during the long voyage from the Cape and while on the run in Europe. It had been enough then to concentrate their minds on the day-to-day problems of sailing and escape. But now the issue was one which could no longer be put aside. They'd arrived in England in a stolen yacht having left a thoroughly disreputable trail behind them. What was the next move?

Jan looked at the saloon clock. 'It's after two. We should go ashore at about six while it's still fairly dark. On the chart Wareham looks to be about four miles from the shore opposite where we're anchored. We can get the train there to Waterloo, via Bournemouth. Should be in London by midday with any luck.'

'And then?' Touching the hair away from her eyes, Pippa looked at him earnestly.

There was forewarning in Jan's smile, as if he knew what he was about to say would not be popular. 'Trafalgar Square,' he said, adding casually, 'South Africa House — home from home.'

'You can't be serious.' André was incredulous.

226

'Whitehall for us.' Pippa looked towards André with proprietorial affection. 'The Home Office. That's going to be our first port of call. We'll find out how we set about getting political asylum. They'll tell us.'

'They won't be able to tell *me*.' Jan was brusquely emphatic. 'I don't want political asylum. I'm going to South Africa House to hand over the microfiche to the Ambassador personally. That document belongs to the South African Government. Krasnov got hold of it somehow. I'm going to see it gets back to where it belongs.'

Pippa gave him a long look, searching and uncertain. 'You know from the *Herald Tribune* what it's about. For heaven's sake destroy the wretched thing. Keep away from South Africa House. It can only mean trouble for us if you go there.'

'Sorry, Pips. My mind's made up.'

André said, 'If the Pentagon rumour was true it means the US Government is going to help Pretoria keep apartheid alive and well. I'd rather give the microfiche to the UK press. After all, why shouldn't everyone know the truth. Anything wrong with the truth?'

Jan's eyes narrowed. 'So you'd like to see a Soviet build-up on South Africa's borders, would you?'

André shook his head. 'Of course not. What I'd like to see is equality for all the people of our country, regardless of race or colour.'

'What you're talking about is one-man-one-vote. The blacks are not ready for it. The majority are still primitive.'

'It's those who think like you who are primitive, Jan.'

'For goodness sake stop it.' Pippa put her hands over her ears. 'Both of you. This stupid cliché-ridden wrangling leads nowhere. It's so fatuous.'

'Right, I will. *But* I'm handing over this microfiche,' said Jan with quiet determination. 'And bear this in mind. We've helped a Soviet agent escape from our country. I know we didn't have a clue he *was* one, but we helped him get out with a secret state document. We left South Africa illegally.

227

We lied about *Southwind's* destination. We were parties to that phoney MAYDAY sent by Stefan. We changed *Southwind's* name and port of registration twice. I know all that was Krasnov's idea. Krasnov the escape artist, who *you* thought was a nice guy called Goddy – but we went along with it and . . .' He frowned, ruffled his hair. 'Where was I? Oh, yes. We landed in Portugal illegally. Stole motorcycles there. Crossed into Spain and France illegally. Stole *Aurore* and brought her here, and now we're about to enter Britain illegally. There's a list of offences a mile long on which we can be charged.' His tone changed, became conciliatory. 'I'm going to hand over the microfiche in return for certain undertakings which will protect us. For that reason it's important that you people come along. I want the Ambassador to see what you're like. That you're not criminals. You're both in more trouble than I am. You *had* to get out. I didn't, but I helped you so I'm involved.'

Pippa looked at him speculatively. 'Was it just to help us that you got involved, Jan?'

'I know what you mean.' There was the shadow of a smile. 'Of course there were kicks in it for me. The action's been terrific, but I want you and André to come with me to South Africa House because that would help us in a big way.'

What he said, the softened manner, lowered the temperature; but it took a good deal more discussion before any sort of agreement was reached. When it was, Jan yawned noisily. 'Now let's get our heads down. Might get two hours' kip if we're lucky.'

'Two hours.' Pippa yawned in sympathy. 'I could do with twenty.'

As it happened *Aurore's* clandestine crew got rather more than two hours' sleep. The saloon clock alarm failed and, exhausted, they slept until after eight when Jan put his head out of the companionway and announced that is was a cloudy day with a cold breeze. Guilty though they were of oversleeping they consoled themselves with the advantages it had conferred: for one thing the tide was still flooding, for another they were able to see the shore where they proposed to land – marsh, farm and woodland with a few distant farmhouses. But they were to learn that waking late also entailed disadvantages.

THIRTY-ONE

Soon after seven o'clock that morning the duty telegraphist on board the coastal minesweeper HMS *Shepperton*, recently arrived in Poole Harbour, reported to the Officer-of-the-Day that Radio Britanny had reported the theft of a yacht, the *Aurore*, from St Jacut-de-la-Mer, a small resort on the Brittany coast.

'So what, Higgins?' The Officer-of-the-Day raised an inquiring eyebrow.

'That yacht we picked up in the searchlight coming in around two this morning had the same name – *Aurore*. Thought you'd like to know.'

'Did it now, Higgins? I was down below at the time. But well done. You'll go far.'

'That's what my Mum says.' Higgins grinned. 'Going to do something about it, are you?'

The Officer-of-the-Day nodded slowly, yawned into a closed fist. 'But of course, my dear Higgins. Theft is a matter for the police. We shall alert the local constabulary at once.'

By eight-thirty they'd washed, tidied and made ready their few possessions for going ashore. Jan and André then went on deck to check the lie of the land and put the rubber dinghy in the water, while down below Pippa got the stove going and set about making coffee.

The two men were about to lift the dinghy over the

guard-rail when they saw a small motorboat heading towards them. Half a mile away, it had just rounded Brownsea Island.

Jan focused binoculars on it. 'Two guys in uniform,' he said, 'and a boatman.' A little later he added, 'Policemen. They've got checkered capbands. Go down and warn Pips. Stay there with her. I'll join you in a moment.'

There were no other craft in the South Deep Channel. Obviously the police boat was making for *Aurore*. Escape now by means of the dinghy was impossible. The outline of a plan began to take shape in Jan's mind. Keep cool, first things first, he told himself as he shut the hatch on the forward end of the coachroof. He picked up a jib sheet, rove it through the grab-rails on either side of the hatch, hauled the loops taut and turned up its end on a cleat. It would now be impossible to open the forward hatch from inside *Aurore*.

The motorboat was within a few hundred yards; he gave it a last look before going below.

In short, staccato sentences he outlined his plan to André and Pippa as he put on a denim jacket, took Krasnov's pistol from a bag and slipped it into an inside pocket. He turned to Pippa. 'The signal, Pips. You drop a pot or kettle or something and shout "oh, for God's sake". Don't forget that. It's vital.' He went through the forward door of the saloon and shut it behind him. Ahead of him was the sail-locker, to starboard the oilskin locker, to port the shower and WC. He went into the WC and shut and bolted the door.

Frowning with anxiety, André watched Pippa. 'Sounds a pretty crazy idea. Typical Jan. But I suppose we'll have to go through with it.'

The sound of a motorboat's engine came down to them through the open companion hatch, faint at first but growing steadily louder. Pippa managed a forced, slightly hysterical laugh in an attempt to conceal her fear. 'I suppose we will. Can't think of an alternative. Can you?'

He shook his head.

'I'm scared stiff,' she said.

'Who isn't? But you don't look it.'

'Nor you, André. Must be suntan.' The noise of the motorboat engine was loud now, almost alongside. A voice hailed. '*Aurore*, ahoy. Take a line.'

As André went up the companion ladder the motorboat bumped alongside. The taller, younger policeman passed up a bow line. André made it fast. 'Hi,' he said. 'What's the trouble?'

The sergeant, a thick-set, red faced man with a black walrus moustache said, 'We'd like to come aboard.'

'Sure.' André pointed to the deck immediately forward of the cockpit. 'Swing over the guard-rail there.'

The sergeant did so, with some difficulty as those unused to yachts do, and his companion, a tall sallow young constable equipped with a walkie-talkie, followed more agilely. The boatman remained behind.

The policemen joined André in the cockpit. 'Have a good journey across?' asked the sergeant with an inquiring smile.

'Not bad,' said André, wondering how much the sergeant knew and what was coming next.

'How many of you on board then?'

André looked him straight in the eyes. 'Just two. Me and my girl-friend.'

'That was her with you on deck just now, was it?'

'That's right, sergeant. She's down below. Making coffee.'

The sergeant peered down the companionway and sniffed. He turned back to André. 'Ah, coffee. It's that all right.' He switched off the smile. 'Now,' he said. 'There's a few questions you and your lady-friend will have to answer.' With slow deliberation and from long habit he took a notebook from his pocket as he spoke.

'Like to come below,' suggested André. 'It's warm there, more comfortable. And the coffee,' he added brightly.

The sergeant turned to the constable. 'Care for some coffee, Harry?' Without waiting for a reply he said to André, 'Right, lead the way.'

André went down, the sergeant followed, then the constable.

'What's all this?' Pippa's forehead wrinkled in a huge frown as she turned from the stove, wiping her hands on her jeans.

'Police,' said André laconically, adding, 'Sergeant . . .?' he looked inquiringly at the sergeant.

'Sergeant Williams and Constable Burt it is.'

'Hi,' said Pippa.

'I'm Jack Hudson. She's Phyll Gray,' explained André with aplomb.

Pippa pointed to the settee. 'Sit down, won't you? It's a bit cramped in here with everyone standing.'

Moving his considerable bulk in sideways behind the saloon table the sergeant settled himself on the settee and took off his cap. Constable Burt followed suit. The sergeant once more took a notebook from his pocket.

Pippa went back to the stove. 'Kettle's boiling.' She turned to them with a seductive smile. 'Coffee all round? Milk and sugar?'

'Ah, coffee. Very welcome,' said the sergeant. 'Milk and three sugars, please.'

'Same for me,' said the constable, who was given to tooth sucking.

André, still standing at the foot of the companion ladder, said, 'The chap in the boat. A bit cold and windy out there. Shouldn't we ask him in for a mug?'

The sergeant looked from the constable to his watch. 'Old George.' He nodded. 'Right. Just for the coffee, mind. Can't have him in here once . . .' a kindly man, he hesitated, mildly embarrassed, '. . . once the questions start.'

André went up on deck. He was soon back with the boatman, an elderly, round-shouldered man wearing a faded yachting cap. He lowered himself on to the settee at the after end of the saloon table.

Pippa put the mugs of coffee, a saucerful of sugar lumps and some plastic spoons on the table. 'Where's yours, then, young lady?' inquired the sergeant. Smiling paternally he popped three sugar lumps into his mug and began stirring. Constable Burt, who seemed to follow Sergeant Williams' every move, did the same.

'Don't take sugar myself.' Old George the boatman shook his head, his eyes troubled as if denying temptation.

Pippa put a milk carton on the table. She gave the sergeant a special smile. 'Now all you thirsty men are fixed, I'll get mine,' she said. 'It's always the women last, isn't it?' She went back to the stove, picked up the kettle and raised it to pour, but it slipped from her hand and clattered to the floor. 'Oh, for God's sake,' she shrieked, jumping aside to avoid the scalding water. She glanced at the sergeant, 'Sorry,' she said. 'I got such a fright.'

'Of course you did,' he said sympathetically. As he spoke the forward door of the saloon opened and she saw Jan, all six-feet-four of him, come through the doorway, Walther pistol in hand.

'Get those hands up quick.' The hoarse command was matched with a villanous scowl. 'No tricks if you want to stay alive.'

The men on the settee, whose attention had been diverted by Pippa and the kettle accident, were taken completely by surprise. Their hands went up, André frisked them. 'No weapons,' he said. 'But I'll have the walkie-talkie.' Constable Burt handed it over.

'This won't do you any good,' said the sergeant in a low voice, shaking his head between outstretched hands.

'Shut up,' Jan glared at him. 'You listen to me. I'll do the talking. No harm will come to you lot as long as you sit there with your hands up. If you don't . . .' his mouth tightened in a hard line as he outstared each of them in turn.

Watching his victims along the barrel of the pistol with the sort of concentration a bird of prey reserves for fieldmice he said, 'Jack and Phyll, get up on deck. Take our bags with you. Call me when you've launched the dinghy.'

They took the carrier bags and clambered up the companionway ladder. While he held the men on the settee covered, Jan could hear his companions moving about on deck as they worked on the rubber dinghy. The only other sounds were the heavy breathing of the sergeant and Old George, and the constable's tooth sucking.

A few minutes later André called down, 'Dinghy's launched. All set.'

Jan directed a final scowl at the men on the settee. 'Now don't you lot move a bloody inch if you value your lives.' Still covering them he went up the companion ladder with his back to it – an unseamanlike manoeuvre but essential in the circumstances.

Jan stepped through the hatchway into the cockpit, André slipped the weatherboards into position and Jan slammed shut the companion hatch. André secured it with a shackle and there was then no way those below could come up on deck.

'It worked,' cried Jan exultantly as they paddled the dinghy towards the shore less than two hundred yards away. 'Empty pistol and all.'

'For the time being,' said André soberly. He disliked violence – and Sergeant Williams, Constable Burt and Old George had seemed rather nice people. After all this was England, they were English and it was to the English André and his companions were looking for political asylum.

'Poor Sergeant Williams.' Pippa sighed unhappily. 'He had such a kind smile. A really nice old boy.'

The tide was high and they were able to get the dinghy well in before it touched bottom and they stepped ashore.

When they'd hauled the dinghy clear of the water they walked through the trees to a farm lane which led to the main road. Once on it they set out for Wareham which they reached within the hour. Before long they were in a train bound for London.

On arrival at Waterloo they made for the public telephones.

Jan dialled South Africa House and after some difficulty with the switchboard got through to a senior official to whom he explained that he wished to see the Ambassador the following morning at ten-thirty. The official was brusque, asked Jan who he was and what he wanted to see the Ambassador about.

Jan said, 'Tell him I have a secret document recovered from a Soviet agent, Boris Krasnov, in Portugal a few days ago. I suggest you check my statement with police head-quarters in Lisbon and with the Security Branch in Pretoria.'

'Ah, I see. What is your name?' The brusqueness at the other end of the line had gone.

'Jan Bretsmar. We must see the Ambassador at ten-thirty tomorrow morning.'

'Unfortunately he is away. On a visit to Pretoria. He'll be there for some time. But his deputy will see you. I'll have to consult him about the time. I suggest you ring back in half an hour.'

'Sorry, that's not possible. We'll be at South Africa House at ten-thirty tomorrow morning.' Jan lowered his voice, spoke slowly. 'I must tell you that a *copy* of the document, a microfilm, is in a sealed envelope in a London solicitor's safe. If any attempt is made to interfere with us it will be handed to the press.'

There was a moment of silence then, until the voice at the other end said, 'I'm afraid I don't like your tone, Mr Bretsmar. Threats are quite unnecessary.'

'It's not a threat. My apologies if it sounded like one. Just a statement of fact. We have to safeguard our position. I'm sure that will be understood.

'You say *we*, Mr Bretsmar. How many are you?'

'There are three of us. Sorry, I must ring off now.' Jan put down the phone, took a slip of paper from his wallet and dialled a number in the City. A woman with a deep voice answered. He asked her to put him through to Mr Harry Morris.

'Who shall I say it is?'

'Tell him it's Gerhard.' There was a click on the line,

then Harry Morris's cheerful voice. 'Welcome to London, Gerhard.'

In the conversation which followed Harry Morris broke the news that Jan's parents had arrived in London the night before and were staying at the Park Lane Hotel. Jan promised to phone them. He then asked for and received an assurance from Morris that he would be happy to keep in his office safe a sealed envelope, to be delivered by Jan that afternoon. News and pleasantries were exchanged, after which the call ended.

While this was happening Pippa had phoned an aunt in Kensington and arranged to spend the next few days with her. André, too, had been on the phone but was non-committal about his call. 'An old friend from UCT,' he said in answer to Jan's inquiry. No doubt one of his anti-apartheid friends, decided Jan privately.

André was delighted to learn that his parents were in London, and particularly looked forward to seeing his mother. Jan, however, was anything but pleased, though he tried not to show it. Harry Morris's news of his parents' arrival had been a shock. The loss of the pictures and, less importantly, of the ore samples was something very much on his conscience. Telling his father what had happened wasn't going to be easy. And he'd have to tell him that Krasnov, alias Goddy, had been on board *Southwind*. That, too, was going to be difficult. It would be an unpleasant meeting but the sooner it was over the better, so he phoned the Park Lane and got through to his father who greeted him warmly. His mother came on the line next, sounding happy but tearful. Then it was André's turn to speak; when he'd finished he passed the phone back to Jan. 'Dad wants another word with you.'

Jan took the phone.

'Are you people coming over now, Jan?' asked his father. 'I've booked a room for you and André. It's a bit late for lunch I'm afraid, but we must have dinner tonight.'

Jan said, 'We'll come across later in the afternoon, Dad. We've a few things to see to first. Got to get some clothes, haircuts and so forth.'

'Of course. Tell me, is everything all right?' There was an underlying note of anxiety in his father's voice.

'More or less.' Jan tried to sound casual. 'Couple of snags.'

'What are they?' snapped Mr Bretsmar.

'Tell you later, Dad. In person, not on the phone.'

That had ended the conversation.

After a snack lunch in the station restaurant they split up, André and Pippa going to Whitehall and Jan to the City. It had been agreed that Pippa would meet them at the Park Lane at eight o'clock that night.

THIRTY-TWO

Jan and André arrived at the Park Lane soon after eight o'clock bringing Pippa with them. Their late arrival and the presence of Pippa, a stranger, displeased Mr Bretsmar, who'd spent an uneasy afternoon worrying about Jan's 'couple of snags'. While he hoped they were to do with political asylum or something of that sort, the unpleasant thought persisted that they might concern the pictures and diamonds. His wife, quite overcome when she greeted her sons in the Bretsmar suite, hugged them ecstatically, but try as she might she could not keep back the tears. Once over the emotional strain, she turned to Pippa and kissed her. 'Welcome, my dear. I've heard so much about you from André I feel we already know each other.' She stood back then and regarded the three young people with moist but happy eyes. 'My, how fit and tanned you all look.'

André grinned. 'Must have been the sea voyage, Mum.'

'Now for a little celebration.' Mr Bretsmar pointed to a

table in the corner where a wine bucket and crystal glasses stood on a silver tray. 'Dom Perignon 1971,' he announced, taking the bottle from the bucket and opening it with a ceremonial pop. When he'd poured the champagne he raised his glass. 'To the crew of *Southwind*.'

Jan made a face. 'Don't forget *Sundance* and *Chicuala*, Dad. They helped.'

Pippa smiled in mild embarrassment. 'Surely we shouldn't be drinking to ourselves.'

'On this occasion I think it's justified.' Mr Bretsmar's small eyes twinkled.

The happy atmosphere was offset for Jan by his father's thinly veiled asides about the charts and Marconi spares.

'When we've had dinner, Dad,' he demurred. 'Not now.'

Frowning disapproval at her husband Mrs Bretsmar said, 'Jan is right, Otto. We're here to celebrate. Let's have a lovely relaxed dinner. You and Jan can chat afterwards.'

With some reluctance he agreed. A little later they went down to the restaurant.

After dinner Mrs Bretsmar took André and Pippa into the lounge for coffee while her husband went upstairs to the suite with Jan. There, over liqueur brandies, Jan began the story of their experiences since leaving Cape Town at the end of June. When Mr Bretsmar realized that the account was to be chronological he quickly came to the point. 'Tell me all that later, Jan. I'll be most interested. But what have you done about the pictures and ore samples?'

Jan shook his head obstinately. 'Let me tell the story in my own way, Dad. It doesn't make sense otherwise.' So he went on with it: explained how they'd picked up Goddy at Rooiels Bay after repainting the ketch.

'I'd never have let you take *Southwind* if I'd known *he* was to be aboard,' was his father's apoplectic interruption.

Jan shrugged, ran a hand through his hair. 'That's why we couldn't tell you, Dad. We had to take him to protect André and Pippa.'

His father frowned, the close-set eyes blinking unhappily beneath the prominent eyebrows, but he was silent. Jan went on with the story: the gale, the fire on board *Sundance*, the rescue by *Island Enterprise*, the landing in Portugal, the meeting with McLean at Pedras Salgadas and the discovery that Goddy was Boris Krasnov, a Soviet agent. At that point Jan produced the cutting from the *Herald Tribune*. Mr Bretsmar read it, muttered, 'The treacherous swine', and passed it back. Jan went on to tell of Krasnov's disappearance with the bag containing the Marconi box and the money, the frantic chase which had followed and finally the Russian's capture in the barn on the hill.

'Thank God for that anyway,' said a shocked Mr Bretsmar. 'I mean, that you caught the bastard.'

'Yes, *and* we got back the secret document. It was on microfilm.' Jan's manner suggested pleasure at the recollection of these experiences.

Mr Bretsmar's on the other hand did not. Dabbing his forehead with a silk handkerchief he came once more to the point. 'So, the ore samples and pictures?' he prompted.

Jan stood up, peered into his brandy goblet as if seeking inspiration, and went to a window. 'The pictures were lost in the fire, Dad. I did everything possible to save them but it was too fierce. That was one of the snags.' He hesitated. 'The other was the ore samples.' He looked across to the street lights bordering Green Park. 'We've lost them,' he said in a faraway voice.

Mr Bretsmar leapt to his feet, his face twisted with anxiety. 'Lost them!' he cried. 'You can't be serious.'

Jan turned back to him. 'I'm afraid I am, Dad. When we landed in Portugal I had to explain to the others why I'd brought along the radio spares on a hitch-hike. So I told them about the ore samples.' He paused, avoiding his father's unbelieving stare. 'Krasnov stole my carrier bag for the money. He didn't want ore samples – bits of rock, extra weight – so, having taken the money, he threw the box out of the car that night while we were chasing him. Somewhere

239

on the road between Loivos and Izei. He couldn't remember where. There was no way we could go back and look for it. We were on the run. I'm awfully sorry, Dad. I know the pictures were worth a packet and how important the ore samples were to you and your syndicate. But at least *they* can be replaced.'

Mr Bretsmar slumped back in his chair, his bulk suddenly diminished, a crumpled desolate figure; he buried his face in his hands and small moans came from between his fingers.

'Don't take it so badly, Dad.' Jan leant forward, patted his father's shoulder. 'It's not the end of the world, you know.'

Mr Bretsmar looked up, his face ashen. 'It's the end of three million rands worth of diamonds and pictures. That's what it is.'

'Diamonds?' echoed Jan. 'What diamonds?'

'They were in the Marconi box.' Mr Bretsmar's voice was hoarse. 'I told you they were ore samples. I thought you might not be – well, shall I say happy – if you'd known they were diamonds.'

Jan looked at his father with sudden distaste, shook his head in a bewildered way and went to the door. 'You're right, Dad. I certainly wouldn't have been happy. I wasn't keen on taking the pictures, that was risky enough, but they'd belonged to the family for a long time and it didn't seem too wrong. And I *knew* about them. But without our knowledge you involved us in smuggling diamonds out of the country for you and your precious syndicate. Diamonds? If you want to know what I think about that – well, it was a rotten thing to do. Sorry, but that's the way I see it.' He opened the door and walked out of the room.

Next morning Pippa met Jan and André on the steps of the National Gallery. It was a breezy autumn day, the sky blue but for wisps of cloud and vapour trails left by aircraft. Beneath the steps endless streams of traffic rumbled round Trafalgar Square, the red of London buses as much a part of the scene as the tourists, pigeons, photographers and peanut vendors who thronged the Square in the shadows of Nelson's Column.

'So what's the drill?' André was surly and resentful.

His brother gestured towards the big white building which occupied the eastern side of the Square. 'We're due there at ten-thirty. Better leave the talking to me. I'm in a happier position than you and Pippa.'

'I think we should know just what you're going to say.' Pippa brushed wayward strands of hair from her eyes. 'You may be in a happier position, Jan, but we're in a much more vulnerable one. Don't you agree, André?'

André said, 'Yes, I do. And I'd like to make one thing very clear. I don't intend to express any regrets or apologies for anything I've done. I'm going to carry on opposing apartheid in any way I can until the thing's dismantled. Just bear that in mind, Jan.'

'That goes for me, too.' Pippa's manner was cool but determined. 'Now tell us what you're going to say.'

Jan regarded his brother sorrowfully. 'You'll never change will you, André?'

'No, I won't.' André frowned in the direction of Nelson's Column as if it were in some way a part of his problem.

Having shrugged his shoulders and spread his hands in a gesture of despair, Jan went on to explain what he had in mind. Among other things, he told them he'd seen Harry Morris's legal adviser on the previous afternoon and discussed their situation with him. Jan then showed them a set of preliminary proposals the solicitor had drafted. These were discussed and agreed subject to certain amendments proposed by André and Pippa, after which Jan looked at his watch. 'Come on,' he said. 'It's twenty past. Let's go.'

THIRTY-THREE

On arrival at South Africa House Jan gave his name to the uniformed doorman on duty at the front entrance and asked for Mr Johan Smit. The doorman signalled discreetly to someone in the foyer above them and almost immediately a man in a dark suit came down the steps. Regarding them uncertainly, as if unable to accept that these were the people he'd been expecting, he inquired, 'Mr Jan Bretsmar?'

Jan, looking down from his considerable height, nodded. 'Yes. That's me.'

Without introducing himself the newcomer said, 'Please follow,' after which he led them by way of a lift, stairs and corridors to an ante-room. There they waited briefly until he ushered them into an office at the far end of which a man with grey hair and moustache sat behind a large desk. The man in the dark suit neither announced their names nor identified the grey-haired man who nodded at them formally through gold-rimmed glasses. 'Good day,' he said pointing to chairs and adding, 'Please sit down.' He turned to the man in the dark suit. 'Stay with us, will you?'

When everybody was seated he opened a file and consulted it for a moment before turning to his visitors. 'My name is Liefveld,' he said. 'I act for the Ambassador in his absence. What can I do for you?' His eyes were unsmiling, his manner cold.

Jan passed him the cutting from the *Herald Tribune*. The grey-haired man read it, nodded as if confirming something to himself. 'Yes, indeed.' He handed it back. 'I take it you are Jan Bretsmar?'

'That's right.'

'And the others?' He examined each of them in turn, his

expression behind the gold-rimmed glasses inscrutable. 'Presumably André Bretsmar and Philippa Brown?'

'Yes. That's so.'

'Good.' He looked at Jan. 'Perhaps you'd like to begin?'

Jan launched into his story, censoring it in some respects but giving a fair though brief account of events up to the capture of Boris Krasnov in the barn on the hill, the subsequent journey across Spain, France and the Channel to Britain, and the encounter with the police in Poole.

As the story unfolded Liefveld's frigid manner changed to one of amused incredulity. 'What an extraordinary story,' he remarked when Jan had finished. 'If we'd not had messages from Pretoria and Lisbon I'm afraid I would not have believed it. Indeed, but for those messages you would not have got in here to see me.' He smiled, then as if regretting the lapse resumed his restrained manner. 'I must tell you,' he said, 'that Krasnov is now in custody in Lisbon.'

'Poor old Goddy,' said Pippa. 'He was only doing what he believed to be his duty for his country. He was . . .'

'Including trying to shoot and stab me,' Jan interrupted.

Liefveld looked up from the paperknife he'd been running through his fingers. 'Are you aware, young lady, that Boris Krasnov is wanted in the Republic on two charges of murder? And is being held in Portugal on one of attempted murder?'

Pippa gasped, half rose from her chair. 'You can't be serious?'

'I'm afraid I am. When he was on the run in the Cape Province he killed an African night watchman in order to steal number plates from a Uitenhage garage. Next day he ran down and killed a traffic officer on Houwhoek Pass. In Portugal he fractured the skull of a woman whose motorcar he stole.'

'Oh, how awful!' Pippa's eyes were wide with horror. 'That's really terrible.'

The muscles on André's face tightened, he pulled at his ear, wriggled uneasily in his chair, but said nothing.

'Callous bastard,' muttered Jan. 'Never really trusted him.' He changed the subject. 'I've told you about the microfiche, Mr Liefveld. I must explain that it's not with us but we intend handing it to you.' He paused, stared with calm, determined eyes at the man behind the desk. 'In exchange for certain undertakings.'

Liefveld sat forward, put down the paperknife. 'What undertakings, may I ask?'

Jan took from his pocket the draft Harry Morris's solicitor had prepared. 'A written undertaking, signed by the South African Prime Minister, fully indemnifying the three of us against all claims or prosecutions of any sort arising from our activities before and after our departure from Cape Town in *Southwind* up to the present time.' He paused, consulted the draft again. 'Secondly, the undertaking must record that no action of any sort will be taken at any time against Philippa Brown or my brother André for their anti-apartheid activities in the Republic prior to their departure in *Southwind*. Thirdly, we must all be free to return to the Republic when and if we choose.' He had another look at the note before going on. 'The South African Government must undertake to return the yacht *Aurore* in good condition to its owners in St Jacut-de-la-Mer, and ensure that the two motorcycles we used to chase Krasnov are returned to their owners in Portugal in good order. Finally the South African Government must ensure that no action is taken against us in connection with our little problem with the police in Poole yesterday.'

Liefveld said, 'That won't be easy. Threatening British policemen with weapons, locking them up, are not the sort of offences that British justice overlooks.'

Jan ran a hand through tousled hair. 'Of course. But the British Government must be as anxious as the South African and US Governments to keep the document in question strictly confidential. I reckon the three of them together can bring enough pressure to bear to have the

Poole trouble overlooked. As a matter of fact,' he added, 'the Walther pistol was empty. No ammunition.'

Liefveld sighed, shook his head. 'You young people certainly seem to have been running wild.'

'Force of circumstance,' said Jan. 'Anyway, Mr Liefveld, those are the undertakings we ask for. The legal document being prepared by our solicitors will be handed to you tomorrow. Once we get it back, signed by the Prime Minister, you'll be given the microfilm.'

Liefveld studied the paperknife with frowning preoccupation. 'What evidence have you that it is genuine? That it *is* a copy of the missing document?'

'That will be for you people to judge. If you decide it's not you can repudiate the undertaking. We don't know what's in it. A microfilm reader would have been necessary for that. And we don't propose to find out. It's not our business to read secret State documents.'

The man in the dark suit gazed at the ceiling as if what was happening there was of paramount interest and pinched his nostrils to stifle a yawn.

'You are asking for a great deal,' said Liefveld coldly.

Jan shook his head. 'The Security Branch must have spent a lot of time and money trying to catch Boris Krasnov on the run with a secret State document. They failed, we succeeded. In the circumstances I don't think the undertakings we're asking for are unreasonable. With respect, I'd say they're cheap at the price.'

The older man appeared to give the point thought. Eventually he said, 'You realize it will take a little time, Mr Bretsmar. We will have to telex the terms of the undertaking to Pretoria. If they agree them, it will take some days to get the signed document back here.'

'We can wait,' said Jan philosophically.

Liefveld got up from the desk. 'Well, I don't think there's anything more we can do today. I can't tell what Pretoria's reaction will be. It is unfortunate that the Ambassador is not here to deal with the matter personally. Don't quote me, but

I'd say you've rendered an important service to the Republic – and to the West generally.' He cleared his throat. 'I can't give any undertakings but I imagine if you people want to return, the authorities will probably take a reasonable view.'

That brought André into the conversation for the first time. 'I won't be going back. Not until the whole rotten apparatus of apartheid has been dismantled.'

'Me too,' said Pippa emphatically. 'I don't want to live in a society with laws which make four-fifths of its people second-class citizens because of the colour of their skins.'

Jan frowned with irritation at these asides. 'Well, for my part I've had nothing to do with apartheid politics. I'll certainly be going back. It's my country.'

Pippa glanced at him disapprovingly. 'It's also the country of twenty-plus million South Africans who don't happen to be white. Perhaps you'll realize that one day, Jan. In the meantime good luck to you in the laager.'

Liefveld went to the window, looked down on the scene below. 'I'm sure you young people hold strong views for and against apartheid – most South Africans do. But if you want a political argument I suggest you have it down there.' He pointed to Trafalgar Square. 'It's a great place for that sort of thing.' He consulted his watch, came back from the window, shook hands with each of them, thanked them for what they'd done and asked for their assurance that they would respect the highly confidential nature of the document they'd recovered.

Pointing out that none of them had read it, Jan said they were quite happy to give that assurance. Liefveld's eyes behind his gold-rimmed glasses regarded him uncertainly. 'One point before you go – I understand you have a copy of the microfiche. May I ask who made the copy?'

'Boris Krasnov presumably.' Jan spoke casually. 'He had one in his wallet, the other in the heel of his shoe. I suppose that's an old espionage trick. When caught you give up the one in the wallet but say nothing about the one in the shoe.'

'I see.' Liefveld was thoughtful. 'I suppose "*The Great Shoe Drama*" put you on to that?'

'That's right.' Jan grinned.

'What will happen to the copy, Mr Bretsmar?'

'It will remain in a sealed envelope in the solicitor's safe. That envelope will never be opened, unless . . .'

'Unless what?'

'Unless, at any time, the undertakings we are given are not honoured.'

'That is quite unnecessary.' Liefveld became frosty again. 'My Government honours its undertakings.'

'Good,' said Jan smiling. 'So do we. So the copy is safe, isn't it?'

From South Africa House they went to a steak house in Leicester Square, settled themselves in a corner, ordered drinks and asked for the menu. All three had forgone breakfast that morning in favour of a late sleep.

The moment the waiter had gone, Pippa said. 'Why on earth didn't you tell us about the duplicate, Jan?'

He leant over, pulled her towards him, kissed her cheek. 'The more you know the more you blow, my lovely Pips.'

'That's pretty trite, isn't it?' André frowned. 'No excuse for not telling us.'

'Sorry,' said Jan absentmindedly. He was thinking of something else he hadn't told them. There *was* no duplicate. But it had seemed a good idea to invent one.

Father Ignatio Gomez, a frail figure in a black cassock, left the Camara Municipal and set off across the square, his long staff tap-tapping on the pavé like the stick of a blind man. He passed the equestrian statue of the first Duke of Braganza, and made for the church of Santa Maria Major at the far end of the square. It was a hot day and he walked slowly, his lips moving in silent rehearsal of the words he would use in the dark of the confessional box. 'Yesterday,' he would say to the Father Confessor, 'walking between

Loivos and Izei I stopped to rest by the roadside. Under the brushwood near me something shone brilliantly in the sunlight. It came from a parcel which lay on the ground, its wrapping torn. Inside there was a broken box from which little pellets of cotton wool had fallen. One of these had opened and I saw in it a glittering diamond. I opened another. In it too there was a diamond. There must have been a great number in that box. What was I to do with them? How had they got there? Thrown away by thieves perhaps? I put the box in my satchel and this morning handed it to the police here in Chaves, explaining where I had found it. But my conscience is troubled, for I did not tell them of the ten diamonds I had left at the orphanage with a note for the Mother Superior. It seemed to me that the man who owned those diamonds must be very rich and well able to contribute to such a worthy cause. The orphanage cares for so many children and the Mother Superior never has enough money for their needs.' That would be his confession. At the end of it he would ask the Father Confessor for absolution. The unsigned note he'd left for the Mother Superior had explained that the diamonds were a gift to the orphanage in the name of Santa Maria, the Blessed Mother.

He went on down the square past the parked cars, the barrows, the ice-cream carts and the people coming and going about their business. On reaching the church he went in by the doors under the campanile. Inside he stopped, faced the high altar and made his obeisances. It was good to be there in that tranquillity after the heat and bustle of the town; as always in the church's dimly lit interior he felt closer to God than at any other time. There were a few people there, some lighting candles, some kneeling, the sound of their prayers lost in the splash of water and the scrape of brooms where men hosed down the flagging and women cleaners worked in the nave, their gaunt faces reflecting the light of stained glass windows.

Father Ignatio went to a pew and knelt. First he prayed for those in the church, asking that their devotions might ease their burdens; next he prayed for forgiveness for his sins and understanding of what he had done. Had he indeed sinned? He was not sure? If he had, would absolution be granted? Would his confession result in the Mother Superior having to surrender the diamonds? For a long time he meditated upon these things, praying for help and guidance. At last, feeling old and tired and confused, he addressed a final prayer to the Holy Mother, asking for her intercession on his behalf. He got up awkwardly, took the staff from where it lay beside him and made his way from the church.

He had not confessed but he felt better, for notwithstanding the canons of his order he had, in his own mind, made his peace with God.

Antony Trew

His novels of action and danger, at sea and on land, have been highly praised. A Royal Navy Commander during World War II, Antony Trew served in the Mediterranean and the Western Approaches, and was awarded the DSC.

His books include

TWO HOURS TO DARKNESS   £1.25
THE WHITE SCHOONER   £1.25
DEATH OF A SUPERTANKER   £1.25
THE ANTONOV PROJECT   £1.25
SEA FEVER   £1.50

FONTANA PAPERBACKS

Geoffrey Jenkins

Geoffrey Jenkins writes of adventure on land and at sea in some of the most exciting thrillers ever written. 'Geoffrey Jenkins has the touch that creates villains and heroes — and even icy heroines — with a few vivid words.' *Liverpool Post.* 'A style which combines the best of Nevil Shute and Ian Fleming.' *Books and Bookmen.*

FONTANA PAPERBACKS

Adam Hall

'This is how the spy thriller should be written: foolproof plot, switchback-fast, every fact ringing right.' *The Times*

'Adam Hall is Top Boy in the spy thriller class.' *Observer*

THE TANGO BRIEFING £1.50
THE MANDARIN CYPHER £1.25
THE QUILLER MEMORANDUM £1.25
THE SINKIANG EXECUTIVE £1.50
THE STRIKER PORTFOLIO £1.25
THE VOLCANOES OF SAN DOMINGO £1.50
THE WARSAW DOCUMENT £1.35
THE PEKIN TARGET £1.65
THE 9TH DIRECTIVE £1.50
THE SCORPION SIGNAL £1.25

FONTANA PAPERBACKS

Helen MacInnes

Born in Scotland, Helen MacInnes has lived in the United States since 1937. Her first book, *Above Suspicion,* was an immediate success and launched her on a spectacular writing career that has made her an international favourite.

'She is the queen of spy-writers.' *Sunday Express*

'She can hang up her cloak and dagger right there with Eric Ambler and Graham Greene.' *Newsweek*

FRIENDS AND LOVERS £1.75
AGENT IN PLACE £1.50
THE SNARE OF THE HUNTER £1.50
HORIZON £1.25
ABOVE SUSPICION £1.35
MESSAGE FROM MALAGA £1.50
REST AND BE THANKFUL £1.75
PRELUDE TO TERROR £1.50
NORTH FROM ROME £1.50
THE HIDDEN TARGET £1.75
I AND MY TRUE LOVE £1.50
THE VENETIAN AFFAIR £1.75
ASSIGNMENT IN BRITTANY £1.75
DECISION AT DELPHI £1.95
NEITHER FIVE NOR THREE £1.95

FONTANA PAPERBACKS

Desmond Bagley

'Mr Bagley is nowadays incomparable.' *Sunday Times*

THE ENEMY   £1.35
FLYAWAY   £1.65
THE FREEDOM TRAP   £1.50
THE GOLDEN KEEL   £1.35
HIGH CITADEL   £1.25
LANDSLIDE   £1.50
RUNNING BLIND   £1.50
THE SNOW TIGER   £1.50
THE SPOILERS   £1.50
THE TIGHTROPE MEN   £1.50
THE VIVERO LETTER   £1.50
WYATT'S HURRICANE   £1.50
BAHAMA CRISIS   £1.50

FONTANA PAPERBACKS

Fontana Paperbacks

Fontana is a leading paperback publisher of fiction and non-fiction, with authors ranging from Alistair MacLean, Agatha Christie and Desmond Bagley to Solzhenitsyn and Pasternak, from Gerald Durrell and Joy Adamson to the famous Modern Masters series.

In addition to a wide-ranging collection of internationally popular writers of fiction, Fontana also has an outstanding reputation for history, natural history, military history, psychology, psychiatry, politics, economics, religion and the social sciences.

All Fontana books are available at your bookshop or newsagent; or can be ordered direct. Just fill in the form and list the titles you want.

_____

FONTANA BOOKS, Cash Sales Department, G.P.O. Box 29, Douglas, Isle of Man, British Isles. Please send purchase price, plus 8p per book. Customers outside the U.K. send purchase price, plus 10p per book. Cheque, postal or money order. No currency.

NAME (Block letters) _____

ADDRESS _____

_____

_____

While every effort is made to keep prices low, it is sometimes necessary to increase prices on short notice. Fontana Books reserve the right to show new retail prices on covers which may differ from those previously advertised in the text or elsewhere.